MW01414677

The Boatwright Chronicles Book One

SUPER VIRUS

What Others Say About This Book

"When Dr. Adam Boatwright, a physician and university researcher in genetics, sets out to prevent his wife's hereditary cancer, he opens a Pandora's Box of possibilities. His manipulation of mouse genes has the potential of freeing humans not only from cancer but from aging, making them virtually immortal. But what will happen when he tries the treatment on himself? And what implications will it hold for the human race, and the Earth, if his experiment succeeds?

Lawrence Lapin writes with clarity and authority. His subject is as current as today's news and every bit as frightening. The story twists and turns like a strand of DNA, its surprising conclusion opening the door to Dr. Boatwright's future adventures. An enjoyable and thoughtful read."

—Elizabeth Lane, Author of *Wyoming Wildfire* and *Navajo Sunrise*
www.elizabethlaneauthor.com

"Dr. Lawrence Lapin vividly and movingly takes the reader into areas of genetic engineering with all its wonders and mysteries. "Super Virus" resonates with unforgettable characters in this fast-paced scientific thriller which makes one wonder what it would be like to never grow old. Meticulously researched and beautifully written, this book is hard to put down."

—Tony Fisher, Retired anatomy and physiology teacher, USPTA tennis professional

"Super Virus is an interesting read…"

—Midwest Book Review

The Boatwright Chronicles Book One

SUPER VIRUS

Immortal Sins

L A W R E N C E L.

LAPIN

Breedwell bwp Press

Lincoln, California

This book is a work of fiction. Names, characters, places, and incidents are a product of the author's imagination or are used fictitiously. Any resemblance to actual events, locales, or persons, living or dead, is coincidental.

Copyright © 2009 by Lawrence L. Lapin

All rights reserved. Except as permitted under U.S. Copyright Act of 1976, no part of this publication may be reproduced, distributed, or transmitted in any form or by any means, or stored in a database or retrieval system, without the prior written permission of the publisher.

Breedwell bwp Press

P.O. Box 1330, Lincoln, CA 95648
Visit our website at www.BreedwellPress.com.

Printed in the United States of America

Book Design by www.KarrieRoss.com
Editing by Arlene Prunkl

First Printing: March 2009
Second Printing: September 2009

Library of Congress Cataloging-in-Publication Data

Lapin, Lawrence
Super Virus: Immortal Sins/Lawrence Lapin—1st ed.

Summary: "This is the first book of the Boatwright Chronicles, dealing with the one man's self-experimentation in find a cancer cure that leads instead to a cessation of aging."

Provided by the Publisher:

ISBN-10: 0-9821020-0-3
ISBN-13: 978-0-9821020-0-8

Introduction

The Boatwright Chronicles

Super Virus: Immortal Sins: is Book 1 in the Boatwright Chronicles. Soon to be published is Book 2, *Boundary Layer:Restoring Life to a Dead Planet.* Being written are Book 3, *Funnel Effect: Genetic Enrichment*, and Book 4, *Megafauna: Back from Extinction.*

Any book in the series may be read independently and in any order.

Details about the series of books and their publication dates may be found on the Internet at:

www.LawrenceLapin.com

Super Virus tells how protagonist Adam Boatwright, a geneticist and surgeon, uses his skills to prevent his wife's impending cancer. The cure would be at the cellular level, guaranteeing that cells divide faithfully. Adam finds a substance to do that and engineers a virus that continually generates the chemical. As the clinical trial, Adam infects himself with that super virus. But the side effect is prevention of aging, and he becomes virtually immortal. Convinced that long lives would destroy the human race, Adam becomes caught in a web of intrigue and conspiracy as he tries to stop profiteers from exploiting the virus.

Boundary Layer begins with the threat from a pending impact by a gigantic meteor. Adam Boatwright faces his greatest challenge: preparing for the collision and dealing with the aftermath of the massive calamity. When all hope of saving the planet is lost, the rescuers hole up in a deep cavern to wait out the catastrophe. Their story deals with worthiness of the human race, family planning, reproductive politics, planned mutations, cloning, animal rights, immortality, sexual preferences, and what life to restore. They encounter betrayal, career crises, shattered dreams, sacrifice, and renewal. The common thread of this book is science, discussed in ordinary language. Subjects include controlled evolution, intelligence enhancements, non-cryogenic embryo storage, expanded animal-human communications, and prolonged cessation of the aging process.

Funnel Effect continues where Boundary Layer left off, with Earth having a handful of people with closely related children. Life restorations are underway, and the genetic material of two groups of surviving humans is pooled. Adam Boatwright leads the genetic engineering necessary to give survival diversity to both animals and humans. The apes have been thoroughly integrated into society and demand that Adam modify their lines to permit speech and bipedal locomotion. The new society begins its long growth spurt and infrastructure building begins.

Megafauna places Adam 500 years into the future. Planet Earth is still recovering from a disastrous meteor impact, bigger than the one that killed the dinosaurs. It tells about the gigantic effort to bring back animals and plants and mankind itself. This new world has a small human footprint, but Adam fears another ecological disaster as population growth continues to explode. But changes are in the works, troubles are brewing, and Adam worries about the directions being taken. He forms a new goal: giving the planet more robust life and a platform for future evolution. In reaching that objective, he will bring back animals driven to extinction by man thousands of years before. These include two megafauna: the woolly mammoth and the saber-toothed cat.

Prologue

Have you ever wondered what it would be like to never age? As long as some disease or accident didn't take your life, you could live forever. You would be *virtually* immortal. What would you be willing to pay for that?

Immortality has been sought after since man walked the Earth. Historical figures, epitomized by Ponce DeLeon, have searched for a Fountain of Youth. Eternal life has been popularized with fictional accounts, like "The Picture of Dorian Gray." Adam Boatwright, the protagonist in this book, even finds himself lusting for it. In the abstract, living forever seems universally attractive.

But some argue that virtual immortality would be a tremendous cross to bear.

Whether or not living things were ever created to be immortal is a deep philosophical issue, best left to religious scholars. Itzak Friedman, a scientist discussed in this book, insisted that the rhythm of life depends on *death* and new *birth*. He maintained it would be tragic if the old never died, because then there would be no room for the young. Old ways would be replaced only at a snail's pace. Itzak claimed that death and birth are essential to evolution itself.

Others maintain that any substance granting virtual immortality would be temporary anyway, because the possessors would inevitably die—perhaps by accident, murder, or from some non-viral disease. Meanwhile, they could live in young bodies for centuries, even millennia. Virtual immortals would see loved ones die, outlive their children and grandchildren, and watch the world decay because of human overpopulation. Trees would all be taken, oceans fished empty, and wild animals all gone, their habitats occupied by man.

It's easy to see why the planet would suffer if people had virtual immortality. Unless the possessor kept his or her status secret, others would find that cessation aging was possible. Some would find a way to achieve it.

It would be a secret almost too strong to keep. A few would likely find it very profitable to dole out virtual immortality to the highest bidder.

Imagine how attractive virtual immortality would be. People now fork over huge amounts just to extend their lives by months. How much would they pay to live indefinitely in youthful bodies? The drug wars would pale in comparison to the greed virtual immortality would unleash. Control of an elixir to stop aging would bring *trillions*, not mere billions.

Sharing the secret would be tantamount to granting six billion people spectacularly long lives, making all but the poorest virtually immortal. All would eventually die some horrible death—but not from old age.

For a person to live with virtual immortality without destroying the world, he or she would be forced to live a lie. She would have to fake her death over and over again. He would live in fear that the secret would be discovered. He could not maintain a career, have no permanent family, nor even keep an identity.

He would spend his life keeping virtual immortality secret and deterring would be profiteers. He would be only a step away from a quagmire of greed, deceit, and unlawfulness.

1

Little Oscar

Adam Boatwright, a medical doctor and genetic researcher, stood six feet tall. In spite of his forty-seven years, his still jet-black hair framed a serious face dominated by large, dark-blue eyes. Even today, the ruggedly good-looking man could still pass as a fighting-trim marine captain.

Adam walked that morning to the Life Sciences Building on the main campus of Central University, moving with a slight limp because of a wound from exploding mine shrapnel. The Vietnam War injury did not slow him as he bounded up the outside stairs to the Life Sciences Building lobby.

Excited, he was about to meet with Dr. Itzak Friedman, the famous Israeli scientist, to plan the next phase of the research project.

Adam was unlocking his office when he was so surprised by a note taped to the door, he dropped the keys. The note requested that he come immediately to Itzak's study. Puzzled, Adam hurried down the long empty hall and pushed open Itzak's slightly ajar office door. He gasped at the shocking scene.

Itzak Friedman was writhing on the floor! The heavy man's eyes were wide with fear as he gasped for air. But the desperate scientist's lungs weren't sucking sufficient volumes. Adam shifted into emergency-room mindset, trying to reach a diagnosis. Itzak's cyanotic skin clued Adam that the flailing man had swallowed something blocking his windpipe. The big man was suffocating, but there was no time to search for the obstruction.

Adam's head pounded from a rush of adrenaline as he rummaged the scientist's neat desk, looking for a sharp object. He grabbed a pair of scissors and quickly made a surgical incision beneath Itzak's larynx. He then carefully pushed and turned until a breathing vent was opened. But the blue-faced man's arms stopped flopping, and his arched back went suddenly limp. Itzak was not breathing through the bleeding hole.

Adam would use his own lungpower to force air into the dying man. Nervous and dripping with perspiration, he grabbed a glass pipette cylinder from the supply cabinet. The glass tube was about twice the thickness of a drinking straw. Adam gently pushed the pipette into the incision and breathed into Itzak's windpipe. The patient's coloring improved, but he soon lost consciousness as blood flowed profusely from the hastily made incision. Adam continued breathing for Itzak, until the poor man's heart suddenly stopped beating.

For several minutes, Adam administered CPR. But it was no use. Itzak was dead.

It was 9:05 a.m. when Adam ran into the Genetics Department office. Nothing about Itzak's death made sense, and he was extremely flustered.

"Quick, Jill," Adam sputtered at the department secretary. "Dr. Friedman's in his office. He just died. Call an ambulance."

Adam paced the halls in shock, his mind again and again reliving those terrifying minutes, wondering what he could have done differently. He always reached the same conclusion—only the tracheotomy could have saved the man's life.

Adam's first research meeting with Professor Itzak Friedman had been just three weeks before. Remembering every detail of that session, Adam let the earlier scene run through his mind, hoping for some clue to explain Itzak's mysterious death.

The two men had exchanged greetings as Adam entered Itzak's orderly study for the first time. A stocky man with long white hair, Itzak looked like a clean-shaven Santa Claus in a lab coat. Adam's attention was drawn to the man's eyes, which seemed to window some deep-seated anguish.

Adam had sat down, startled to see the man's lab coat almost fly apart. A white rat sprang out of the pocket and scurried onto the man's shoulder. Itzak scooped up the acrobatic animal and kissed it on the forehead, explaining, "This is Little Oscar. He's the guiding light for the cancer project."

Moments later, Itzak was prying the mobile rodent off his chest. "I'm ready to share my great secret. It all revolves around this little fellow." Itzak held Little Oscar up high, smiling like a father marveling over his baby.

Adam shared Itzak's obvious love for animals. But bonding with a rat! How odd. Although highly intelligent animals, rats led short lives and simply couldn't provide companionship like a dog or cat.

"Where does your pet fit into your cancer research?"

"I'll say this as simply as possible," Itzak answered, looking with clear admiration at the animal. "Little Oscar is *ten* years old."

"That's impossible. Rats hardly ever live beyond three years. The rodents usually die of cancer. But *ten years!* Never! That's like a human living to be two hundred."

Itzak grinned at Adam, obviously enjoying the drama. "Precisely. But as long as I continue treating him, Oscar will never get cancer. He'll live until one of the escaped boas from herpetology finds him."

"Oh my God! How did you manage that?"

They were interrupted by a phone call.

Adam waited for Itzak, mulling over cell physiology. Body cells divide naturally, their regeneration being a normal part of life. Most cells are short-lived and constantly have to be replaced. Difficulties arise when the new cells fail to duplicate the originals, and the resulting freaks sometimes become cancer.

Adam smiled, distracted by Little Oscar's antics. The rat had climbed on top of Itzak's head, running its paws through the man's long hair, as if trying to make a nest. Itzak never budged until Oscar jumped down to the desk.

Finally, Itzak replaced he phone and resumed the conversation.

"Now I can answer your question, Adam. I've been keeping Little Oscar alive by giving him I-complex. That's a group of special chemicals employed by the body for fighting viral infections. My research proves that I-complex also maintains cell-division fidelity. That's how it prevents cancer."

Adam felt confused. "I've never heard the term *I-complex*."

"It's my name for a substance I discovered," announced Itzak, looking proud. "It came from bodily fluids taken from Little Oscar's older sibling while fighting a viral infection."

Itzak went on to say that he and a deceased biochemist colleague separated identifiable substances from the rat's liquids, including dead viruses and various metabolic products and antibodies. The leftover concoction—which he called I-complex—defied any traditional description. Itzak confessed that he knew little other than that it did the job. It had been an arduous exercise to synthesize the I-complex.

"In Israel," said Itzak, "we exposed Little Oscar to every rodent virus known. So far he has never caught a viral infection."

"Do you use the same complex on your liver cells?"

"No. We found human I-complex from the lymphatic fluids of volunteers, all suffering from various varieties of flu, colds, and worse."

Itzak explained that they had used similar chemistry, separating the critical disease-fighting chemicals and amalgamating them into the final substance used in the liver-cell experiments.

"It remains a mystery how it works," Itzak said.

Adam could hardly contain himself. "If you did it all over again, would you obtain the same I-complexes?"

"No," Itzak replied, "we've tried to replicate the human substance with different volunteers and a new mix of viral infections. The resulting chemicals don't foster cell-division fidelity. The same is true of rat I-complex."

Adam mentally summarized those strange findings, merging them with what he knew regarding the body's immune system. "Let's see if I have it. During an active viral infection, the body produces a host of chemicals, some of which we can lump together. Those are your I-complex. Your hypothesis is that this substance is what conquers viral infection. Further, I-complex helps cells properly divide and thereby prevents cancer. The substance is present only until the virus is conquered, when the body stops making it."

"You're absolutely right, "Itzak said, grinning widely. "The chemical must *always* be present to accomplish those miracles. That's why I use *synthetic* rat I-complex, manufactured outside the body. Little Oscar receives daily transfusions. We insert analogous synthetic human I-complex into the growth medium of the liver cells being cultured in dishes."

Adam absorbed Itzak's intense stare. "Rat or human, the same principle applies. Synthetic human I-complex eliminates errors in cells dividing *outside* the body. That's how the whole line of research was started. My animal experiment was the second step. My main goal is preventing cancer in a *live* person. I'm just about ready to launch the next phase."

"It's too soon for that! You can't do live human research until the FDA has seen the animal results and gives its approval."

Itzak was quick to reply. "I'm taking a few shortcuts. I can't wait a quarter-century for every approval."

"I hate delays, too. But what's your hurry?"

Itzak stared at the picture on his desk. "My wife Hannah has melanoma. It has metastasized into several organs, and she has only a few months to live. I'll treat her myself once I perfect the cancer cure."

"Your research is certainly promising," said Adam, struggling to be nonchalant. "But you're far from a cure for cancer."

At that point the conversation was interrupted by Little Oscar, who jumped onto Adam's shoulder and sniffed at his ear. Adam laughed and gently picked up the animal, patted his belly, and cuddled him between his palms. Within seconds, the energetic rodent squeezed out from the confinement and scampered across the desk, jumping into the pocket of Itzak's lab coat.

"Where do I fit into your plans?" Adam asked.

"It takes lots of synthetic I-complex to keep Little Oscar going, equivalently more than a healthy human can absorb."

"So the treatment won't work in people?"

Itzak's steady stare outlasted the researcher's reply. "I'm convinced it *will* work. We just have to administer human I-complex in manageable doses. That's why I wanted to consult with you."

2

A Glimpse of Immortality

Still pacing the hallway, Adam looked at his watch. It had been only minutes since he'd first found the gasping Itzak. He continued to let his mind wander and was soon dwelling on his research.

Adam's thoughts were interrupted by a tall, well-dressed stranger entering Itzak's study. He assumed it was an official investigator and decided not to interrupt. Adam resumed his rhythmic gait, recalling his second encounter with Itzak Friedman.

Dressed casually in plaid shirt and jeans, Adam had arrived that day at the mouse research laboratory, a few doors down from the Genetics Department office. An early riser, Adam often breakfasted at work. Mandy Rogers always had hot coffee and Danish ready for his team of mouse researchers. Mandy was a "Jill-of-all-trades." One of Adam's favorites, she had been Life Sciences secretary before taking early retirement. Bored and missing her work, she returned on a temporary basis. Mandy assisted on all of Adam's projects.

Mandy greeted her boss. "Hello, Dr. Boatwright. Brrrr—it's cold out there. I nearly froze my tail."

"Hi, Mandy. This is a tropical heat wave compared to the chill from my nightmares."

"You're such an early bird. Aside from Dr. Friedman, you and I are the only people on this floor now. Dr. Friedman was like a schoolboy with a new toy. He just picked up the latest cell replication slides. He said he was on division fifty-five."

Since the door was open, Adam entered Itzak Friedman's office without knocking. The big man was busily writing on the blackboard covering the north wall.

"Hi, Itzak. I hear you've reached the fifty-fifth successive division of your cultured cells. That's incredible!"

"Yes, especially with human liver cells," he answered in his impeccable Oxford English, spoken with a distinctive Hebrew overtone. "These cells faithfully only divide about thirty times over a normal lifetime. Even in laboratory Petri dishes, untreated cells replicate only about thirty-five times before onset of gross carcinomas. It's impossible to find normal ones after about forty divisions."

Adam watched admiringly as Itzak sat down behind his very neat desk. "You've stumbled onto something! Cell-division limits are the root cause of aging. If Little Oscar is any indication, you've discovered the Fountain of Youth!"

Itzak's eyes fixed on Adam. "Definitely not. The high split counts are due to *synthetic* I-complex, and the latest cells are riddled with errors. A real person's liver would reach this same point after 155 years, but she would soon die of cancer."

"Your therapy would have doubled her natural life span."

Itzak stared at Adam with a hopeful expression. "As I already told you, I-complex injections in live humans aren't feasible yet. Did you have time to think about a possible solution?"

"Another agent could act as a *catalyst*," replied Adam, bubbling with excitement. "Ascorbic acid—vitamin C—comes to mind. Remember Nobel laureate Linus Pauling? He claimed mega dosages of vitamin C could prevent the common cold. Perhaps lower quantities of I-complex can be fortified with that."

"It might allow us to duplicate laboratory results in a functioning body. Then we'd really be onto something."

Adam reflected the man's enthusiasm. "Imagine the long-term implications! My God, man, you might end aging as we know it."

"I only want to ensure a complete life, not a long one," Itzak replied, his voice suddenly taking a somber tone. "It's *cancer* I'm fighting, not aging."

Adam totally missed the flip-flop in Itzak. "Right. But the lucky person who takes your 'elixir' would be immortal!"

"Damn it Adam, that's not a blessing! Men were not created to be immortal. Can you imagine what would happen if people don't die?"

Adam was caught totally by surprise.

Itzak bounded from the chair as if propelled by a coiled spring. "The rhythm of life depends on *death* and new *birth*. It would be tragic if researchers didn't die. There would be no fresh thinkers, because there wouldn't be room for the young. Old ways would never be replaced."

Adam tried to put a positive light on immortality. "Yes, but couldn't longer-living scientists still bring advancements?"

Looking like a professor from an old Hollywood movie, Itzak glared. "Only at a snail's pace, Adam. You know the best thinkers in your field are still in their thirties. When a molecular biologist reaches fifty, he's hardly capable of original thought. In physics, the creative life is even shorter—main idea makers are in their twenties."

Adam remained unconvinced that immortality was bad. "We scientists are just a minority. What about humankind in general? Wouldn't we all benefit from prolonged life?"

"No," Itzak's voice rose to almost a yell. "Definitely not! Change never seems to come from the old. The old *must* make way for the young."

Adam extended the debate. "But surely, a race of beings should benefit from prolonged life?"

Itzak's face turned beet red. A chill ran down Adam's back, as he feared the man was about to attack. Itzak stood up and pounded on his desk. "Damn it, Adam, I've never heard such stupidity. Your statements border on heresy. The whole basis of evolution is death and birth, death and birth! Without genetic diversity, of course, there can be no evolution. And you know that's absolutely necessary for survival in a changing world. And where do we get the genetic diversity?"

"Okay! Okay!" Adam surrendered, feeling like a scolded schoolboy. "I still think it would be grand if *humans* could live very long lives."

Itzak's original normal coloring returned as he continued, like a rabbi talking to his congregation. "The death of some *individuals* is tragic, especially when they die early. Look at Gershwin, Kennedy, and Jesus Christ. They all died young, and the world would be better if they had lived longer. But who can predict who will live and who will die? And what if Hitler had not grown prematurely senile and instead lived a full life? It works both ways."

On an intellectual level, Adam could accept Itzak's arguments against the notion of immortality. But he was still attracted to long life. Immortality had pulled at Adam, like some kind of sexual attraction.

Itzak's old-fashioned rotary telephone interrupted the heated discussion with a raucous ring. It was from Hannah Friedman.

"Hello. Of course, dear. Have you been taking the pain pills?"

"Yes—"

Adam waited for Itzak to get off the phone, anxious to continue the debate. But instead Itzak had dismissed him curtly. Without even waiting for Adam to leave, Itzak opened a worn lab book and started making handwritten entries.

Adam left Itzak's study feeling a bit used. He resented being abruptly dismissed without thanks. Although Itzak was clearly a genius on the level of Crick, Leakey, and Darwin, the man seemed to deserve his reputation for being as cold as ice.

3

Virtually Immortal

Adam continued pacing the LSB halls, waiting for the authorities to come and take charge of Itzak. Unable to rehash a new explanation for the man's death, he pondered over the cancer research project, dredging deeper into his mind.

Adam recalled the morning after that second meeting with Itzak. That unusual day had also begun with a dramatic scene in front of the Med Center, where he was about to lecture his class of medical students.

The three women wore only strips of carpet to simulate animal skins. The artificial pelts were covered with bright red paint. Their otherwise complete nakedness was obvious for all to see. The tall, mature blonde carried a sign: "Stop the Killing." She was followed by a longhaired twenty-something Asian holding a placard: "Free the Animals!" Rounding out the circle was a heavy-set woman with very long gray hair. Her placard showed drippings of simulated blood running through the words, "You could be next!" As they marched on the sidewalk in front of Central University Medical Center, they chanted in unison: "Stop the killing. No more animal research. Stop the killing."

A group of ironworkers had left their perch on a nearby high-rise and were whistling, making catcalls, and clapping to the rhythm. A large-bellied one cut into the circle behind the older woman and started to wag his ponytail in unison. Two grinning city police stood by watching the spectacle.

Adam had to snake his way through the crowd of gawkers blocking entry to the hospital complex. He used animals in his research and deplored the demonstrators' tactics. Animal rights interruptions had proven very costly.

The med school protestors should have known that the lion's share of animal-based research was done on the main campus of Central University. That was where Adam directed laboratory work carried out by a team of genetic researchers. His experiments sometimes involved using catheters to remove semen from mouse testes. Although the fluid extractions were painless, the mice did suffer considerable fright. Animals were essential to medical science, and their suffering was kept to a minimum.

That morning, Adam was working at his other job, professor of medicine.

Adam had trained as a surgeon. But prolonged periods of standing aggravated his leg, and lack of movement inflamed the nerves surrounding the scar tissue. Forced to leave surgery, he maintained his medical career on a part-time basis teaching.

Adam wore a coat and tie as he entered the cozy, round auditorium where ninety-three second-year medical students anxiously waited to hear their professor lecture. Standing behind the podium at the bottom of the bowl, Adam's pangs of stage fright disappeared as soon as he spoke.

"Today, we will talk about the human immune system and its role in fighting infection."

Adam immersed the students in technical details. They were especially interested when he described how the body copes with long-lived viruses from the herpes family.

No cure was known for the most common, *herpes simplex*. That virus causes recurring cold sores, or fever blisters, around the lips of most people. During periodic flare-ups of those surface infections, victims' bodies create chemical defenses. Those substances eventually force herpes back into a dormant state, although most immune systems never kill the stealthy virus.

At the end of a very exhausting hour, Adam invited questions.

One impatient student asked, "Dr. Boatwright, why do we have to study this? I won't use this stuff when I become a heart surgeon."

Adam gave the student a sympathetic stare. "Are you sure you'll be doing heart surgery? I was a surgeon, too, but now look what I'm doing! If we could predict exactly where you'll end up, we could customize the curriculum just for you. You could get your MD in months."

"Yeah, and then anybody could become a doctor," said an older student, as she glared at her smart-alecky colleague. It was Bonnie Burton, who worked part-time in the Genetics Department as Adam's research assistant.

Adam was the only joint professor at Central University who taught medicine and a separate science. He felt comfortable with that dual role, and remaining with medicine had made him a better geneticist. The reverse was also true, and he had a much broader perspective on the human condition than most physicians.

Adam was currently working on two major genetics projects. The first involved changing mice reproductive DNA, thereby altering their subsequent offspring. He hoped such procedures would someday eliminate hereditary diseases, such as cystic fibrosis.

Doing that required a detailed knowledge of what part of the DNA to change. Those molecules were huge, with billions of four elementary building blocks strung together in seemingly random patterns. But there was little randomness about those sequences. All plants and animals had their own distinct DNA molecules. Except for identical twins, individual people had unique variations.

Mapping human DNA was the focus of Adam's second area of research. He wasn't concerned with finding whether a particular segment characterized humanness as opposed to apeness. Rather his focus was more detailed, such as determining whether piece of human DNA might represent blue-eyedness or brown-eyedness. Each segment had to be tested and retested, a mind-boggling task. Researchers all over the world were working on that. Adam led a team that was developing computer software to find shortcuts and avoid blind alleys.

Later, Adam waited for the shuttle back to the main campus, his primary work place. The animal rights demonstrators were gone, but their paraphernalia and signs still cluttered the med center mall.

"Quite a scene!" a student had remarked as they waited at the stop. "There was a brawl between construction workers and the animal rights people—the men. It started when one of the hard-hats tried to grope the naked blonde with the big boobs. The cops joined in the fray. Two paddy wagons were used to haul them all downtown."

"Those people are nothing but terrorists," Adam muttered as he climbed into the bus.

Adam was still pacing the hallway. He remembered the afternoon following the Med Center protestors.

Adam had been excited at the prospect of seeing his wife Vera walk off the jet from Seattle. A concert violinist, she was returning from a guest appearance with the Seattle Symphony Orchestra. His affair with Vera Sokol had been a torrid one, and their relationship blossomed into a most unusual marriage in which Vera was his intellectual match.

The anxious husband had pulsed with excitement when Vera finally appeared. Her tallness had been imperceptible in the striking pink suit, so perfectly complementing her milky skin, blonde hair, and green eyes. Although Adam had always thought she was beautiful, Vera's demeanor had the most appeal.

Adam replayed the scene, remembering all details and every word of their ensuing conversation.

Vera was traveling light, one costume bag and her Stradivarius violin, which she always carried personally. They entered the first taxi in a long line of cabs.

"Oh Adam, I've missed you so much. God, it's great to see your gorgeous face. I've been thinking about you constantly."

"I've been thinking about you, too. Especially about Wednesday night."

"You horny sex maniac. I've got something even better in mind."

"So, how was the concert?" asked Adam, needing to change the subject.

Because Vera and Adam were best friends as well as lovers, she could talk with him about anything, in the minutest of detail. She answered his question as if she were speaking to another violinist. "I was a little bit off with my Sibelius. The drums were way too loud. They're supposed to create a haunting counterpoint for the violin, not a thunderstorm! But the conductor was sweet, and the strings didn't have the squeaky sound that can ruin a performance. The audience ate it up."

Although he was fascinated with music talk, Adam struggled to stay at her level. "I love your reading of that concerto. Sibelius sure had a big impact on Sweden."

"You're a little off," Vera gently corrected. "Jan Sibelius was a Fin and composed *Finlandia*, their national anthem. He was a very interesting guy. Did you know he was about ninety when he died?"

"At least he lived a full life. I was talking yesterday with Itzak Friedman about George Gershwin. He died way before his time. Gershwin might've had a similar impact on America if he'd lived until ninety."

Vera gave Adam a curious look. "Do you really think so? Wouldn't he have spent his last fifty years resting on his laurels?"

"Itzak Friedman would've answered with a big *yes*," Adam said.

Adam seized the moment and redirected the conversation, hoping for her analysis of the bothersome conversation with the Israeli scientist.

"Itzak doesn't think long lives are beneficial. We had a very heated discussion yesterday."

Adam admired Vera's ability to instantly tune in to his wavelength. He continued, letting his words sink in. "It's ironic that Itzak may be on the track toward longer life. Yesterday he reached a new milestone in the liver cell-division experiment. We should start calling him Ponce De Leon."

Vera grasped the heart of the issue. "Do you really think he can extend human life?"

Adam had expected her response. "Preliminary results are pointing in that direction."

Vera continued, precisely on target. "My goodness! If you can prolong life beyond seven or eight decades, where do you stop? Couldn't life go on without ever ending?"

Getting more than he expected, Adam responded in kind. "Theoretically, yes. But you're talking about cessation of aging, not immortality. Even a person who doesn't age would die someday—by accident, murder, or from some disease."

At that point Vera became visibly discomforted. "But, how long would that take? A person could live for centuries. That'd be awful."

Adam didn't perceive his wife's strong negative reaction. He was beginning to enjoy the conversation. "Some hardy soul could live for hundreds or thousands of years. The modifier is a bit overused, but the lucky guy would be *virtually* immortal."

"He wouldn't be lucky," blurted Vera, appearing irritated. "He'd see his loved ones die. He'd outlive his children and grandchildren. He'd watch the world decay because of human overpopulation. No more trees. No more fish. No more elephants."

Adam countered, "You're being melodramatic. The immortal's journey would be the most fascinating experience imaginable. To watch the changes, to see if your prognostications come true, I would welcome that."

4

Itzak Friedman

Born in 1948, shortly after Israel's independence, Itzak Friedman had been an excellent student. Before age ten, he won a government scholarship to study in England at Eton. From there he was admitted to Oxford, after which he completed graduate studies at Cambridge. He earned accolades for his pioneering research in the chemistry of physiology, helping to form the evolving field of molecular biology.

Itzak was a sabra, or second-generation Israeli. His father, Jakob Friedman, had survived World War II in the infamous Treblinka concentration camp. After the war, Jakob was smuggled into Palestine and joined the resistance. On the kibbutz Yelna, he met Itzak's mother, Ruth Weisenberg, child of Zionist settlers who arrived in the 1920s.

Itzak Friedman was a very private person. This closedness spilled over into his work, where he managed his research team with strict lines of authority. His staff members were like workers in an automobile assembly plant, knowing only those bits and pieces absolutely essential to their tasks. Although he directed them very knowledgeably, some felt that he was impossible to please.

Except for that day when Itzak told the secret of Little Oscar's longevity, Itzak had told nobody his secret agenda. His public objective was to study cell division and determine if it could provide a long-range cure for cancer. But Itzak's private agenda was curing his *wife's* cancer, and soon.

Itzak was envied by molecular biologists worldwide and admired by the entire Israeli scientific community. Consensus was that he would someday win the Nobel Prize. Itzak had never sought fame or fortune and felt his successes in molecular biology drew excessive attention. They were just natural extensions of his daily research. He didn't feel special—quite the opposite. Itzak believed himself to be unworthy. Indeed, he considered himself to be a *fraud*. His notoriety reinforced his fear of falling hard when the truth became known.

The "I am a fraud" syndrome is a common trait among high-achieving people with deep-seated feelings of inadequacy. They are motivated to hide their missing talent. Public perceptions are diametrically the opposite, but the "frauds" know better.

But there was an inexplicable, darker side to Itzak. He had never wanted to have children. He didn't even want close friends. His marriage was more a personal convenience than a product of love.

In his youth he underwent psychological counseling on recommendation of his employer, upset over Itzak's verbal abuse of colleagues. In two cases, he shouted loud and made threats. The psychologist never could explain the interpersonal difficulties. They seemed related to Itzak's relationship to his father, his banishment to boarding school at a tender age, and Jakob Friedman's experiences in Treblinka.

In response to misguided belief in his own incompetence, Itzak had kept his best research private, unwilling to suffer a public failure. All live-animal experiments had been conducted personally, with results recorded in secret journals, handwritten in Hebrew. Before his untimely death, he planned human experimentation. He did not want to wait for permission or possibly be denied the right to do it.

Ten years earlier, while still in Israel, Itzak had begun studies with I-complex and rats. He would have remained in Israel, except that a science writer got wind of Itzak's secret research. Fearing discovery, he accepted a visiting professorship at Central University Medical Center. One condition was that privacy be guaranteed. That was why the Physiology Department located him away from the main center of med school activity.

Adam recalled his last meeting with the healthy Itzak Friedman. It had been an impromptu get together at the Central Medical Center cafeteria.

Adam had been waiting for his hot sandwich, when he spotted Itzak, sitting alone. Adam watched with a hero worshipper's admiration as the scientist poked disinterestedly at his plate, like a child forced to eat his liver and green beans. The white-haired man looked more like a bored bookkeeper than a renowned scientist. Adam's eyes followed Itzak's every move, like a biology student watching Charles Darwin chalk theories on the blackboard.

The power of Adam's stare must have brought Itzak back to full consciousness, because he looked up and saw Adam gazing at him. Itzak frowned as he raised his arm to greet Adam and beckon him, as if summoning a child.

"Hello, Itzak. How's it going?"

"Another week, another round of dividing cells. I'm starting to get a little bored."

Adam shared his own research results and thoughts. "I wish my work was as boring as yours. Today we started to make implants in mouse testes. I'm hoping to start taking semen samples soon."

Itzak started to redden, blurting in a very loud voice, "Why are you interfering with an animal's reproductive organs?"

Adam was quite taken aback. "You're a scientist. You know everything we eventually do with people must first be tried on animals."

Itzak became even more excited. He shouted, "What you're planning to do is monstrous. It's ungodly to manipulate a man's sperm!"

"For god's sake, calm down," Adam begged, as other lunchers stared at the outburst.

But Itzak was a raging bull. Totally surprised and embarrassed by the commotion, Adam left the table.

"Come back here," Itzak yelled. "You charlatan! You're no better than a common murderer."

The entire cafeteria was hushed, all eyes pointing toward the source of the ranting. Adam wanted to hide. Never in his life had he been so embarrassed.

It took several minutes for Adam's equilibrium to return as he sat on the shuttle back to the main campus. On that ride, Adam wondered why Itzak had been so upset. The man had simply gone berserk.

Adam's memory of that encounter brought to mind the frenzied aftermath. Scenes of that pivotal noon hour were still vivid in his mind.

Adam had left the shuttle in a flustered state. To find solace, he went to see Mildred Rose, an adjunct professor and staff psychologist. Mildred and Adam had met years before while serving on the sabbatical leaves committee. She had helped him cope with several difficult events over the years. But those sessions had been more than mere visits to a shrink. Adam had sensed that Mildred was becoming strongly attracted to him.

Since the death of his first wife and until meeting Vera, Adam had been uncomfortable with romance and sex. For nearly fifteen years he had no love life, and his rare sexual encounters involved nobody connected to him professionally. A very handsome and charismatic fellow, Adam had attracted many women. Not savoring the chase, it was Adam himself who'd been pursued. Thus, he only dated brazen women. Invariably they, not Adam, had made an early break.

Adam had been tempted by Mildred, but nothing ever happened. Since remarrying, he had resolved his own feelings about Mildred in particular and women in general. That day, all he sought were insights regarding Itzak's strange behavior. Adam took advantage of their friendship, hoping for a quick professional opinion.

Mildred had been eating lunch at her otherwise bare desk when Adam barged in. Her maroon dress perfectly complemented her long, dark-red hair.

"Mildred, I need your help," Adam pleaded, skipping all preliminaries.

"It's good to see you too!" she'd said in a mock indignant tone.

"I'm sorry for being such a clod. I'm very upset."

"I only have fifteen minutes until my afternoon sessions begin," Mildred continued, leaving her food untouched. "What on earth is going on?"

Adam told Mildred about the confrontation with Itzak in the cafeteria. He briefly described his professional relationship with Itzak. She seemed to struggle maintaining her professional demeanor, as the facts about Itzak unfolded.

"What do you know about Dr. Friedman's personal life?" she asked.

"All I know," replied Adam, rubbing his neck, "is that he's married. He's visiting from Hebrew University and is possibly the most famous Israeli scientist. His father spent the war in the Treblinka concentration camp."

She put her finger on it instantly. "That's it! I've worked with survivors of the Holocaust. They're guilty about still living, after six million Jews died."

"But Itzak was born in 1948. His *father* was the one at Treblinka."

"I know," Mildred emphasized, looking pensively at Adam. "Parents transmit their pain and guilt to their children."

"Well, I think Itzak won't trust my further assistance. He'll probably never speak to me again,"

Adam remembered squirming, as she had looked him over. But she had been very professional with her reassurance. "Of course, Itzak will continue your relationship. It's typical with survivors' syndrome to have seemingly irrational outbursts. I think Itzak feels terrible about his treatment of you. I predict he'll soon make amends."

Mildred looked at the clock and announced, "I'm terribly sorry, Adam, but you have to leave. My next appointment is ready."

Adam stood, smiling. "Thanks, Mildred. You're a great shrink."

"Hey, just give me a call anytime."

5

Adam

The ambulance crew had just arrived when the tall stranger introduced himself. Detective Dick Reilly was a big man with a prominent nose, giving him a hawklike face. The cop's raptor image was reinforced by thin legs protruding from the brown trench coat. Like a bird of prey guarding its kill, Reilly directed the paramedics not to touch the body until the coroner arrived and then placed yellow tape on Itzak's door, warning that the premises were sealed.

Reilly commandeered an empty office and invited Adam to answer some questions. Adam had just begun to tell the detective what he found and what actions he took, when they were interrupted by the medical examiner.

Reilly talked with the coroner in the hallway, out of Adam's earshot. He returned with a grim expression. "It appears you slit his throat, Doctor."

"No. No. I performed an emergency tracheotomy. Itzak's windpipe was blocked and he couldn't breathe."

The hardened cop glared at Adam through steely eyes. "I'll check your story. Please let your secretary know where you'll be at all times. We'll talk again."

Adam left the hallway, and sat down in the empty staff lounge. Now that the police suspected foul play, Adam's worries magnified and his puzzlement grew.

Adam needed a diversion. He had to get away from the office. Away from the police and thinking about Itzak. He decided to go on a drive in his Porsche.

As he crawled out of town and away from the busy roads, Adam let his mind drift, grabbing memories from a lonely childhood.

His life would have been very different if his father had not been killed in the Korean War during the Inchon landing. His mother never recovered from the loss, and after long bouts of depression, she ended up in a sanitarium. Adam shuffled between relatives until he was eight, when Aunt Elizabeth placed him in St. Bartholomew's, a boarding school ran by the Brothers of Hope. His visits with family trickled down to nothing, and he was just ten when he last saw his mother, not long before she hanged herself in a sanitarium shower. Shortly thereafter, his aunt passed away and Adam became a permanent ward of the Brothers.

With the exception of religion classes and sessions with Brother Jonathan, Adam had enjoyed school. His smiles and eagerness to please won the hearts of his teachers.

Adam's workaholic tendencies had started with the *Daily Bugle* paper route. He fondly remembered rising in the dark and the long quiet bike rides over deserted streets. Outside jobs were special perks for top students, and he could spend paper-route earnings as he saw fit. They mostly financed his Four-H project.

Adam had an early love for animals. He began by raising pigeons for St. Bartholomew's animal husbandry program. Eventually, he bred racing pairs, which the school sold to raise funds for the remainder of its Four-H activities.

Adam took an early interest in mating his birds to produce superior offspring. He liked to sell the older birds, forming new pairs with the younger pigeons. He bought birds from outsiders, and his pigeons suffered little from inbreeding. He'd kept a detailed breeder's book, evidence that he had guided fourteen generations of racers. Hobbyists from all over the state sought the school's birds.

Adam was startled by wailing sirens and pulled to the side of the road. As he watched the small emergency caravan pass by, his thoughts fast-forwarded a few years.

After graduating from LaSalle High School, an all-boys' high school run by the Christian Brothers, Adam won a scholarship to Harvard, where he double majored in chemistry and modern languages. He arrived knowing French and German and reading ancient Latin and Greek. He soon added Russian and Hebrew to his repertoire.

Adam's main physical activity was climbing—beneath the ground, rather than on mountains. He started the hobby to strengthen his leg muscles, and it led to numerous caving expeditions to such places as Carlsbad Caverns.

His various hobbies and professional activities intersected with his love of animal paleontology. Animal evolution is a natural concern of geneticists, and he was particularly fond of dinosaurs, their physiology, and their world.

Like so many life scientists, Adam was concerned about environmental issues. He deplored deforestations and killing of endangered species and was ashamed of man's mindless onslaught against wildlife habitats. Adam feared the future, believing that even if men did not run out of food, they would certainly take all the wood, burn all the fossil fuel, fish the oceans empty, warm the planet, and destroy the ozone layer.

As much as he hated this depressing trend, Adam held a strong love for life and people in general and was totally committed to their betterment. That was his main reason for going into genetics after leaving surgery. He was content to let others deal with concerns about the planet. People were his major interest, with animals a close second.

That was paradoxical, because Adam had killed men in Vietnam. He had been a good marine and would have been a career military man, but for the tremendous personal tragedy before his second war tour and the calamitous injury suffered there. Like many veterans of that awful war, Adam had been changed by the experience. But unlike many ex-soldiers who no longer could cope with life, the war had been an annealing process that made Adam stronger.

The Vietnam experience had turned Adam into a pragmatic humanitarian. During convalescence from the shrapnel wound, feeling a strong need for atonement, Adam decided to become a doctor. Upon discharge from the Marines, he returned to Harvard, whose the medical school was happy to accommodate the disheartened war veteran.

Adam sailed through the program at an accelerated pace, landing a residency at Mt. Sinai Hospital in New York. A star intern, he was accepted for surgical training. But the physical demands were too great. He happily left medical practice for a new career in teaching and pure science.

Genetics was a comfortable choice and a field for which he had demonstrated an early aptitude. It was a science where he could use all of his medical training and could help tens of thousands of people, eventually millions, through genetic intervention to correct or prevent hereditary disease. That work brought inner satisfaction he had never before known.

6

I Get It, Dr. Frankenstein

The Boatwright's luxurious apartment was located on the tenth floor of Falcon Tower. The entry hall led into a spacious kitchen spilling into the large dining-living room. In one corner sat an oak table where Adam and Vera often ate. They sometimes enjoyed weekend breakfast on the adjacent balcony, all furnished in white wicker.

When not eating or working, Adam and Vera often spent hours leisurely sprawled on the long blue couch that vividly contrasted with the off-white Berber carpet. The oversized sofa dominated the living area and gave an easy view of the elaborate entertainment center. That electronic obelisk was topped by a sixty-inch screen TV, fed by video disk and old-fashioned cassette players. A complete sound system was integrated into the giant open-faced cabinet and had the appearance of a NASA control center.

The rest of the apartment was dominated by a master bedroom containing an open Roman bath with Jacuzzi. An adjacent bedroom housed personal computer, office equipment, a musician's stool and stand, an oversize cabinet full of sheet music, and a small stereo. That separate sound system allowed Vera to practice her violin in synch with recorded symphonic accompaniment. The entire room was acoustically insulated and had walls pocked with rubber tiles of varying thickness to soften outside noise and shield neighbors from bombardment by Vera's vibrating strings.

Across the short hallway was a guest bathroom and third bedroom. The Boatwrights referred to the latter as "The Orpheum," after the old famous vaudeville and movie theater chain. It contained their massive electronic film library.

Adam and Vera watched several movies each week in their home. The Orpheum's film archives contained over five thousand complete recordings, stored along the walls in floor-to-ceiling shelving. Those were tightly packed with ten layers of video cassettes and video disks. The closet was jammed with oversized filing cabinets, each drawer stuffed with movies recorded in various storage mediums.

Adam never acquired TV habits common to his generation. But he did develop an early taste for movies. The Brothers of Hope never allowed television in the orphanage. Instead they showed movie classics in the dining hall on Saturdays, using an antiquated movie projector aimed at the large white wall. A St. Bartholomew's alumnus loaned the free movie prints from his film distributorship.

In college, Adam quenched his thirst for film entertainment by attending revivals at the Boston colleges and patronizing regular theaters. While in the Marines, he paid a quarter for admission to see at least five movies per week. Years later Adam started renting movies. At "pennies on the dollar" he bought the entire inventory from a closing video store. Swapping from that hoard, Adam amassed his large collection.

Adam ordered a large sausage and pepperoni pizza. While they waited for delivery, he and Vera sat on the living room couch, sipping from glasses filled with a rich Cabernet. Adam was still in a state of disbelief over the previous day's traumatic event.

"It's terrible about Itzak," Vera said. "Will you ever find out if he had a cancer cure?"

"I think so," Adam replied. "It all seems very plausible. I want to investigate it myself."

"You're not taking over Itzak's research, are you? You're already so overloaded."

"I'd like to take it over. I've never been so fascinated with a project. You know my staff does the heavy work. My projects don't require my complete attention."

"So, it's already a *project*. I knew it. I'm sick of talking about cancer and immortality. Tell me about your current projects."

"Where do I start?"

"Start with the mice. But keep it nontechnical. Okay?"

Adam began, his voice animated. "I love that aspect of my work. We're making good progress on our germ-line intervention experiments."

"Wait a minute. You're always tossing technical words around. I understand a lot, but jargon gets in the way. What in blazes is a germ line? I keep visualizing a string of tuberculosis bacteria marching down some derelict's windpipe, looking for a cushy home."

Adam chuckled. "Sorry, honey. By germ line, I'm using the word in the same sense as in 'germinate'—what plants do when they grow from seed. Only it's more like the creation of the seed."

"Now I'm really confused. Germ line is plant sex? I thought you dealt only with the animal kingdom. Horny mice, not promiscuous plants."

"We're talking about sex, but not the physical act. Think of a germ as an animal's essence, as mirrored in her DNA. The germ line is like a family tree contained in the DNA. Modifications to the germ line don't change the animal itself. They involve revising its *reproductive* DNA, so that only the offspring are affected. Think of germ-line intervention as *planned mutation*. The change is permanent. All of the animal's future family tree will reflect the modified germ line."

Vera smiled maliciously. "I get it, Dr. Frankenstein. You don't create one monster. You create a whole line of monsters, father to son to grandson, and so on, ad infinitum."

Adam gave his wife a pained look. "You've got it. But our changes are beneficial. It's not fair to use the connotation 'Frankenstein.' Besides,

I'm dealing with mice—human experiments are a long way off. Also, if changes are bad we'll break the line—"

Vera interrupted, reflexively completing his dangling sentence—"by killing all the creatures on that family tree. What if you make a mistake with a real person?"

Adam found it challenging to keep up with Vera—especially with issues not totally settled to himself. As usual, he gave considerable thought before responding.

"We won't work with humans until we experiment with animals. We'll start with some innocuous trait, like ability to roll the tongue. We'd take a man who is a non-tongue-roller, change his reproductive DNA to activate the tongue-rolling gene, and wait and see if his children inherit the gene."

Vera pounced. "That could take years. And, suppose your change causes the kid's tongue to turn out malformed. What then?'

"That'd be highly unlikely. We first have to know exactly which gene location to tinker with. I have a team working to determine that."

Vera kept going. "That's your human genome mapping project. What's a human genome? When I hear those words, a little elf-like gnome comes immediately to mind. A mouse genome sounds like an incredibly cute creature, like those on Christmas ornaments."

Adam laughed vigorously, trying to give a straight answer. "It refers to the collection of human genes. Our goal is to identify physical location on DNA molecules for a gene's activator. These are chemical switches, most of which direct development of the fetus. A few will also direct various aspects of body chemistry, such as hormone production."

"So your map of the genome tells you where to change reproductive DNA. Do I have it right?"

"On the button. But it's not a map in the geographical sense. It's a listing of DNA locations of important genes. My group is developing software to speed up and simplify the process."

"Wow! And I though Mozart was complex. You win the prize."

7

Dave Wiley

Adam was downcast as he parked his car. He usually enjoyed the ten-minute drive to campus over tree-lined streets evoking scenes from a Manet painting. But Itzak Friedman's untimely death hung over him like a dark cloud.

It was a five-minute walk from the parking lot to Adam's office in the Life Sciences Building, the largest complex on the Central University campus. Today he had an appointment with Dave Wiley, chairman of the Genetics Department, to lay out plans for the upcoming budget review. Adam would rather visit the dentist than haggle over funding details.

Adam entered the building, its halls filled with the hustle and bustle of students. The clamor always reminded him of his undergraduate days at Harvard. One young couple was having a heated discussion, triggering a flash in his mind about an old girlfriend. That memory quickly faded as Adam switched thoughts to his meeting.

All biology-related classrooms were on the first floor, along with instructional laboratories. As Adam climbed the stairs, it felt like stepping into another world. At the top, he was now in the "Monastery," the student nickname for the upper floors of the LSB, where very serious activity took place.

Adam stopped at the third floor, where the Genetics Department was located. Few younger students ever went there, since Central had only one junior–senior course in genetics. The genetics program had a sprinkling of older, more serious genetics graduate students, many having made the two-mile shuttle run from the medical school. Most were working on a master's in genetic counseling, hoping someday to give advice to potential parents having histories of Tay Sachs or sickle cell anemia.

Adam entered the department office, wearing slacks and a tweed coat, his blue shirt making a tasteful backdrop to his striped tie. He felt overdressed, but appearances worked wonders with his dapper boss.

"Hello, Jill," he greeted. "I trust you've recovered from the shock of Itzak's death."

"What a mess," Jill replied, obviously still disturbed. "That poor man. I hardly knew him."

"Neither did I. I presume Dr. Wiley's already in."

Jill Yamamoto epitomized the department secretary. She did all the real work, while her boss played academic politics. Whenever instructors wanted to change schedules, they went to Jill. Whenever they wanted to set up a special display, Jill was there to help. She was good at her job and liked Adam Boatwright because he was down-to-earth and always treated her with respect. Few staff knew she had a master's degree in Asian history. In many ways she was intellectually superior to the scientists, who mostly were outrageous prima donnas stuck in extremely specialized ruts. But Adam was different with her, nearly always able to engage in a round of intelligent conversation.

"Watch out," Jill warned. "Dr. Wiley's grumpy today. But you're the best therapy for him. Your visits always seem to rejuvenate him."

"I'll do my best. Wish me luck," Adam said, feigning cheer as he reached for the door to the chairman's inner office.

"Ah, Adam. I've been itching to see you. Take a seat."

"Hi, Dave," Adam greeted apprehensively. "Jill's still shook up about Itzak's strange death."

"Terrible, Adam. That was a great loss."

"I hope everything's okay with you otherwise.

The chairman was ten years older. Slightly balding, Dave Wiley was a short, heavyset man with bushy eyebrows protruding from under his strong glasses, giving him an owl-like look. He was dressed in his "uniform," a conservative, gray three-piece suit.

"Just the usual earth-shattering problems and forest fires," Wiley replied in a serious tone as he stood and paced around the room.

"The congressional oversight committee is looking to cut the National Science Foundation budget. I think we'll be unscathed, but they're responsible for 20 percent of our funded research."

"Is this a bad time to request increases in staffing?"

"On the contrary! You're my most productive researcher. I'm not writing blank checks today, but I'm willing to hear you out. I get a double-whammy out of you. You're the only guy here directing *two* major research projects."

"Thanks, Dave. Will the NSF grants adversely impact our computer programming for genome mapping?"

Wiley continued to pace, and Adam found his constant movement annoying. It was easier to gaze at the red-haired lady in his oversized Toulouse-Lautrec poster.

"No, no," Wiley replied nervously. "NSF knows the importance of mapping DNA."

Adam shifted his eyes back to Wiley as he spoke. "We're making great progress. Jude Ojukwe's program pinpoints DNA sources of hereditary disorders like Alzheimer's and Huntington's disease. It'll considerably narrow our search for their genetic markers."

Political animal that he was, Wiley always had the right thing to say. "Wonderful. Your software project is safe."

Adam had never felt entirely comfortable with Wiley and was compelled to touch all bases. "What about funding for mouse germline intervention? That's where the real genetics take place."

Wiley sat down, tapping his fingers on the big oak desk. "They accept the brilliant connection of your computer programming and mice. I've juggled funding so that the National Cancer Institute will sponsor it."

Adam responded diplomatically. "Your alchemy in turning sentiment into dollars is amazing. You have such a grasp of the big picture."

Wiley smiled proudly. "That's what I'm here for."

Adam stared intently at Wiley. "I gather you've conveyed the importance of our animal experiments. Physical intervention is essential for getting concrete results from the DNA mapping exercise."

"Indeed, I have, Adam," Wiley answered, sitting now and rocking in his chair. "They know 'hands-on' genetic engineering is essential."

Adam took this opportunity to make an announcement. "Good, because we're close to breakthrough. We're about to alter the germline in white-eared males so they produce black-eared offspring."

Standing erect, as if speaking to an audience, Wiley replied. "That's great. Our sponsors know genetic diseases can't be cured without modifying DNA itself. But I couch it in sexier terms. You are in charge of planned mutations, which you accomplish using sperm cells as the medium."

"*Mutation* is the layman's term."

"I get a kick telling bureaucrats that Dr. Boatwright is not exactly Dr. Strangelove, but he is certainly a doctor of stranger love."

Adam resented being the butt of jokes, but instead of showing displeasure, he took advantage of the interlude to make his pitch. "Here's the bottom line. I need two more programmers and one new lab technician."

"Your request couldn't come at a worse time," Wiley replied with semi-feigned somberness. "But you do get results, and you're highly visible. Your fallout attracts money for the entire department."

"Thanks. I appreciate that."

In an official tone, Wiley gave his pronouncement. "The best I can do is one programmer and one tech. That's only if you don't tell Charles or Fred. I don't want those pests accusing me of favoritism."

Adam had got what he wanted. "Don't worry, Dave. I'll say my new staff are on loan from the med school."

"Yeah," Wiley said in a teasing tone, "and I'll bet you tell the doctors downtown we buy your fancy equipment there. Your MD status gives you immediate acceptance by the medical fraternity. But your Berkeley genetics PhD is more helpful getting grant money."

Ever cautious around his boss, Adam tried hard to stay in his chairman's good graces. "I guess I made a good choice, leaving surgery and going back to school."

Wiley was mercenary and a very superficial scientist, and Adam disliked him. Why was Wiley being so nice to him now?

Wiley sat again, gazing curiously at Adam. "While we're on the subject of med school, there's something I've been meaning to ask. You've been working with their hotshot, Itzak Friedman. What a tragic death. How old was he?"

"We were the same age, but he looked ten years older."

"Well, I've been very curious about him, even before his death. Every time I passed his lab, there was a beehive of activity."

Adam was primed to report on Itzak. "He let me in on a few secrets."

Wiley's curiosity was transparent. "Great. Friedman was just a tenant here. I didn't want to be a snoopy landlord and peek inside his office. I know Friedman was a molecular biologist with a PhD, not an MD, but I have no details. What's been going on?"

The question was just for show. Adam knew that nothing happened in the LSB without Wiley's knowledge.

"Itzak's research involved cell division. He wanted to nip cancer in the bud, at the cellular level. You know that carcinomas result from faulty cell replication, which can trigger wild growths instead of normal cells. Itzak found an agent to help dividing cells make perfect copies. He may have found the cancer cure we've been hoping for."

Wiley reminded Adam of a cartoon character having flashing dollar signs for eyes. "This is impressive stuff. I wish we could inherit his funding. Do you think he would have gotten results?"

Adam breathed deeply, trying hard to hide his annoyance at Wiley's tone. "Yes. Itzak had artificially duplicated human liver cells and reached the fifty-fifth successive split."

"My God, Adam! Wouldn't a living person be two or three hundred years old for his cells to survive that long?"

"You're thinking of muscle tissue. This is liver. A female would be approximately 155 years old after her liver cells divided that many times. But the experiment isn't over. Itzak was getting a new cell generation every week."

"Adam, we have to move that project to *our* department. What a gold mine!"

Wiley jumped up and walked briskly to the door, opening it to signify the end of their meeting.

Dave Wiley stared at Adam as he left. Although the department chairman thought Boatwright was a bit of a boy scout, Wiley was jealous of his intellect. He wished he had the personal talent for vacuuming up the grant money the way Boatwright did. But Wiley had few equals as puppet master, and he loved to pull strings and watch his professors jump. Boatwright was his favorite pawn, a man whose tremendous energy might be tapped to considerable advantage.

8

Go Indy!

It had only been two days since Itzak's death, and Adam was still putting the pieces together. Walking briskly that morning on the main campus, Adam would be meeting with his mouse research group.

Adam was wearing his winter "uniform"—slacks and a long-sleeved striped sports shirt. He was snugly covered by an old brown-leather naval aviator's flight jacket, with a collar of synthetic fur and festooned with many zippered pockets, now stuffed with a random assortment of ticket stubs, old shopping lists, receipts, and lab notes. Giving further protection against the cold was the wide-brimmed, brown hat. In the rain, Adam preferred that hat to his ungainly umbrella, which pulled him off balance as he carried the usual arm-load of books and folders.

Adam was not surprised when a carload of teenagers passed by, one of the passengers yelling, "Go Indy!"—a tribute to the Indiana Jones movie character. There was more than a superficial resemblance between himself and Professor Jones. Like that character, Adam loved physical adventure, which he primarily acted out in his caving expeditions. But otherwise, Adam's gymnastics were strictly *mental*. His own job gave him tremendous psychological thrills, and Adam had no craving for Indiana's dreadful chases—being pursued by snakes, head-hunters, or worse.

Indiana Jones' on-screen close calls were tame stuff compared to Adam's own goblins and mental challenges. The demons inside were a mental drain, and he found the best therapy was to take off every few months for an exotic caving adventure that could rival those of the movie hero. Adam craved physical demands, because only they could completely crowd out everything else from his mind. He had chosen an activity filled with desperate thoughts—such as getting from one crevasse to the other side, how to climb a sheer rock wall, or whether he would finally crawl out from the confines of a narrow passageway, barely thicker than his rib cage. Two weeks of caving, and he would be refreshed for more months of mental challenges at work.

The mouse germ-line intervention group included several well-established scientists, with a few junior people serving as technicians and research assistants. The meeting opened with a round of nonscientific gossip. Adam heard his name mentioned together with Itzak Friedman's and confronted the issue head-on. "I guess everybody has heard about Dr. Friedman's untimely death."

"What exactly happened?" somebody asked.

"We won't know until we get the coroner's report. I found Itzak choking and performed an emergency tracheotomy. He died shortly thereafter."

Adam shifted gears. "Did anybody witness the spectacle last week in front of the med center?"

"Three naked animal rightsists were accosted by blue collars," a women technician responded. "I hope the protestors don't come over here," she said shaking her head.

Adam stood up, as if about to make a speech. "We have to make contingency plans for just that."

Adam told about a similar incident, years before at Berkeley. Months of research were lost when animal rights protesters desecrated his lab. The vandals took every cage outside and released all the animals, including infected ones. He lost an entire genetic strain of mice, specially reared for their susceptibility to anthrax. "It's fortunate no cattle were nearby," he said. "They all would've been shot to prevent a hoof-and-mouth disease outbreak."

Laboratory mice are special genetic strains, carefully reared for hundreds of generations. Let loose, they would suffer a fate similar to that of a Chihuahua released in wilderness full of wolves and grizzly bears. Most Berkeley mice experienced their only hours of freedom being eaten by owls or cats.

"There would be lots of white-spotted mouse babies if our little sex maniacs get out," a post-doctoral fellow joked, alluding to coloring the laboratory mice would pass to offspring from mating with their wild cousins.

Everybody except Adam chuckled. He usually liked such raw humor and even tolerated the staff's practical jokes—as long as they didn't cut into project productivity.

"That may be true in the tropics," Adam said. "But our little guys wouldn't last one cold night outside. I'm more concerned about disruption. I know from sad experience we can't stop terrorists from breaking into the LSB. That's why I plan to duplicate important experiments at a remote site."

"My parents' ranch is just twenty miles from here," perky lab tech Sylvia Beckwith announced. "We have a spare shed where I raised rabbits for Future Farmers. They'd be happy to rent space to us—cheap."

Adam was grateful for the surprise offer. "Great. Why don't you ask them?"

Adam continued with his plea. "Some of you will have to shuttle to the remote laboratory. It'll be taxing, but in the long run we'll all benefit."

The two research associates reported next. First was Jack Chin, a fourth-generation Chinese American who, like Adam, was a Berkeley PhD specializing in molecular biology and genetic engineering. On a small scale, Jack had cloned DNA molecules and made minor modifications to the DNA itself.

After giving a very detailed progress report, Jack concluded with thoughts about working off campus. "We can manage with what we have, even at the remote site. But, all bets are off if protestors pour buckets of blood on the equipment."

"At least, blood will wash," remarked Adam, his face reflecting dread. "These guys only simulate blood with red paint. That's much worse.

"Okay, Rita, update us on your progress."

Rita Morales had a doctorate from the University of Texas at Austin. Proud of her Mexican heritage, she was wearing a bright red-and-green blouse from her grandmother's village in Oaxaca. Her brown hair framed a handsome face, its seriousness intensified by the penetrating look from her dark eyes.

Using special computer software from Adam's programming group, Rita's job was finding which DNA segments to replace. She had some success to report. "I've located the coordinates for black ears. I'll be working with Jack to verify them."

"Great! We can accept the germ-line hypothesis if we actually get black-eared offspring from white-eared parents."

Adam reminded the staff that black-earedness wasn't present in the parents' original genes. They were about to alter the papa's germ-line DNA, so that half his pups from white-eared mothers would be born with black ears. Black-earedness would become be a permanent trait of all descendants from those mice.

"Okay everybody, back to work."

Adam thought about the project's next phase as he watched the team disperse.

Others had proposed the original idea of germ-line intervention. The black-eared mice would improve the technology for passing along altered genes. Adam's team was almost ready for human experiments.

Since the genetic markers were well established for Huntington's disease, its carriers were promising subjects for experiments. Adam planned to remove Huntington's from the DNA of volunteer fathers who feared having children. Their sperm-generating cells would then be permanently altered. Months later, he would test sperm samples to ensure absence of the Huntington's marker and give the patients worry-free clearance to become fathers.

Some felt it was sexist to concentrate on *male* germ-line intervention. But all eggs are formed in baby girls, before they are born, and it would be impossible to alter a mother's germ lines. That would require surgical modification of every individual egg. Adam took comfort that the *daughters* and sons of a father with altered sperm would carry germ lines reflecting his changed reproductive DNA.

9

The Treblinka Connection

The med school Physiology Department directed Adam to gather loose ends from Itzak Friedman's untimely death. Since the office was under police quarantine, Adam was only allowed to enter under escort.

An African-American policeman carefully peeled back the yellow tape sealing the premises. Together, they entered the study and hop-scotched around the chalked edges where Itzak's body had fallen. Adam was surprised at the amount of caked blood spread over the Persian carpet.

He was dismayed to see several extended drawers poking out of Itzak's four large filing cabinets. In their search for evidence, investigators had thoroughly scrambled the files, some of which lay askew and spilled on the floor. Adam opened the third drawer of the first cabinet, searching for Itzak's records of Little Oscar.

Itzak had believed computers to be unsafe havens for important results and had confessed to having visions of some hacker gobbling up his life's work. Adam himself once lost six months of effort because of a mysterious computer accident.

As the bored officer watched, Adam meticulously scoured the files, arranging and sorting them as he went. After two hours of flipping through the pendaflex file holders, his fingers stuck on the gum of a badly stained manila envelope. He scanned the printed message:

Official Copy
Trial Depositions
Nuremberg, February, 1946

Nuremberg was where the Nazi war criminals were tried after World War II. There, the victorious allies prosecuted top German officials and death-camp operators.

Adam opened the unsealed envelope and removed a stack of papers. The top page was handwritten in Hebrew by Itzak Friedman. He had no trouble translating:

11-15-95

My poor father. How could a human endure what he did? By all rights, he should never have survived. I am strictly a fluke. What absolute degradation!

The first few court forms listed the remaining pages as depositions for the war-crimes tribunal. They had been used in prosecuting the infamous Nazi doctor, Hermann Kistlring. Adam knew of the man's chilling reputation at the Treblinka concentration camp.

Adam scanned through the pages of Jakob Friedman's testimony, presented in journal form. There was no need to translate from the original German. The images flowed through his brain as if he were watching a horror movie.

Jakob told of cellmates who had mysteriously disappeared. There was the grisly tale of Sebastian, one of whose toes had been amputated each day. When the Nazis started to cut off fingers, he hanged himself. Adam was just about to leave the room to stem the upsurge in his stomach, when he came to Jakob's narration of his own experiences.

I am placed in a warm room. The doctor enters and asks me to ejaculate into a bowl. He leaves. It is impossible for me to do as he asks, as I cannot even get an erection. Although I am young, I have had very few erections since arriving in Treblinka. He returns and is very angry when he sees the empty bowl. He says, "I'll make sure you give me the sample."

After a few minutes, the doctor enters the room with a young woman prisoner. He says, "I know you can fill the bowl to the brim with her help." He gives a wicked laugh and leaves.

We talk in Yiddish. She has a two-year-old child who is being kept in a special nursery compound. She will do anything to keep her child alive.

I explain my problem, but I cannot bring myself to ask for her help. She says, "You must do as they say. My daughter's life depends on it."

She then gently messages my manhood. I am extremely embarrassed. I have never done such a thing with a stranger. But nothing happens. She begins to cry, sobbing, "Oh, what am I going to do? My lovely Natalia."

She tries again, telling me that she has only done this with her husband, and she kisses me there. I feel terribly guilty, and concentrate on my last sexual encounter. I try to blot out the present. It isn't easy for me to do. I am so ashamed.

Finally I reach orgasm. There is no pleasure in it. I might as well be pissing into the bowl. She thanks me profusely. I feel like a combination of whorehouse customer, pimp, and prostitute. She leaves. I never see her again.

Adam scanned through page after page of similar recollections. He wondered what the semen collections were used for. He choked when he read Jakob's last record.

When I get back to my cell, the fellow prisoners jeer and call me a sex pervert and worse things.

One of them tells the rest to shut up. He says he knows what the Nazis are using my sperm for. He says it is being used in the animal experiments. He knows because he has to clean cages and dispose of the dead creatures. They gave him this job because he used to teach medicine. He says that at first the doctors injected sperm into the vaginas of rhesus monkeys, trying to get them pregnant.

He describes how one poor monkey actually did have a fetus grow inside. One veterinarian remarked that she would be the mother of a human mule. The monkey spontaneously aborted a one-kilogram fetus impossible to describe. The monkey weighed only ten kilos herself. It finally dawned on the Nazis that it would be impractical to make monkeys pregnant. But they never gave up.

Instead, they mixed monkey eggs and the sperm in an attempt to get an embryo. A few took. These they implanted into human females in the hope that a full term pregnancy could be achieved.

The prisoner did not know if they succeeded.

I feel more horrible. Not only am I responsible for degrading those women, but I am also a participant in human bestiality and the deaths of numerous animals. Who knows how many mothers carried my bastard monkey offspring. If I were a braver man I would have followed poor Sebastian. I vow never, ever to become a father.

Adam noticed that the sheet was crinkled and stained, as if it had once been out in the rain.

The poor souls!

The New York Times was lying on the table beside the Falcon Tower mailboxes. Adam picked it up, got the mail, and took the elevator to the tenth floor. Vera would soon be home from rehearsal. In need of cheering, Adam was extremely anxious for her presence.

He began to read the paper, usually a favorite pastime but now overtaken by dread. He did not exude his usual confidence and sense of accomplishment. Not today.

Adam skipped to the Tuesday science section. The first-page story told how DNA might be used as a high-speed "computer" for solving the famous mathematical conundrum—the shortest routing for a traveling salesman visiting every customer. As he read the article with fascination, Adam started to feel better. Continuing with the story, he turned the page and felt a kick in the stomach. The story below blared the headline:

Ethicists Wary over New Gene Technique's Consequences

Adam skipped to that story, which discussed germ-line gene therapy. The story quoted a Dartmouth ethics professor, who referred to type of research that Adam was doing with mice experiments. The article criticized changing peoples' reproductive DNA, claiming that altering germ cells might actually cause harm. Adam felt more physical pain when the article questioned if any good at all could come from such change—even if the target disease were eliminated. Adam could barely finish the article, which questioned the right of parents to control the characteristics of their offspring.

Adam couldn't quell his pangs of anxiety. Beginning to question his own philosophy toward biological science, he poured himself a generous serving of Scotch. He took the first sip just as Vera arrived home, wearing a black "matador" suit. Her long blonde hair was braided and wound into a decorative bun. Adam hardly noticed her striking appearance.

"Thank God you're home! We have to talk," Adam blurted with a troubled, agonized tone.

"I guess this Itzak thing still has you down. Oh, darling. All day I've been wanting to hold you, to comfort you."

Adam stared at Vera with a pained expression. "Yeah. I still can't believe what's happened. But time marches on. Itzak's body had been cold just a day when I was directed to tidy up his affairs."

"What ghouls!" Vera exclaimed, her expression showing disgust. "But that's not why you're upset, is it?"

"Physiology's haste was stressful. But you're right. Something is bothering me, and it's not directly related to Itzak," Adam replied, doubting his own sanity. "I'm having serious doubts about my entire research plan."

"What prompts this?" Vera asked, her face showing deep concern. "You're the most together person I know."

Adam told Vera about the Nuremberg testimony. After she had read the papers, he showed her the *Times* article.

Vera warmly presented a logical evaluation. "Adam, what's done is done. You're overreacting. I agree with the article's Dr. Brinster when he says we can't put the genie back in the bottle."

Adam responded with despair. "Although I'm not trying to impregnate monkeys, I am 'monkeying' with the genes of mice. I don't throw away their lives frivolously, but some animals do die. Nobody is coerced, but we do modify semen. I have a lot in common with the Nazi doctor, Kistlring."

Vera began to smooth out the rough spots. "No, Adam, you don't. He was a monster whose goal was to kill and to experiment in a sadistic way. Your goal is the noble one of eliminating diseases and saving lives."

Vera's words were like a balm to Adam's ego and he began regaining composure. "But are my ends any better? Will humankind really benefit in the long run from my research?"

Vera continued, spicing her logical deduction with feelings. "Adam, only God can answer that question. You should feel good about what you're doing. It's grossly unfair to compare yourself with Nazis. One reason I love you is my deep respect for your work. Ninety-nine percent of the world would agree with me. Why should we care about the other one percent?"

Adam felt warm again and his stomach stopped churning. He stared into Vera's eyes, and in an upwelling of emotion told her, "And you're always there when I need you. I love *you* so much."

"I love you too, more than you'll ever know," she said before kissing her husband passionately.

10

A Tale of Two Wives

It was opening night of the Central Symphony Orchestra. Adam beamed with pride as Vera entered the stage to receive loud and long applause. Perched in his dress-circle seat wearing a formal tux and white tie, he felt like a stuffed penguin on display. Adam was grateful the ordeal only happened once a year. But for now he was thrilled at the prospect of hearing his wife.

Adam loved classical music, especially the violin. And Vera was an exquisite player. Already a world-class performer, the portents for Vera were very positive. Her agent expected she would eventually join ranks with Itzak Perlman and the immortal Jasha Heifetz to become one of the top violinists ever.

Vera played the Brahms with much emotion, her vibrating fingers gliding up and down the strings like a hummingbird sampling flowers on a hanging vine. Her bow moved in quick broad strokes, the sway of her body driving the rhythmic motion. And the sounds emanating from her centuries-old Stradivarius violin were like haunting chords from a human spirit voice, at times quickly rising from a throaty moan to a shrill banshee's wail. Those pulsating sounds seemed to resonate from Vera's body itself, instantly magnified by her Strad and then enhanced by the eighty-five musicians on stage.

Watching Vera play in concert gave Adam a psychic high, as if he had taken a mind-altering substance. Tonight, the music and Vera were almost too much for Adam to bear. His own body and mental chemistry began to pulsate with the music, as Vera led two thousand people through this charismatic Brahms' piece. Several times, as he gazed into Vera's straining face, Adam had to rub tears from his eyes.

Vera dawdled the next morning, savoring her memories from the night before, especially Adam telling how much her Brahms had moved him. Adam had fun at the banquet, proving groundless fears of an evening spoiled by fallout from Itzak's death.

Always standing tall, Adam's brave attempt to save Itzak's life raised her husband to a new pinnacle. It was painful to hear him question his own ethics. A break would do him good.

Vera blocked out two weeks in late spring for a vacation. She wanted a sun-filled visit to the Bahamas for snorkeling and scuba diving. But Adam convinced her to help him explore the recently discovered Lechuguilla Cave in New Mexico. That incompletely mapped complex of hollow limestone was open only to expert cavers and their closely supervised novices.

Vera had little time for hobbies, even as a young girl. The violin had consumed most of her childhood free time. Things improved after finishing college at the Julliard Institute, when she took occasional trips to Massachusetts. A school friend had a summer home on Cape Cod, where they beached the days and enjoyed evenings in coffee houses of Provincetown, the trendy commercialized village at the cape's tip.

Her thirst for espresso extended into the present, and she usually drank it at Father Nature's, a local hangout for the players from Hillary Hall, home of the Central Symphony. Today, Vera was ordering a cup of latte, when she spotted Marty Sweet, the chubby cellist with a disposition to match his name.

Joining him, she teased, "Hi 'Pablo,' how's the arm?"

"Hello, beautiful," Marty smiled. "Not so bad today. I have to exercise it every fifteen minutes when I play. The doc says I have

Carpel Tunnel Syndrome in my right wrist, even though I hardly move it to push the bow. I ought to switch hands and bow with the left."

"Then you'd be the only switch-hitting cellist to play the Shostakovich. I squeeze a rubber ball every ten minutes at practice. It would be weird doing it in the middle of a concert, although I'm tempted."

"My exercise would look more ridiculous. Imagine me swinging my right arm like a blimp's propeller. I'd blow Nancie's music off the stand. Remember the Disney cartoon with Clara Belle, Goofy, and the gang playing Von Suppes' *Light Cavalry Overture*?"

"Boy, do I!" She laughed with gusto.

Their talk turned to more serious matters.

"Your poor husband had quite a time over that Israeli scientist," Marty said. "How's he taking it?"

Vera was grateful for the opportunity to unload. "Adam's a tough cookie. It's ironic that he'll inherit Dr. Friedman's project. That'll be *three* major projects, plus a full teaching load. He has over a dozen people working for him now."

"And I only have the one job," Marty noted.

"Yes, but you're so good. You could do the concert circuit."

"I would, if I didn't hate flying," Marty admitted.

Changing the subject, Vera asked about the upcoming concert. "What do you think of the Lalo piece?"

They had talked shop for about ten minutes, when Vera looked at her watch and excused herself. "Got to run. See you tomorrow."

"So long, beautiful."

It was pleasant outside, and Vera decided to walk to Falcon Tower. The rhythm of her steps caused her mind to drift back two and a half years.

It was on a side trip to Boston that she'd met Adam, who had been attending a conference on genetic engineering. Vera and Lucille had gone to a movie, *Dangerous Liaisons.* As they were navigating on their way to seats in the crowded theater, she stepped on Adam's foot.

"Ouch! I didn't know the Viet Cong were coming," she could still hear Adam saying. Vera had been terribly embarrassed. But it was he who apologized first for being so sarcastic. She soon learned she had stepped on the foot of Adam's war-injured leg. After the movie, they accepted his invitation to join him and a colleague for a beer.

Vera and Adam spent their first real date walking the beaches of Cape Cod. She was intrigued by the deep sadness he covered with a veneer of humor and forced cheerfulness. At first she went with Adam out of curiosity, but she soon became very attracted to him. For Adam, it was love at first sight.

Vera had just entered the Falcon Tower apartment when the phone started ringing. It was her sister, Nora, who was undergoing chemotherapy for breast cancer. Vera's mother had died of breast cancer when she was only ten, and her aunt Candice had died from the same disease. Vera wondered if she would be next.

After talking with Nora, Vera's thoughts returned to Adam. Vera and he both lost their mothers at a young age. She thought that was quite a coincidence. But Adam's losses had been much greater. She remembered his sad story.

Adam had met his first wife in his senior year at Harvard, thirty-two years before. Like Adam, Judy Boatwright was a student of languages—in written form only, since scarlet fever had taken her hearing when she was eight. It was from Judy that Adam learned American Sign Language.

Judy and Adam were married soon after platoon leader's training, during his first months in the Marines. They had two children, Anne and Janet. Adam enjoyed parenting, sharing all the child-rearing chores equally with Judy.

Before Adam was to leave for a second Vietnam tour, Judy was driving with the children to their rented home in the South Carolina countryside. She was crossing railroad tracks, yards from the spot where kids had placed a piece of metal roofing, obscuring the crossing signal. She never heard the frantic wailing of the train engine's horns just before it slammed into the car at sixty miles per hour. All three of them were killed instantly.

Out of compassion, the Marine Corps offered to remove Adam from the Vietnam docket. But he insisted on going anyway. He was in such deep despair that only the ultimate catharsis—war—could restore his soul and dull the memories. It was the day-to-day coping in Vietnam that pulled him through. While not exactly suicidal, he did take lots of chances and risked his life leading to safety a squad of marines otherwise certain to die. For that act of heroism Adam received the Navy Cross. Only a month later, he stepped on an exploding mine.

The Vietnam experience had ruined so many lives and left many survivors' minds irreparably damaged. It was paradoxical that the war strengthened Adam as a person. But even he did not come back emotionally whole.

It was while in medical school that Adam decided not to have more children, believing he never could survive another loss. Over the years he wandered in and out of relationships, but he just didn't have any more love to give.

Vera's thoughts switched back to her own relationship with Adam. Not long after that first walk on the beach, she spent every other weekend with him in Central City, and he came to New York on the other weekends. Within months, they were married in a simple civil ceremony. She kept her maiden name, Sokol, and enjoyed watching people squirm when they found out she was living with a Dr. *Boatwright*.

Adam's not wanting more children suited Vera, who felt that it would be impossible to be an outstanding mother and continue her demanding career.

And Vera was too much of a perfectionist not to do everything well.

11

The Crunchers

Adam was taking the bus to work on Monday after leaving his Porsche at AutoHaus Krugger for some scheduled maintenance. The car was his one luxury. Not a flashy person, Adam bought it neither to impress people nor to demonstrate his double-income lifestyle. Rather, he liked to take short, fast drives in the countryside and over the hilly roads east of town. Along with caving expeditions, sporty maneuvers in the Porsche satisfied Adam's craving for physical adventure.

Adam rarely allowed himself to become bored, and he found ways to entertain himself during occasional trips on public conveyances. His favorite perch was the side seat, directly behind the driver. From there, he could watch people as they got on and off the bus. It was a perfect spot to play his little game of guessing occupations.

At Maple Avenue an impeccably dressed man, about seventy years old, climbed aboard carrying a briefcase. *A lawyer*. Adam smiled as the man took out a long yellow tablet favored by attorneys. At the next stop, the new passenger was a woman in white pants and top. *A doctor at County Hospital.* She would be a first- or second-year resident; that would be consistent with her age and general demeanor of fatigue.

Adam left the bus near the Life Sciences Building. The grounds were almost deserted in the early morning, when a few lab technicians and department secretaries were beginning to arrive. But by ten o'clock the LSB would be like an anthill crawling with activity.

Adam had scheduled a meeting with the DNA mapping software team, who were all waiting in the conference room. The "Crunchers" were a motley collection of non-conformists.

The lead programmer, Timothy Miller, was slurping obscenely from a mug just filled from his large thermos of coffee. Still in his twenties, the scraggly-bearded Timothy looked like a punk rocker with a short haircut. The young man had never graduated from college, and Adam had to fight for Timothy's appointment. Adam prevailed, even though most university researchers have at least a master's degree. Adam needed Timothy's great experience with graphical interfaces, a skill honed developing violent video games.

"Hello boss," Timothy greeted.

"Hi gang," Adam began. "I just wanted to chat informally about how things are progressing."

"I hope this'll be short," Timothy pleaded. "I'm on the verge of a breakthrough graphically representing DNA. Until now, it has been looking like two coiled ropes."

"More like the stuff you smoke," Dutch Smeidhoffer teased. The heavy-set young man was working with ballpoint pen on a crossword puzzle. Dutch was the database expert and a PhD dropout from Carnegie-Mellon, where he had been working on artificial intelligence.

"I worry about what he's drinking," said Sandra Wickham, taking a sip from her cup of herbal tea. Sandra—don't ever call her Sandy—had double-majored in computer science and zoology. Standing at five-eleven, she was the resident debugger and troubleshooter. Her expertise with animal physiology was handy for planning computer programs.

"Herbal cocktails can damage your psyche," Timothy shot back. Dutch and Timothy laughed as Sandra blushed out of irritation and embarrassment.

All the while, the fourth Cruncher, Jude Ojukwe, was clicking a song through his teeth while reading a book of Isaac Asimov's essays. His black skin contrasted sharply with the whiteness of the others. A totally bald Nigerian, he was a PhD candidate in mathematics and full-time team programmer. Jude's specialty was algorithms—basic rules that govern computer programs.

"Hey, Jude," Adam gave his customized greeting, stolen from the Beatles.

"Oh, hello sir. I want to tell about my genetic search algorithm for locating genes."

"You can after we've seen Timothy's demonstration. Ready, Timothy?"

They formed a semi-circle around Timothy's workstation, with its extra-large twenty-four-inch monitor screen.

"This is the DNA molecule for *E. coli* bacteria," Timothy said. The helixes rotated slowly, like two snakes in a mating ritual. He showed how to change the magnification, reducing the screen image down to one component molecule and expanding it back up to several hundred, all done using a game joystick. Each of the four basic DNA building blocks was shown in a different shape and color. At further reduction in magnification, individual molecules disappeared, replaced by colored bands representing genetic markers already identified.

"This is the best part!" Timothy said. "You all know M.C. Esher, the famous artist. Tell me, if he were painting this scene, what he would add to the picture and what activity would be represented?"

The image showed about ten molecules on the DNA strand. With a slightly tinny sound, the computer played the "Marine Corps Hymn." In time with the music, the helixes slowly rotated, with each molecule serving like a step on a ladder. Meanwhile the strand itself was moving slightly, new parts appearing gradually at the top and disappearing at the bottom.

"Ants on a Mobius strip!" Dutch exclaimed. "We're the ants, and the DNA helixes form our stairway. We're crawling up the DNA molecule."

"You win the prize," Timothy grinned.

"Amazing," Adam said, shaking his head. "I assume that researchers can actually use this feature to full advantage."

"The music is just for you guys. There's a complete menu bar at the top so that the user can control movement and read descriptions of segments shown on screen."

"This is going to be a hard act to follow," Adam said, shifting gears. "Okay Jude, tell us about your *genetic* algorithm. I don't understand it myself. We can use more details."

Jude gave an elegant summary. "We use the biological model of *evolution* to hunt for gene locations. My program uses a set of rules that imitate the evolutionary process by giving 'birth' to possible DNA coordinates for, say, the color-blindness gene, starting from two 'parent' locations. Millions of 'births' and 'deaths' take place inside the computer each second. All the while, the program breeds new candidate gene coordinates, saving the fittest of these for future generations. At the end, we have a few choice spots, all highly likely to be the gene's true location."

"I see," Adam said in awe. "Your method might make genome mapping hundreds of times faster. Check it out by taking trial runs. See if your program can find correct coordinates for genes whose locations are already known."

"Now, Dutch, how's progress in cataloging DNA-mapping research?"

Dutch grinned as he described his work. "I've developed a new keyword search procedure. It makes it easier for field researchers to find who's doing what. I think it'll help to avoid experiment duplication."

"It might also make it easier to identify new areas to research," Adam replied. "Keep up the good work."

"Sandra," Adam continued, "I'm relying on you to keep these guys productive. Help them with their code-testing protocols."

Sandra replied with a serious expression. "I'm always available. But Jude's program bugs are so juicy that I'm almost a full-time pest controller."

Adam smiled as he announced: "We've been generating sufficient good stuff for Wiley to increase our funding. He's budgeted a new programmer to help you, Sandra."

Adam was home alone, already missing Vera, who had left earlier for a New York concert. His Saturday breakfast was interrupted by a loud knock. Looking through the peephole, Adam was surprised to see Detective Reilly with a burly uniformed policeman standing behind him.

Still in pajamas, Adam opened the door. "Detective Reilly, what a surprise! Please come in."

"I have bad news for you," Reilly replied. "The coroner's report on Dr. Friedman was misplaced for several days, and we just received it. The medical examiner could find no object in his throat. We need you downtown to help sort this thing out."

Shocked, Adam forced a calm exterior. "Sorry. I've got deadlines. I can't spare the time."

Reilly replied in a stern voice. "You don't have a choice. Please get dressed."

The police station was a large office complex with half the people wearing blue uniforms. With no parade of colorful characters, like in a cop movie, the place reminded Adam of the motor vehicle office. The police and staff looked like bored bureaucrats. Adam was almost disappointed by the lack of official activity.

Reilly ushered Adam into his partitioned cubicle. The detective's desktop was immaculate, containing only a nameplate and picture of his family.

"Please sit down, Dr. Boatwright," Reilly said, pointing to a faded chair in front of the desk. "Can I get you some coffee or a soft drink?"

"No, thank you," Adam replied nervously. It felt almost as though he was waiting for a job interview instead of a police interrogation.

Reilly sat behind his desk, pulled out a yellow note pad, and began. "How long have you known the deceased?"

Adam was taken aback by the term "deceased," as if Itzak were some strange body pulled from the morgue. "I knew him for about six months. But I never had a serious conversation with Itzak until about three weeks ago."

The interview proceeded with more mundane questions for about ten minutes; all the while Adam's impatience was rising steadily until he interrupted. "Why are you going through all this? I was simply trying to save the man's life."

"Dr. Boatwright," Reilly said sternly, the pupils of his eyes dilating down to the size of a dull pencil point, "I'm the one asking the questions here."

"Sorry," Adam said obediently, biting his tongue.

When Reilly paused and busily wrote notes, Adam watched the people. Two women were busily typing, while a well-dressed young man sat at his computer playing solitaire. A couple were having a heated discussion by the drinking fountain. The man touched the woman's derriere and was rewarded with a wallop on the chin. The blushing man slinked to a nearby desk, ignoring several cheering kibitzers. That was more like a police drama.

Adam had never been in trouble with the law. But he lived on the edge, and he had several harsh encounters with his superiors. The Marines nearly court-martialed him twice. The first occasion was a trumped up charge of fraternization, what today would be sexual harassment, brought by a major whom Adam had inadvertently embarrassed. The last charge was abandoning his station in battle; that event led instead to a medal for bravery.

Adam had once been sanctioned for violating research protocols. The university was fussy about proper documentation, and Adam was often too busy to file reports. Those problems disappeared after he hired Mandy Rogers, who made sure that all documentation was perfect.

Reilly resumed the interview. "How did you slit Friedman's throat?"

"I used his scissors," Adam replied, barely able to contain himself. "But I actually made a surgical incision in his windpipe—what we call a tracheotomy. Itzak was struggling for air."

"Yes, yes, I remember now. Tell me doctor, is it common for a tracheotomy patient to bleed so profusely?"

"Ordinarily, there's very little blood. It all depends on the physician, the patient's condition, and a host of factors."

Reilly looked deeply into Adam's left eye for several seconds, before asking, "Did you like Professor Friedman?"

"I worshipped him," Adam confessed, somewhat embarrassed. "In the scientific community, he was a superstar."

"Yeah, yeah, but weren't you just a little bit jealous?"

"No, I was *very* jealous. I wished I had a fraction of his talent."

Reilly seemed surprised at Adam's frank response, and his demeanor softened. "Why would anybody have it in for Dr. Friedman?"

Adam took a moment to respond. "Itzak Friedman was a cold person. I don't think he had any friends. But I can't imagine him having any enemies—certainly none who'd want him dead."

Reilly left the cubicle and returned with his boss, Lieutenant Bert Lewiston, a stern-looking African-American man. With a red paisley tie hanging neatly from the collar of his immaculate, tailored shirt, Lewiston had the aristocratic look of a young U.S. senator. The lieutenant introduced himself, but did not extend his hand to meet Adam's outstretched palm.

"We're booking you on suspicion of murder. Anything you say can and will be used against you. You have the right to remain silent ..."

In total disbelief, Adam was escorted to a room where he was photographed and fingerprinted. Although his prints had been taken in the Marine Corps and when he applied for his medical license, it was different this time. Now the ink stung his skin terribly.

Adam was relieved when he could finally put his hands in running water. He scrubbed like preparing for surgery, trying to wash away the thick ink. In a daze, He looked at his fingers as if they were harbingers of something much worse. He fought pangs of nausea as he gradually realized that the stains on his fingers were just temporary, that this dreadful business was just beginning, and that the permanent stains would be to his reputation.

When the draining police interview was finally over, Adam called his lawyer. But he was not permitted to leave. At 3:00 p.m., his attorney, Tom Essinger, finally showed up.

Essinger was a tall, thin man with a commanding presence. It took some doing, but he managed to convince the police that Adam was definitely not a flight risk and would show up for arraignment in the morning.

“This is really a nightmare,” Adam said to Essinger as they left the building. “I can’t understand why they think I’d harm Itzak in any way.”

“I don’t know either,” Essinger replied. “The police were influenced by the superficial evidence that you cut the man’s throat. Tomorrow we’ll find out where this thing’s going.”

Adam couldn’t wait to get home and call Vera with his news.

12

Grabbing the Reins

Adam arrived on campus feeling like a student who crammed all night for a suddenly postponed examination. That morning, Tom Essinger had reported a forty-eight-hour postponement of the preliminary hearing.

Adam vowed not to let that nonsense interfere with his work. There was much to do. Under National Cancer Institute pressure to continue Itzak's project, the Physiology Department had transferred directorship to him. Fortunately, Itzak's team knew exactly what to do, and managing the project would be like flying a plane on autopilot.

Still, Adam was uncomfortable stepping into the dead man's shoes. Although the murder suspicions were preposterous, he couldn't stop worrying about being accused. Essinger had warned there might be a university disciplinary hearing if he were indicted. Adam was angry that the university might give credence to a cockamamie police theory, possibly suspending him—even before a trial.

Adam still needed a police escort when he entered Itzak's sealed office. He proceeded to the filing cabinets and continued rummaging, beginning where he found the Nuremberg deposition. But he saw nothing about Itzak's pet rat, except staff instructions for feeding Little Oscar and giving him daily therapy.

He stepped for the first time inside Itzak's cell-division laboratory, where an assistant was busily inventorying supplies. Adam was startled to see Little Oscar perched on the man's shoulder. The rat's whiteness contrasted starkly with the thin man's long salt-and-pepper hair and matching full beard.

"Congratulations, Dr. Boatwright," the man greeted, extending his hand. "I'm Saul Lowenstein. Welcome to your new job. Wish you were coming aboard under different circumstances. We're grateful you tried to save Dr. Friedman's life."

"I couldn't have changed the situation," Adam replied, shaking Saul's extended hand. He reached out to Little Oscar and gently rubbed the rat's tummy.

Saul Lowenstein grinned at the rat and then looked inquisitively at his new boss. "What do you think caused Dr. Friedman's death?"

"Your guess is as good as mine. I'm here today to pick up the pieces. I searched Itzak's study for records of your research."

"All of our research records are stored there."

"I didn't find much about Little Oscar."

Saul gave some details. "Everything should be there. As for our star boarder, we have instructions only for the daily intravenous diet supplement."

Diet supplement! The man seemed to know nothing about the significance of Little Oscar and the miracle of his very long life.

Adam was perplexed as he looked at Saul. "Where do you get his IV solutions?"

Saul shrugged his shoulders. "I don't know. Every Friday Dr. Friedman would bring a vial of supplement. In three days we'll run out. Then we're going to switch to fortified saline."

Little Oscar would probably die soon without receiving the real solution—what Adam knew to be the rat's own synthetic I-complex. Although the rodent had served its research purpose, Adam decided to intervene on Little Oscar's behalf—at least until learning the details of Itzak's project.

"Did Dr. Friedman take work home?"

"Oh yes. He always left and returned with a full briefcase."

"Thanks, Saul. I'll leave the lab in your good hands. Don't change Little Oscar's IV solution until we've investigated further."

Adam needed Hannah Friedman's permission to search Itzak's apartment. She had returned to Israel months before, hoping the dry air would help her recovery. Physiology had given him the Israel address and cell phone number, and it was a good time to place the call.

Adam's knowledge of Hebrew proved essential when Hannah Friedman's mother answered. After Hannah took over, they continued speaking in Hebrew. She told Adam about Itzak's journal, updated daily from notes brought home, and gave him permission to borrow whatever would help continue Itzak's research.

Mandy Rogers assisted Adam at the dead man's apartment. Like Itzak's office, the place was stark—no decorations on the wall, no pictures on display. There was absolutely no clutter, and the apartment looked and felt like a freshly made hotel suite. Mandy busied herself taking notes for the movers.

Adam went directly to the master bedroom, opened the armoire, as Hannah had instructed, and lifted the false bottom panel. There were ten thick lab books, handwritten in Hebrew, which Adam placed in a suitcase.

Physically and mentally exhausted, Adam turned on the TV news. The lead item followed up on the death of Itzak Friedman. The reporter stated that police had arrested a murder suspect and that the Pan Palestine Freedom Alliance had claimed credit. A few highlights of Itzak's life were given, followed by a brief statement by the Israeli counsel. Within hours of Itzak's death, the body had been flown to Israel, where Itzak received a state funeral.

Adam couldn't believe what was happening. His mind spun frantically as he attempted to analyze his situation.

13

Similar Scientific Perspectives

Being a murder suspect would have incapacitated a lesser man. But paradoxically, the stress intensified Adam's fascination with the victim's work. Like switching attention from one project to another, Adam ignored the murder investigation and focused on Itzak's cell-division research.

Adam examined Itzak's handwritten journals covering observations and conjectures dating from his years at Oxford. Hannah should have them placed in a museum. Adam winced when he remembered that she was dying of cancer. Itzak's wish to save Hannah would not be fulfilled.

There it was—in Itzak's most recent journal—from an entry made just before his death. Itzak was going to be the *Guinea pig* and administer fortified I-complex to *himself!* He planned to proceed without waiting, as if he had already discovered a cancer cure.

The scientist in Adam was indignant, even shocked. But as a fellow human who had also suffered great loss, he understood. Itzak wanted to save his wife and was grasping at straws. The man's unselfishness and honorable intentions raised Adam's adulation to a new level.

Hoping for fresh insights, Adam thumbed the opened journal pages. He stopped at an entry made as the cell-division research began at Hebrew University. Adam read with fascination.

Itzak had been meticulous, reporting all key assumptions, describing all experiments, detailing results, and interpreting them. Along the way, he interjected his thoughts about where the project was heading and conjectured long-run implications.

Five laboratory rats had been involved. The first two had experienced slight improvements in longevity, as Itzak perfected I-complex dosages and regimens. The third rat was already dying of cancer when treatment began. From that experience, Itzak concluded that I-complex might stop new cancers, but it was useless against older cancers. The substance would actually help existing cancer cells duplicate indefinitely.

Reading further, Adam learned that the fourth rat was a sister of Little Oscar. The last two rats reached the age of fifty months when, once accidentally, the female was given distilled water instead of I-complex. She became infected during the short pause in viral immunity and died of pneumonia.

It seemed like Adam and Itzak had very similar scientific perspectives. That was uncanny. Adam would soon discover that he had much more in common with Itzak Friedman.

Adam was leaving the Falcon Tower lobby on his way to Dela's New Delhi Deli, when a young woman jumped in front of him, blocking his path.

"Dr. Boatwright, can you comment on Dr. Itzak Friedman's death?" She spoke loudly into a microphone. Adam was startled by the shuffle of feet behind him, as a TV cameraman hurried to position himself.

Not knowing whether to cooperate, but dreading looking stupid on TV, he answered truthfully. "Dr. Friedman had a blockage in his windpipe and couldn't breathe. I performed an emergency tracheotomy, but he died shortly thereafter."

"The police suspect that you murdered him," the reporter shouted. "What can you say about that?"

"I really don't know—don't know what to say," Adam stuttered. "It must all be a terrible mistake. Excuse me."

Adam pushed his way through the small crowd of curious bystanders, ignoring the frantic pleas of the reporter. His heart was beating like a timpani during *Beethoven's Fifth*.

Sitting at a corner table in the delicatessen, Adam eagerly resumed reading Itzak's journal. He discovered that the rat I-complex had been synthesized by the Israeli branch of Millner Laboratories, using a patented and secret process. The local facility of Millner had continued to provide Itzak with the substance.

Adam considered the implications to live humans. If their own I-complex could be administered in the same way as the rat's chemical, they could live without viral infection and cancer. Itzak, of course, had been thinking the same thing from the beginning. But rat experiments suggested doing so would be impractical, because *gallons* of liquid daily would be needed for a person. Itzak had consulted with Adam in hopes of finding a better way.

Just before he died, Itzak was about to experiment with vitamin C, following through with Adam's suggestion. Itzak had planned to sacrifice Little Oscar, if necessary, by reducing the rat's I-complex allowance by 95 percent in the hope that the leaner solution would still work when fortified by a mega dosage of the vitamin. Itzak had deduced the exact dosages required.

Adam decided to perform Itzak's vitamin-C experiment himself.

The journal said little regarding human liver-cell division. The replicating cells were still growing abnormally in their Petri dishes. Adam agreed with Itzak that I-complex could best maintain cell-division fidelity only when generated *inside* the body.

Adam's thoughts were interrupted by the classical music tone of his cell phone.

"Adam, Dave Wiley here. I just saw you on TV."

It must have been the noon broadcast. Adam was appalled that they processed his interview so quickly. "Hello, Dave. They caught me totally by surprise."

"It's really bad. You looked guilty as hell. A nurse said Itzak Friedman called you a murderer."

Adam felt a pang of panic as he realized the TV interview had been interspersed with other footage. "That's all out of context. When he said that, Itzak confused my intervention in mouse testes with his father's experience at Treblinka."

"You'd better come up with a better explanation," Wiley replied sternly. "I'm under a lot of pressure. You know I believe you. But President Wentworth is bothered about this. The university can't sponsor anyone under criminal investigation."

"Rest assured, there's no basis for concern," Adam said, struggling to sound diplomatic in spite of his aching stomach.

Adam paced the apartment, trying to calm himself down. It took considerable psychological strength to suppress this murder stuff and get back to the nitty-gritty, back to continuing Itzak's research.

Adam wondered about Hannah Friedman, who would probably die from cancer within months. That got him thinking about Little Oscar's experience, and he wondered if the same therapy would maintain faithful cell division in a person—perhaps by using I-complex with the vitamin-C boost. Like the pampered rat, that person would never get cancer. *Never age!*

Adam would be an *old man* before government regulators allowed the use such therapy. Adam's mind wandered over the steps needed. First, the vitamin-C regimen must work with Little Oscar—that was a very big *if*. Then, some systematic process must be found to get I-complex that would work with live people, not just a bunch of liver cells. There was no evidence that Itzak's human substance would even work on living people. Moreover, there was no record of how the first human I-complex had ever been created to begin with. Even if the process became known, it might not even be practicable to manufacture the substance with current technology.

Those hurdles aside, suppose that a sufficient and workable human I-complex was available. The FDA would insist it be statistically "proven" harmless through phase trials and experimentation. That would require administering the human chemical to animals and checking for toxic effects. Then extensive human trials would be needed to show the substance actually worked. Effectiveness would have to be demonstrated through double-blind studies involving hundreds of patients.

No wonder Itzak planned to take shortcuts.

14

Scientific Objectivity Overwhelmed

The day had arrived for Adam's delayed appearance in court. Adam and Tom Essinger arrived at the steps of the courthouse, scurrying through a cordon of reporters, photographers, and TV camera crews.

"We have nothing to say," Essinger shouted, actually pushing a cameraman out of their path.

Adam resented the interruption and was anxious to get back to work. He was confident his attorney would quickly resolve the issue.

When they finally reached the sanctity of an empty jury room, Essinger warned in somber tones. "Be prepared for preposterous charges. I believe your story totally, but that won't cut any ice with the judge."

The court was called to order, Judge Roxanne Wheeler presiding. She was a small gray-haired woman, looking like a church choir member. The judge glared sternly at Adam as he sat at a front table. He looked across the courtroom at assistant district attorney Marvin Smithline, who frowned back at him. Adam squirmed in his chair.

"Your Honor," Smithline announced, "the State will be seeking a grand jury indictment charging Dr. Adam Boatwright with the murder of Professor Itzak Friedman."

"Your Honor," Essinger protested, "my client was only trying to save Dr. Friedman's life."

Judge Wheeler asked the prosecutor to present his *prima facie* case.

Smithline began. "Adam Boatwright slit Dr. Friedman's throat."

Essinger stood up. "That was a tracheotomy! Friedman was not breathing and about to die."

The DA's face looked like he'd just spotted a cockroach crawl across a restaurant washroom floor. "Yes, he was about to die, and Dr. Boatwright killed him. We have an entire cafeteria full of witnesses who heard Friedman and Boatwright yelling. Several heard Friedman call him a murderer."

Adam couldn't restrain himself. "I never yelled at Itzak. He was the one doing the yelling."

Judge Wheeler stopped him. "You'll get your chance to speak, Dr. Boatwright. Now I only want to hear from counsel."

The DA continued. "The State will show that Dr. Boatwright was jealous of Dr. Friedman's cell-division research. He wanted Friedman out of the way so he could steal his ideas and obtain grants to continue Friedman's work. His Genetics Department needed fresh funding, and Dr. Boatwright thought this would save his other projects."

Adam's flustered attorney jumped up. "Preposterous. Your honor, this contrived story has no foundation."

The judge seemed bored with it all. "I'll take it under advisement. Now, Dr. Boatwright, will you speak or will your counsel speak on your behalf?"

"I'll explain," said Adam. He blurted it all out." I never intended Dr. Friedman harm. I found him on the floor of his study, gasping for air. He must have had a temporary mental aberration in the cafeteria after I told him about my interventions in mice reproductive systems. Why would I murder him in his own office, just doors away from mine? Why would I then call for help? The entire argument is patently ridiculous."

The judge avoided Adam's insistent eyes. "I think we'll have to send this to the grand jury. In the meantime, Dr. Boatwright is released on his own recognizance."

Adam left immediately with Essinger. As they paused on the courthouse steps, Adam asked weakly, "It doesn't look good, does it?"

"I'm not sure," Essinger replied. "I'll have to give it some deep thought. I'm disturbed by the cafeteria incident and need to speak with witnesses." Essinger told Adam that at the very least, the process would take months, even years, to clear up. That was true whether he was guilty or innocent.

Frustrated and angry, Adam blurted: "You think I might be guilty, don't you?"

"No, but I have to play devil's advocate. You've got to let me handle this. I can minimize the disruptions to your life and the damage to your career."

"My boss has hinted at sanctions if I'm investigated. Is there anything you can do?"

"Don't worry, Adam. I'll make sure nothing happens before this goes to the grand jury."

Vera and Adam were walking in the park. There were occasional pockets of Canada Geese resting from their migration flights south. The afternoon sun still provided comfortable warmth in contrast to the brisk chill in air as the fall day ebbed. Squirrels romped in the grass looking for acorns to store for the approaching winter. For a short time the setting magically suppressed all cares.

"I had a call from Nora," Vera announced, breaking the spell.

"How's the chemotherapy going?" Adam asked.

"Not very well. The cancer has spread to her lungs. I'm afraid this will be her last Christmas."

Adam couldn't hide his alarm. "I'd like to talk with her doctor."

"Why? It'd be pointless. Oh, Adam, the women in my family are cursed. My mother, her sister, and now my sister—all getting breast cancer at an early age. My mother and aunt both died young. I'm so scared."

Adam pulled Vera toward him and hugged her. She clung to him like a child, choking back the tears.

"I'm so sorry, Vera. I didn't realize Nora's cancer had progressed so far. I've been too preoccupied with my own problems."

Adam thought about Nora's prognosis. She would probably die within six months. The disease's rapid progression could be explained by the Sokol women's predisposition to the cancer. The trait was one of the hundreds of hereditary conditions he hoped one day to eliminate. But such a "cure" wouldn't help persons having the inherited dysfunction. It would only prevent their *children* from inheriting the problem, breaking the chain forever.

They were startled by a group of geese honking overhead. They paused to watch.

There was a high probability Vera would get the virulent breast cancer killing her sister. Would preventing Vera from getting the cancer just become a wild-goose chase? Adam couldn't bear the thought.

"You ought to preempt the cancer," he suggested. "A lot of women in your situation have their breasts removed *before* they can get the disease. That improves their life expectancies considerably."

"I won't be butchered," Vera said passionately. "I'd have to stop playing the violin. And what about us? You deserve a whole woman."

"You're the most complete woman I've ever known. I wouldn't love you any less if you had artificial breasts. I've seen some of the reconstructive work following mastectomies. It's amazing."

Vera's eyes were filled with tears, and she almost choked on her words. "Oh Adam, I wouldn't want to live under those circumstances."

"Don't be so selfish," Adam spouted, regretting his words as they were coming out of his mouth.

"I mean it!"

Adam was hurt and felt rejected. But the momentum of their passions dictated the direction of the conversation.

Adam stopped and pulled Vera so she was facing him. "*You* couldn't live without your *breasts*. *I* couldn't live without *you*. I didn't marry two tits. I married a warm, thinking human being. I love the whole you. To me, losing your breasts would be no more serious than if you lost your pinky."

"I couldn't play the violin without my pinky."

There it was. It seemed Vera's violin career was more important than her life with him.

Not showing his pain, Adam concluded the discussion. "It was a lousy metaphor. Sorry. But I've made my point."

They finished their walk in stony silence. Both were angry. Both were frightened.

Although Adam regretted his abruptness, it was the necessary first step. It would take a series of shocks to prod Vera into accepting preemptive surgery.

Halfway home, a thought popped into Adam's mind. *I can follow Itzak's example!* All along, Itzak's hidden agenda had been to somehow accelerate getting the proper I-complex and use it as therapy to cure Hannah Friedman's cancer.

Adam let his mind play out the possibilities. He would use his genetic expertise to somehow get a workable I-complex. He could do that so much easier than Itzak. He could then treat himself with that chemical, and if he was successful it should work on Vera.

But Adam had to admit that was not yet science and currently just a daydream.

Yet the pending doom overwhelmed his scientific objectivity. Adam was willing to break all rules to save Vera. He continued to play out the scenario, laying out all steps that would be needed. The list was a long one.

Was it all just wishful thinking? If any one step didn't work as planned, none of it could come to fruition. And what about scientific protocols? Scientists don't experiment on themselves.

Like a kid on a treasure hunt, Adam's mind went back and forth in circles. He was totally absorbed with his fantasy cure for Vera's cancer, an illness she did not yet have.

15

Bloody Mary's Cocktail

Adam entered the mouse laboratory, spotting Bonnie Burton looking out the window, her brown hair cascading over her white lab coat. For the first time, Adam noticed how strikingly beautiful she was.

Bonnie Burton was the only single mother in her class at Central University Medical School. She had dropped out of high school in her junior year, giving birth to her son Michael, now ten. While still living with her parents, she had passed the high school general equivalency test. She then attended the local community college, majoring in science, getting straight A's while working nights as a waitress. That led to a full scholarship at Rice University, where she completed her major in chemistry. After Rice, Bonnie and Michael had moved to Philadelphia, where she took a job selling pharmaceuticals. She learned much about medicine from making sales calls to doctors, and that experience culminated in her decision to become a physician.

Adam gave Bonnie instructions. "Contact Millner Laboratories. Tell them I'm assuming Dr. Friedman's project. They've been genetically cloning a substance of his for several years." He gave her the control number from one of the miniature IV vials, careful not to say what the substance was. For now he would maintain secrecy about what was in those containers and how it would be used.

Within minutes Bonnie reported back to Adam. "I've just talked to Dr. Friedman's contact at Millner. He was curious about the substance they've been making. But I knew no details and couldn't help."

"Say nothing to anybody about the chemical. Itzak wanted to keep it confidential. We'll do the same for now."

"Okay. The next shipment arrives by Federal Express tomorrow morning. They'll deliver it directly to your genetics office. Same quantity as before."

"One more errand, Bonnie, and then you can shuttle back to med school. I want to administer two thousand units of vitamin C intravenously as an additive to another fluid. Can you have that ready for me in the morning?"

Adam was following the last plan of Itzak Friedman. If Little Oscar maintained his immunity after receiving a thinned I-complex solution fortified by vitamin C, the first step would have been taken toward human application.

Next, Adam visited Rita Morales, who was busy examining a new brood of baby mice.

"Hello Adam," she smiled as he walked into the cage room. "Cute little guys. No fur yet, but their skin color indicates they'll all have black ears."

"Are these the second generation, Rita?"

"No. They're the third. Their great grandfather is Primo, the subject of our first successful germ-line intervention."

"Imagine! Primo's only fifteen months old and he's already a great-grandfather!"

"Mice are so nice," Rita said, gently stroking a pup. "They breed so fast we can make genetic changes a hundred times faster than we could with people."

"Make that a *thousand* times faster. With mice, we don't have to worry about the FDA."

"True. So, what's up, stranger?"

"I'm taking over Itzak Friedman's show," Adam sighed.

Rita stared at him with her dark eyes. "You've sure got your fingers in lots of pies!"

Adam regretted being away from the lab for so long. “That project brings me to you today. We want to test immunity to viral infections in rats. Can you make me a 50 milliliter vial containing about a dozen rat viruses?”

“That’s an odd request. If you mix them, you can’t tell what virus belongs to which symptom.”

Adam admired her quickness. “I know. But I just want to see if global immunity is working. I don’t care which infections take, if any. I need a cocktail lethal to an ordinary rat with normal immunities.”

“Can do, boss,” Rita said, scrunching her face and hunching over, as she joked, “I feel like Bloody Mary. I hope the animal-rights people don’t have spies here.”

Adam was no expert in law. But he knew that criminal trials took a lot of time and energy, even for innocents. And sometimes, the innocent get convicted. He might even be incarcerated before or during the proceedings. He worried that the next few days might be his last free ones for months, until the trial and acquittal. Although the DA’s case was weak, Adam couldn’t tolerate the uncertainty.

He had to solve the crime *himself*, and quickly.

Adam called the laboratory. “Hello, Mandy, this is Adam. I need your help. Listen, this is what I want you to do...”

Fighting Friday afternoon traffic out of town, Adam inched along behind a van full of kids. A small boy made faces through the back window. Adam smiled and waved at the boy, who quickly hid from view.

As soon as he passed the main suburbs, Adam left the freeway, turning down a country road. Sylvia’s directions were easy to follow, but Adam was taking an indirect route to the Beckwith ranch. He didn’t want anyone following him, especially the police. He pulled into a turnout and waited. No car could be seen, and none passed for about five minutes. Adam backtracked to the main road. After a mile, he pulled off again, waiting. After ten more minutes, he drove back to the main highway leading toward the ranch.

It was dark when he arrived. He could tell from the parked cars that they would be meeting in the building behind the main ranch house. It was as large as a normal house, with insulated metal exterior walls and concrete floors.

They were all waiting. From the germ-line intervention team there were Sylvia Beckwith, Jack Chin, Bonnie Burton, and Mandy Rogers. Adam wanted Bonnie because of her knowledge of the pharmaceutical industry. Two Crunchers, Dutch Smeidhoffer and Timothy Miller, were included because Adam would need their computer help.

Adam began the emergency meeting. "Except for Mandy, most of you have little in common, only your connections to me. As you know, I'm going to be charged with the murder of Itzak Friedman. Of course, I couldn't possibly have killed him."

There was a short round of nervous laughter. Adam then told what he had found, the coroner's conclusions, and what the DA had surmised.

Adam somberly concluded, "If I have to go to trial, some of you will lose your jobs. Our projects will die, and the remainder of my team members will be reassigned. Time does not wait for an innocent person on trial. I've called you here so we can meet with absolute secrecy. Please tell no one about this. We're going to share information on a strictly need-to-know basis. That includes what you tell one another. Is that understood?"

"I like the melodrama," piped Timothy. A few others smiled wryly.

Adam continued. "I want to find the killer. The police think he or she has simply murdered Itzak, but they won't look for anybody while I'm the suspect. If the real perpetrator knows we're all trying to solve the crime, we could all be targets. We mustn't get in the way. My secondary concern is the authorities. They're more benign, but they can slow us down."

Suddenly the room became quiet; clearly everybody was becoming frightened, especially Bonnie. Finally she asked, "What do you think really happened?"

Adam gave a complete answer, including his own hunches. "At least one person from a terrorist group very carefully murdered Itzak. My first guess is the Pan Palestinian Freedom Alliance. The PPFA has actually claimed credit. But I'm not sure, since terrorists have a history of bragging about other's dirty deeds. It could instead be a domestic group—possibly the animal rightsists or the right-to-lifers."

"This sounds so paranoid," Jack interjected, unable to shift gears from his usual professional demeanor.

Adam looked at him sternly. "Jack, it's not just my imagination. *Somebody* murdered Itzak. If any of you can think of further suspects, let me know."

"Maybe it was a jealous lover," offered Dutch. Nobody laughed.

"How do you think it was done, Dr. Boatwright?" asked Sylvia.

"Poison. He made it look like I slit Itzak's throat and covered with the tracheotomy story. My actions normally should've saved a choking person."

"But why do the police think it was murder?" she asked.

"The day before his death, I had a heated public discussion with Itzak."

"I was in the cafeteria and saw and heard it all," Bonnie offered. "Dr. Friedman was doing all the yelling. You appeared very embarrassed by his unprovoked outburst."

"Thanks for the vote of confidence, Bonnie. The DA has even given my motive. He claims I wanted to steal Dr. Friedman's research and bring the funding to the Genetics Department, which he wrongly purports to have fallen on hard times."

That made Jack angry. "Oh, how *stupid!* Itzak's research was physiological, not genetic."

"True, but that's a subtle distinction. I was officially a *consultant* to Dr. Friedman."

"Your plate is full! Why would you want more?" asked Mandy rhetorically.

"I'm glad you all see that. But you all *know* me. How long would it take to convince a jury?"

"Too long, I'm afraid," Dutch said, his dejection obvious to all, "especially with the DA inventing preposterous falsehoods."

"What kind of poison was it?" Bonnie asked, moving the discussion in a constructive direction.

"Actually, I think there were *two* substances. The first made it appear as though Itzak was choking on something. Whoever planned this knows I'm a surgeon and must have guessed how I would react. But even if I hadn't performed the tracheotomy, a second poison actually killed him. I think the first was just a ruse for me."

"The autopsy should give clues," Jack said.

Adam shook his head slowly. "Unfortunately, Itzak now lies buried in Israel. For religious reasons, he had a speedy funeral, before foul play was even suspected. There was no autopsy. Even if we could get permission to exhume the body and have the autopsy performed, that would take too long."

"But we need something from Itzak's body before we can proceed," Jack insisted.

"There's a crust of blood on the carpet in Itzak's study. Can you do something with that?"

"Damned tootin' he can!" said Timothy excitedly. "That was my standard protocol for *Murderer's Row*, a video game I've created. This is like a video game come to life."

Scowling at Timothy, Jack answered Adam's question. "I can do a forensic analysis of the dried blood. As a student I worked part-time at the Oakland criminology lab."

"Very good! I knew you guys could come through."

Adam paced the room, thinking about the use of blood. It only took a minute to put a plan together.

"The blood's our only shot. For starters, I want a spectroscopic workup to help identify chemicals in the blood residue. Even if we have to do it molecule by molecule, we've got to find any suspect substances."

"Some foreign chemicals may have metabolized in the victim before he died," Jack complained. "There'd be no trace left in the blood."

"Let's hope not," Adam replied. "Dutch and Timothy have computer codes that will trace any compounds back to their source. Right, fellows?"

"You betchya," Timothy replied.

"We can't do it!" Mandy exclaimed, almost bursting into tears. "Itzak's study has been sealed."

Adam had been in the office twice since Itzak's death, each time under police escort. He couldn't get at the blood without their permission, and sensed it would be futile to even try. It would be very damaging—even incriminating—to tamper with evidence for his murder trial.

Again Adam paced, letting his mind play freely. A plan soon popped into his fertile mind.

16

Brainstorm

It was 11:00 p.m., when most of the campus was deserted. Under any other circumstances, Adam would have found it pleasurable to climb four stories to the LSB roof, but his mind was preoccupied. He rigged a drop line and platform above the window to Itzak's third-floor office, one story below. The LSB had old-fashioned windows that actually opened from the outside. Itzak's had been painted over many times and was completely stuck. That was fortunate, because the window latch was in the unlocked position.

With a few simple tools, Adam chiseled away at the layers of paint along the woodwork holding the windowpane. He tried not to make a mess that might attract police attention. After an hour of patient gouging, he was able to pry the window open and enter the study.

Adam shone his cavers' lantern on the floor, covered with an ancient red Persian carpet. It took seconds to locate the cake of blood where Itzak's neck had rested. He was surprised at how much blood had been lost. The incision had been small, and the wound should have clotted naturally.

Adam scraped just enough crusted blood onto a filter paper and poured the contents into a sample jar, carefully destroying all evidence of scrapings.

He climbed back down to the ground, removing all his equipment and stashing it in nearby bushes. Then he unlocked the main door to the LSB, ran up the stairs to the third floor, and entered the main laboratory, not far from where he'd been just ten minutes before. He left the dried blood for Jack Chin to analyze in the morning.

Adam refused to let his own informal murder investigation stop any work. He continued to delegate, relying on his ability to juggle several hot irons at the same time. As urgent as solving the crime was, that was a mere nuisance. Continuing Itzak's research was far more important.

First thing that morning, Adam proceeded to Itzak's laboratory, where Saul Lowenstein was strapping Little Oscar onto a small pad, on which the rat had willingly positioned himself, waiting for the usual cheese snack. The animal had a miniature IV permanently implanted in his back, so he suffered no pain while receiving fluid. The rat was to about to be injected with the first of four daily rations of 10 milliliters of vitamin-C enriched I-complex. The entire procedure took only five minutes, after which Little Oscar jumped off the table and into Saul's coat pocket.

Later, Adam took Little Oscar to his private study, where he punched the rodent's hind end with a hypodermic syringe loaded with Rita's "Bloody Mary" mix. The animal squeaked in protest. "That's all right, little fellow," Adam purred. "This is your last shot. I hope you stay well."

If the rat survived Rita's viruses, it would prove enriched I-complex worked. That should prove that a similar substance would protect humans from viral infections and cancer.

Adam joined Jack in the genetic engineering laboratory. The scientist had spent most of the day rigging equipment for the relatively mundane task of analyzing Itzak's blood. Adam helped patch in testing equipment borrowed from the med center hospital. He watched as Jack first dissolved a gram of solid blood and then began to filter out natural organic materials. After a couple of hours, they had syrup containing only compounds normally foreign to the body.

The sample was given a spectroscopic analysis. That process examines the light reflected by chemical compounds, each of which yields distinctive colors and intensities. Like a person's fingerprints, every substance had its own telltale signature. But like identifying suspects from a pane of glass touched by dozens of people, it would be difficult to separate the compounds, especially with contamination by floor dirt and strange dies from the Persian carpet.

The two men worked into the night, sustaining themselves on coffee and stale doughnuts leftover from morning. After a few more hours of detective work using a diagnostic computer program, one by one they eliminated various identified chemicals, erasing them from the composite spectral signature. At last, only one compound remained to be identified. Finally, Jack announced, "there is definitely a trace of *warafin...*"

"Wow!" howled Adam. "That's rat poison! How ironic!"

In small doses, warafin was also given to stroke victims to keep their blood thin, dissolving any clots before further damage. In larger quantities, warafin caused rats to bleed to death, their blood oozing out of the tiniest pores. That agent caused Itzak to bleed until his heart failed from insufficient supply.

The DA had been partly right. The tracheotomy had probably caused Itzak's death, but only because of the warafin. And that substance would have caused internal bleeding eventually followed by death, even without Adam's neck incision. But the blood anticoagulant had not caused the choking and breathing impairment, apparently a severe allergic reaction to some unrelated agent. Whatever other substances the killer had employed, there was no trace in the blood.

At sunrise the tired scientists left for home.

Adam's cell phone jingled as he was eating lunch at the med center cafeteria. He grabbed it from its case, wrapping his sandwich in a napkin at the same time. The hospital operator told him to call Saul Lowenstein.

"Little Oscar is warm and lethargic," Saul spouted over the phone. "I think he has an infection!"

"God, I feel awful," Adam replied. "Put him in his cage. I'll check as soon as I return."

"Damn!" Adam cursed silently, tossing his sandwich in the trash.

Little Oscar could not be saved. Vitamin-C fortification had just been proven unworkable, dashing hopes for a quick route to human therapy. A ludicrous vision flashed in Adam's mind of a person tied to an IV taking a gallon of unfortified fluid every hour.

Adam was too depressed to progress normally through the rest of the day. At these times a good walk was the best therapy, and he wandered on city streets toward the main campus, thinking about Vera.

Her sister Nora was only three years older, and Vera's genetic time bomb was ticking loud and fast. Although not certain that Vera would get the same cancer, Adam judged the chance quite high.

The trait was transmitted through mitochondrial DNA, making it comparable to a more typical hereditary disease. Adam mused that his germ-line intervention in *male sperm* would never eradicate this disease from future generations, since the trait passed only from mothers to daughters.

If Vera got the cancer and it was caught early, there was a 70 percent chance she would live. But only after a radical mastectomy. That would weaken her arms and upper torso, which would likely ruin her violin career. But at least she could then lead a normal life.

The walk was good, allowing Adam's mind to flow freely, meandering wherever it happened. Images of meals, childhood, war, and sex popped in at random. He didn't force the issue.

Suddenly, the thought exploded in his head: those chemicals giving rise to I-complex are generated naturally to fight viral diseases. They are only present in the body while the infection is active.

Of course! Rather than introducing a synthetic from outside, he would coax the body into manufacturing its own I-complex and related chemicals. He didn't need the illusive I-complex itself to get the job done. The only challenge would be preventing the crucial substances from metabolizing and disappearing entirely. That could be done by maintaining the *infection* itself.

Adam was bursting with excitement.

In all infections that healed, the conquering chemicals always disappeared with the cure, usually eradicating the underlying disease source. But for some infections the fighters disappear before the job is completed.

Adam recalled his lectures on *herpes simplex.* As with most virus diseases, body chemistry stops the infection, and then the body quits making the virus-killing substances. But the body pushes that particular scourge into dormancy only. The stealthy virus is still there, ready to re-infect. Herpes is not killed and its symptoms reoccur throughout the host's life.

That was it! He would find a herpetic virus that never goes dormant and remains constantly active.

Adam shuddered at the thought of permanent fever blisters. His virus must have no debilitating symptoms. Where would he find such a virus?

Adam's mind raced in a manic burst. He was, after all, a geneticist, and one of the few people who could create life forms on demand. He vowed to engineer that virus.

It would be no small feat. His mutant herpes would have to be altered to withstand forces pushing for dormancy. The host must continuously fight but never conquer its active infection, generating nonstop I-complex-type chemical flows. To engineer such a virus, he would have to create different mutations, trying them out like new shoes. None could bring horrid effects nor be virulent enough to infect others.

There would be tremendous dangers in such tinkering. An experimental volunteer could end up with permanent shingles, chicken pox, or worse. At the first sign of trouble, the engineered viruses must be shut down, killed to save the patient and to prevent their spread. All of Adam's mutated viruses would need a stopping mechanism for doing that.

Keeping the body infected was a radical thought for a physician. Medicine traditionally shows little concern for what happens in a healthy body, one that had won its battle with the disease. Furthermore, medicine always has fought disease. Adam now planned to do the direct opposite—*create* a new disease, one that could *never* be cured.

To that end, he would convert Itzak's cell-division project into a genetic engineering effort, beginning with animal studies.

But even if everything worked as envisioned, and the proper mutated virus was found, it would be many years before *public* trials could begin. Slow-paced conventional research would not satisfy Adam's immediate need to prevent Vera's imminent cancer. He would accelerate the process and conduct the human experiments clandestinely, using *himself*.

As Adam reached the LSB, he had it all worked out in his head. His plan would require systematic deception of the highest order. He felt a strange mixture of guilt, fear, and elation.

But his euphoria evaporated when he remembered about his pending murder indictment.

17

The Hidden Agenda

Adam hadn't spoken to Dave Wiley since his attorney, Tom Essinger, had intervened over the genetics chairman's veiled threats to discipline him prior to trial. Wiley had acquiesced when the attorney promised legal sanctions.

Adam confidently marched into the Genetics Department office. "Hi, Jill. I need to see Dave Wiley."

"He's on the phone with NIH. They want to cut funding."

"Cutbacks always happen when I need more," he said lightly. "I'll wait."

Adam admired Jill's blouse. Inspired by a Japanese silkscreen, it depicted a couple sitting under a magnolia tree beside a lake.

"So how are your parents?"

"They're doing okay for eighty-year-olds. Like many traditional Japanese their age, they spend mornings meditating. They're preparing themselves for death."

"I thought they were younger."

"That's a natural assumption, since I'm only thirty-two. But I'm the baby of the family. I have a brother twenty-five years older."

Life and death, Adam thought. He had difficulty reconciling with death. Although the new obviously requires the old to step aside, it would be an incredible waste to lose the Yamamotos' 160 years' worth of collective experience, only to have their spots taken by new babies.

"I guess it's normal for Japanese to prepare for death. They're so orderly and efficient in all aspects of their lives."

Jill felt comfortable with Adam and was not shy about displaying her intellect. "Not all Japanese are so acquiescent. Acceptance of death follows from the Shinto-Buddhist cultural influence, which unfortunately is on the wane. Japanese are becoming more like us. Teenagers now think themselves immortal, just like American kids. Many rich Japanese act as if they'll be taking their money with them after they die."

"Jill," Dave Wiley shouted through the closed door. "Call Dean Boucher's secretary and arrange for lunch."

"Yes, sir." Opening his door a crack, she told him, "Dr. Boatwright is here to see you."

"Send him in," he barked.

Adam quickly collected his thoughts as he entered the department chairman's office.

"Hi, Adam. It seems like yesterday that we last talked."

"It *was* the day before yesterday, on the phone," Adam replied, grateful Wiley had not mentioned Adam's role in Itzak's death.

Adam proceeded directly to essential business. "In our last face-to-face, we spoke about bringing Itzak Friedman's project into the Genetics Department."

"He would have been a real attractor of funds," Wiley said sadly. "What's the Physiology Department going to do now? They informed me you're in charge."

"That depends on what you and I cook up. I'm hoping we can bring project control here. This is where the work's being done."

Dave Wiley perked up noticeably, seeming to salivate at the prospect of taking over Friedman's project. Curing rat cancer seemed unimportant to Wiley, in and of itself. For him, it was only a means to obtain grant money. But Adam needed Wiley and would manipulate his boss to get what he wanted.

Adam gave Wiley the essential details.

His boss absorbed it all, nodding his head energetically at each of Adam's key points.

"Man, oh man!" Wiley finally exclaimed. "We have a blank check here."

Adam had been careful to avoid mentioning Itzak's hidden agenda of self-experimentation. Secretly, Adam had now modified the problem from one of chemistry to one of genetics, and with different players, and saving his wife from cancer had now become his own private goal. Adam's formal proposal would be animal research exclusively—engineering a new *mouse* disease to cause the mouse's body to continuously manufacture I-complex-type chemicals. That investigation should suggest human counterparts.

18

Staring into the Abyss

Adam finally had time to search med center files for information about Itzak. He was pleased to find only the night clerk on duty. He smiled at the clerk without stopping on his way to check the patient records.

Adam entered the large cabinet-filled room and walked to the personnel files. Fortunately, the employee medical records were unlocked, and he was able to look up Itzak Friedman's information.

There it was! "Allergies to drugs: streptomycin, penicillin, amoxicillin."

Any one of them would send Itzak into shock, causing his stupor just when Adam had found him, and eventually driving the victim to lose consciousness. Itzak's body would have processed that drug while he was still alive. No traces would have appeared in the sample used to find the blood thinner. "We have it!" he whispered excitedly.

Adam was in his jeans and T-shirt, reading the paper, when Vera entered the apartment with a takeout dinner and groceries. She was wearing her hair down and free, the way he liked it.

"Hi honey. Are those ribs I smell?" Adam asked hungrily.

"Tony Roma's. You're home early."

"Short day, long story. Let's eat now. I missed lunch."

Adam would eventually tell his story. He thought she was willing to wait patiently and join him in a quiet dinner, making light conversation. He took a few moments to watch her prepare the plates for dinner. After a dessert of hot apple pie, Adam and Vera would sip their coffee.

They began talking as Vera unpacked the rest of the groceries. Vera seemed eager to hear more and didn't wait to start probing. "Now, Adam, tell me about your day."

He told her about analyzing Itzak's blood.

"How on earth did he consume rat poison? Wouldn't the murderer need a gun to force him to eat it?"

"The killer *injected* him with the substance. It works as a blood-thinning agent."

"So he bled to death?"

"Yes."

"It doesn't look good, does it?" asked Vera, her voice trembling.

"Yes, it does," Adam answered in an upbeat tone. "Another substance caused him to choke, and I know what it was. Itzak was allergic to several antibiotics. One was administered by the killer, causing the suffocation spell."

"A health professional must have done that. Oh Adam, I'm worried about your safety."

Her words sent a chill down Adam's spine.

Adam hadn't finished.

"There's more to my day," Adam said at last.

"Do I want to hear it?" she asked, putting the lukewarm ribs into the microwave.

"It's not about Itzak's death," he reassured her in a calming tone.

Adam told her of Itzak's planned self-experiment to prove I-complex works on humans, just as with rats. Adam explained about

Little Oscar's injections. That test proved that I-complex with vitamin-C enrichment would have failed.

"Why would Itzak want to experiment on himself?"

Adam told of Hannah Friedman's cancer and how Itzak was desperate to find a cure.

"Wouldn't it be terribly unethical for him to experiment on himself?" she asked, taking a big logical leap.

"It definitely would be. Itzak was going to bend all the rules."

Adam discussed the impediments to medical advances. "If Louis Pasteur were developing the rabies cure under today's rules, he would've died of old age before it was implemented. Walter Reed would've never been allowed to use his treatments for Yellow Fever—even after infecting himself—without double-blind studies taking decades to complete.

"I empathize with Itzak," Adam continued. "In fact, I colluded with him, although in a minor way."

"How?"

"I kept his secret. I told him about vitamin-C enrichment. I followed through with Little Oscar. Only you, I, and Dave Wiley know the full story about Itzak's pet rat."

"Wiley!" Vera sneered. "I wouldn't trust him as far as I can toss a bass violin."

"Wiley's okay. He's too preoccupied with funding and power to care that Itzak was about to violate the rules. I need Wiley."

Vera removed the dinners from the microwave. "What do you mean, you need Wiley?"

"I'm going to step in Itzak's shoes, *literally*. I'm going to find a cure for cancer."

"Oh Adam, you must know that's not possible!"

"It *is* possible, and I'm doing it for the same reasons," he said in a reassuring tone. "But I'm making a midcourse correction."

Adam then described his general plan to genetically engineer a mouse virus that would continuously infect the host, permanently generating I-complex-type chemicals.

Vera interrupted. "And you plan to use that as a cover to engineer your own human virus, using yourself as a Guinea pig. That would be a crime."

"What I'm planning is *subterfuge*, for sure. But it's hardly a crime. It's for the greater good of humankind. I'm sure it'll end well."

"Okay, out with it," Vera erupted. "Why are you in such a hurry you can't go through normal channels?"

"The truth is—I want to prevent your getting breast cancer," Adam blurted. He caught his breath, almost gasping, "I can't live without you."

Vera responded shrilly. "I'll never let you ruin your career—possibly go to jail—just for me!"

"It's not for you to decide. I've already set the wheels in motion."

The dinner sat on the table, getting cold.

Vera's eyes filled with tears. "I'm concerned for your safety. You could get a terrible disease."

"I'll have protection. I'll build a stopper mechanism into the viruses created. That way, I can quickly destroy any that give bad effects."

"If one of them doesn't kill you first."

She had pinpointed the greatest risk. Some viruses are very fast acting and can kill within hours. But he would stay within the herpetic family, making incremental changes to DNA. It was a tremendous gamble with long odds.

Adam stared into Vera's eyes, wishing he could mesmerize her. "Imagine if the procedure did work. You'd never get Nora's cancer, and neither of us would die from cancer of any type."

But Vera remained practical and logical. "Yes, that might be nice. But wouldn't our bodies stop *aging*, too?"

Adam hadn't confronted the aging issue since those early days with Itzak. Of course, she was right again.

"Yes, all bodily cells would divide perfectly," Adam answered in a fluster. "That would guarantee our bodies wouldn't age."

"We'd be virtual immortals!"

"We could survive until some bacterial infection got us or until we had an accident," Adam replied, feeling the tug of the debate going her way.

"For thousands of years?"

"I think so, but I can't say for sure," Adam sputtered.

"Not just us, *everybody*!"

Adam had clearly not thought it through completely. Curing cancer for the human race would be tantamount to granting over six billion people spectacularly long lives, making them virtually immortal. He didn't want to think about that. But Vera persisted.

"You're not God, Adam. Once you let the genie out of the bottle, you'll have to share it. First thousands, then millions, and finally billions of people would infect themselves with your magic virus. That can't be stopped, once your secret gets out."

"I don't want to stop it."

"We've been over this ground, Adam. Fewer deaths and insufficient birth control will cause the planet will fill up twice as fast as it's doing now."

"There are still limits," he protested. "People will still not live forever."

"Of course they won't!" Vera exclaimed. "Some will have to die *anyway*, of starvation, of murder, of drowning, of any accident. But *never* from old age!"

"People will still die from disease. The I-complex chemicals will not control poisons, bacteria, parasites, fungi, or more esoteric biota."

Vera's points cut like a hot blade through butter. "Precisely! Some people must die. All people will die with young bodies, since there would be no old-age, as we know it. Their deaths will be horrible. Is that what you want?"

"Of course not," said Adam, looking pained.

Vera finally gave the *coup de grace*. "Here's your moral dilemma. You cheat and discover a cure for cancer. We become immortal, or virtually so. You have to then decide whether to share the secret or not.

The answer from where you're coming is to *share.* To do otherwise would violate everything you stand for. You will cure one disease, give everybody youth, but in the long run you'll guarantee them horrible deaths."

In silence, they ate cold ribs. Then they spent the rest of the evening quietly with their chores and reading. Adam's head was spinning.

They held each other tightly in bed. Both eventually drifted off to sleep.

Adam was crawling down a tunnel, leading to a cavern. He could see a red glow. Magma, he told himself. But it wasn't in a limestone cavern. The walls were of hot granite. "Welcome to hell," Brother Jonathan's voice echoed.

Adam brought himself awake with a shout, "No!" he hollered, waking Vera.

"That dream again?" she asked knowingly.

"Yes," he cried. "Nothing in my life bothers me like that dream."

Vera knew better, telling herself: *Poor Adam. I hope he'll never find that virus.*

19

Quest for a Super Virus

Genetics chairman Dave Wiley and Dean Robert Boucher, head of Life Sciences, were teeing off at the tenth hole at Fox Trails Country Club. The sun was warm in the November Wednesday afternoon. Both men had the tanned patina of summer sun worshippers. Avoiding extra exertion, they sat beside the fairway in an electric golf cart.

"I really like golfing in the middle of the week," Wiley smiled. "I use weekends for errands and light chores. I hate crowds."

Robert Boucher was sixty, a tall, thin man, bald at the top, with a neatly trimmed beard and mustache. "I like Monday and Wednesday afternoons, if I can find partners. It's impossible to arrange a foursome, except after Dean's Council meetings."

Wiley stared down the deserted fairway. "I have the same problem. Few faculty ever play golf. I guess we work them too hard. I mainly golf with retirees, doctors, or lawyers. They're practically strangers."

"I guess you envy their incomes," Boucher said, seconds before driving his ball 150 yards in a high parabolic arc.

"Fortunately, I inherited a substantial sum from my father," Wiley replied. "He was chairman of Millner Laboratories. I always had a job there as a student. I learned the value of a buck early."

Wiley smartly set himself in position for a powerful swing. Like a ballet dancer, he twisted his whole body in a continuous smooth motion, transmitting so much force to his club that it sent the ball flying nearly two hundred yards. "I still consult for Millner and they do small custom jobs for some of our research projects."

"When you retire, you can replace the Fox Trails golf pro."

After the eighteenth hole, the two scientists retired to the lounge.

"I had a call from the med school dean yesterday," Boucher announced, sipping his Dewars. "He was mad as hell about losing the liver cell-division project. That was the first I heard of it."

"Sorry, boss," Wiley apologized, "I had to act fast."

"You went over my head, straight to Wentworth. I felt like some cuckold."

Wiley smiled faintly, telling himself that wasn't far from the mark. Deans didn't have much power. The real stakes were with the departments, closer to the work, closer to the sponsoring agencies.

"That won't happen again," Wiley promised, mentally crossing his fingers.

"Tell me about the project."

"It's not much, really. Just some cancer experiments with mice."

Wiley was stingy with information, parceling it out where advantageous. There was nothing to be gained by telling the figurehead dean any more than absolutely necessary. Besides, Boucher was a botanist and knew little about zoology.

Within hours after the cell-division project had been transferred, the Genetics Department assimilated Itzak's three staff members. Saul Lowenstein would be reporting to Rita Morales, director of animal activities. The other two technicians would begin collecting and organizing Itzak's original cell-division data, inventorying, and shutting down the liver-cell activities.

The focus of the group's activity was the mouse laboratory. Connected to it was the cage room, where several hundred mice were quartered in sanitary warrens. With the temperature controlled and plenty of food, the animals lived out their pampered lives free from predators.

Every research group has its own genetic strains of test animals, with crossbreeding strictly controlled. The closest human equivalent to those inbred mice was nineteenth-century European royalty. Only a few generations of closed marriage among those princes and princesses had led to high incidences of hereditary diseases, including hemophilia. More extreme examples took place in Hawaii and ancient Egypt, where brothers and sisters sometimes married.

Laboratory mice were inbred much more extensively than any other creatures in human experience, creating large populations of weaklings. The near-clones had limited genetic diversity. That brought efficiency in comparing experimental groups to the controls, the latter receiving just placebos or normal treatments.

Rita brought Saul into the cage room. "It'll take some adjustment to work with these little guys. Mice aren't as hardy as rats."

"You look like you've just come from a funeral," Rita said.

"I had to put our pet rat to sleep," he replied. "I'll miss him terribly. But I've worked with rodents of all kinds. At the San Diego zoo I tended capybaras, beavers, and marmots. We had little ones too—kangaroo rats and field mice."

Rita had been happiest working mainly by herself. She was wary at the prospect of working with Saul, but vowed to make the best of it. "It'll be great to work with someone who shares my love for animals."

"I'm okay, except for the euthanasia," Saul said as he petted one of the mice.

"You and Adam! Don't worry. Putting mice to sleep is my job." She wondered if her virus cocktail had killed Saul's pet.

Adam had begun tapping his staff for inputs for his urgent project to engineer the special virus. Just three of his staff would be the leaders of that secret effort. So far, only Adam knew the real objective: getting a mouse virus that continually infected its host, thereby constantly generating I-complex inside the animal itself. That virus had to be harmless. It was a tall order.

For their special skills, Adam had selected Rita Morales, Jack Chin, and Sandra Wickham. A common bond was that they already worked for Adam, and each had demonstrated complete loyalty.

Rita Morales would be collecting mouse viruses that displayed obvious symptoms. That was very odd and backward from standard procedure. Usually a *known* virus is tested, and the investigator determines how mice react under various treatment regimens for killing the virus. Rita had never searched for a virus that gave a particular symptom.

Extremely curious, Rita was nonetheless reconciled with being patient. Adam would fill in the details when he was ready.

Rita continued to indoctrinate Saul, who would assist in both the old and new projects. "Your tasks will include animal maintenance, injections, and drawing samples. These little guys are part of a genetic experiment involving germ-line intervention. The young ones all have a black-eared trait. We'll be importing a new strain of mice reared especially for their quick response to viral infections. Those will be your responsibility."

Jack Chin had been asked to help on the new mouse experiments, switching from changing mice genes to altering their *viruses*. Virus DNA was easier to reproduce because of its relative simplicity.

Jack easily propagated viruses in his lab, where he could clone one individual into thousands of exact copies within hours. These small quantities would be sufficient for mouse studies. Greater volumes of viruses would be needed for human research. Those would have to be grown in a commercial laboratory.

The real challenge was getting an original mutated virus. Adam planned to implement the changes using software developed by the Crunchers. (The three men in that group weren't involved in the new project.) Jack would then be responsible for the chemical part of the genetic engineering. They had refined that technology on mouse DNA for germ-line intervention. Since DNA of the *mouse* itself was far more complex than DNA of any mouse *virus*, Jack was confident they could make needed changes.

Jack wondered why the new project would focus on the mouse *virus* rather than on the mouse itself. He would eventually have the answer. His present concern was only with the *how*.

Sandra Wickham thought deeply about Adam's new virus project. Participation would be independent of her continuing work with DNA mapping software and the other Crunchers.

Sandra was to write a new computer program to identify the DNA coordinates for controlling cell division within a mouse virus. Adam also wanted to create a gene to interrupt that process on command. This *stopper* gene would be dormant until triggered by a special vaccine injected into the mouse. The vaccine would activate that gene, disabling the ability of the virus to reproduce itself.

Sandra accepted at face value Adam's request for secrecy and didn't worry about why he needed it. She supposed it was simply a normal part of finding a cure.

Today the secret task force was meeting in the Genetics Department conference room, under the auspices of one of the conventional cancer studies. No outsiders knew the true agenda.

"I'm glad you made it on such short notice," Adam said, launching the first get-together of the new task force. "Our goal is to engineer a virus that keeps a mouse constantly infected while causing no serious problems."

"That's backward," said Jack Chin. "There aren't any good viruses. You're saying that instead of fighting a virus, you want to ensure its permanence?"

"Exactly," Adam said, congratulating himself for picking Jack. "I have a long story to tell. You're all familiar with Itzak Friedman's cell-division experiment. Well, Itzak found that his I-complex guarantees faithful replications in *live* animals, although an analogous substance gives limited benefit to human cells cultured *outside* the body."

"How did he make animal cells divide faithfully?" Rita Morales asked.

"He did it with chemical injections. His subject was his pet rat, Little Oscar. The rodent lived over *ten* years."

"Impossible!" Rita exclaimed. "Rats live about three to five years, max. They nearly always die of cancer."

"My reaction was the same," Adam admitted. "But it's true. Little Oscar would still be alive today, and maybe last for another ten years too, if you and I hadn't killed him."

Rita gasped. "My Bloody Mary cocktail!"

"So Itzak's I-complex injections prevented the rat from ever getting cancer?" Sandra asked, incredulous.

Adam turned to face Rita. "That's right. And Itzak wanted to do the same with humans. I suggested an alternative, which we tried on the rat. Unfortunately, Little Oscar died."

"I didn't know any of this," Saul said, shaking his head.

Adam started to pace nervously. "Itzak showed us that I-complex stops cancer in rats. We want to do the same thing for humans. But instead of injecting a human substance after cloning it outside the body, we'll generate the human counterparts naturally. That's why we need a continuous infection—"

"I'm missing something. Aren't we working with mice?" Saul interrupted.

"We can't experiment directly with humans until much later," Adam explained. "We must always start with *animals*. If we only wanted to save rats or mice from cancer, we already know what to do. But eventually we'll require a *human* virus to coax the body to generate *human* I-complex-type chemicals. Outside injection won't be practical on people."

"Got it! Thanks," Saul replied.

Jack found it hard to contain himself. "This is so unnatural. We're going to create a *super* virus that keeps the mouse infected?"

"Precisely. But the new virus must be harmless. We need a mechanism for quickly killing any test virus that doesn't work properly. We have to engineer a chemically-triggered stopper gene."

"Okay," Rita interjected. "I need to clarify things. During the animal research phase, you need *two* sets of mouse viruses. The first batch will be more Bloody Mary cocktails for testing the stopper gene. We won't even look at the second group until the stopper is perfected. Those will be your candidates for the mutated virus. Do I have it right?"

"That's close," Adam answered gratefully. "But once we have a general idea of how a stopper gene must work, we'll customize it to *each* candidate for the super virus."

Adam paused. "I love that name—*super* virus. Thanks, Jack."

"Now I see where you were headed," Sandra said. "You want me to do the computer workup for engineering a stopper gene, followed by workups on the various super-virus candidates themselves. Then, you and Jack will use my recommendations to make the actual DNA changes."

"Precisely," said Adam, content that his project appeared to be in good hands.

20

Tainted Evidence

Adam had awakened Bonnie Burton with a morning phone call, telling her about the blood results and Itzak's drug allergies. He asked her to meet him at the Crunchers' computer lab in the LSB. He placed similar calls to Mandy, Timothy, and Dutch. When Adam reached the lab they were all there and had exchanged information. Adam handed still sleepy Bonnie a cup of black coffee.

"Warafin is a generic blood thinner and can be manufactured by anybody," Bonnie said. "It's distributed in the U.S. by Jacobsen Labs under the name Actifin. The antibiotics causing Dr. Friedman's allergic reaction could have come from a dozen manufacturers."

"Okay, Timothy," Adam said, "find which nearby customers received shipments of Actifin from Jacobsen. We'll be waiting in the staff lounge."

It took just ten minutes for Timothy to report back. "Within the last six months, only two places received Actifin—Central University Medical Center and Good Hope Hospital."

Adam thought for a moment. "We should stay with the med center for the time being. It's your turn, Dutch. I want you to find all persons who have obtained Actifin from central pharmacy."

While Dutch tapped the university databases, Adam and the other Crunchers enjoyed a coffee break. That lasted less than five minutes.

"You're not going to like this," Dutch reported. "There are three names—Dr. Goodwin, Dr. Miller, and *Dr. Boatwright*."

"That devil! The killer was indeed framing me."

It was standard practice to supply the professor's name as the requesting physician. Although neither Adam nor his students had requested Actifin, the actual recipient's signature would be on a prescription form filed away.

Adam was extremely discomfited his name had been used, a fact the DA could use as evidence in a wider murder investigation. But that didn't slow him.

"We're running out of time. We'll have to pursue the Pan Palestinian Freedom Alliance hypothesis. Dutch, get a listing of all foreign staff and students at the med center."

The others continued sipping their coffee while Dutch ran that errand. It took him only a few minutes to generate a three-page printout. Grabbing the list, Adam shook his head in dismay. "This had to be a person familiar with drugs. A pharmacy student, a med student, a nurse, perhaps."

The three staff members each took a page, crossing out any names that were not of Middle Eastern origin or unlikely to have checked out Actifin.

Bonnie was the first to speak. "I think I've found her," she said. "A pharmacy student, Nesti Aziz from Cairo."

Adam frowned. "Let's do a crosscheck on her. Dutch, see if this Aziz has ever drawn any of the three suspect antibiotics from the med school pharmacy."

Dutch went to his computer and typed and clicked for a couple of minutes.

He soon came back with the news: "Two days before Dr. Friedman's death, Nesti Aziz requisitioned 50 milliliters of liquid amoxicillin for a lab experiment."

That drug was ordinarily administered orally in pill form, rarely injected as a liquid. And the dosage was extraordinarily large.

"It fits!" Adam exclaimed gleefully. "She must be the one. Hers is the only likely name.

Mandy took only two hours tweaking her network of contacts to compile a biography of Nesti Aziz.

Nesti was a Palestinian, originally from Gaza, where she had spent her childhood. Her parents had emigrated there shortly after Israel was formally established in 1948. Her father had prospered as a druggist, and he became a pharmaceutical importer for the entire Middle East. The family moved to Cairo in Nesti's teen years. Her politically oriented brother had joined Hamas. He was killed by Israeli soldiers shortly before Nesti went to college.

Nesti's father had been devastated by the loss of his only son, whom he had wanted to take over the family business. A modern thinker, he had shifted that responsibility to Nesti. After taking her degree in chemistry from Cairo University, Nesti had won admittance to Central University's pharmacology program.

After hearing Mandy's report, Adam felt totally vindicated. He needed only to call his lawyer to put a stop to further nonsense.

The Essingers were just finishing breakfast when Tom answered his cell phone. "Adam, what's going on?" asked Essinger, his mind not yet fully operational.

"I've solved the crime," Adam proudly announced, relieved at his vindication. Adam related to Essinger the story about the break-in, the blood analysis, and the med center pharmacy records.

"Stop right now!" Essinger ordered. "What you did is illegal. You can't steal evidence that way. We have to go through channels."

"What do you mean?" Adam asked incredulously. "We've solved the crime."

Restraining himself, the lawyer replied, "Yes, but your evidence is *inadmissible*. Everything you found is tainted, because there was no warrant to get the blood sample."

"Nonsense! I broke into Itzak's study, but I'm entitled to be there, since I now run his project. Why do I need a warrant?" Adam asked, beginning to get very angry.

The attorney continued, using the tone of a stern father. "Once the study was sealed, in the eyes of the court it was no longer yours to enter unescorted. You could be prosecuted for tampering with evidence."

"So what should we do?" Adam shot back impudently.

Essinger spoke like an officer of the court. "I'll see Judge Wheeler in the morning. I'll tell her nothing about your shenanigans, but I'll suggest a blood workup. She can direct the DA to have the police perform it in their crime lab. I can say nothing about what you know."

Adam couldn't believe his ears. "But, the chemistry is complex. It took my best genetic engineer to decipher the blood. I don't think the police can do it."

"They have the best forensic labs available."

Adam had no confidence that the crime labs would find anything except Persian-carpet vegetable dye. "And how long do you suppose that'll take?" Adam asked, seething inside and struggling to control himself.

"Maybe two or three weeks."

"By which time I'll have been indicted for murder," Adam replied with disgust.

"Yes, but the wheels will be turning. We have a good case."

Adam tried one more time. "Why can't I just go to the police, who'll arrest the culprit and obtain a confession?"

Essinger sprinkled more cold water. "Because they know that confession would be inadmissible, since it was based on the illegally obtained evidence. The police wouldn't do it—even if they believed you."

"But the confession would clear my name, wouldn't it? It would prove my innocence."

"Yes, but the police won't ruin any case against your suspect just to clear you."

"Then we have a Catch-22 situation," Adam sighed, feeling like a helpless child.

"I'm afraid so."

"I'll get her to confess. I'm not bound by rules of evidence and legal protocol."

"Don't do it!" was the last Adam heard before angrily clicking off his phone and leaving his apartment.

A dark-haired stranger got onto the elevator with Adam. Noticing the roughness of the man's hands and his sun-darkened skin, Adam guessed he was a landscaper visiting neighbor Willard Emerson about the gardens at the Emerson country home, East of town.

But why did the man look so troubled?

Adam's mind shifted back into gear as the elevator reached ground level. But he didn't notice the landscaper, who was observing Adam get into his car. He paid no attention as the stranger followed him across town in a gray Volkswagen.

21

Gone to Graveyards, Every One

For several nights Nesti Aziz had restless sleep, haunted by memories of recent events, starting with the Pan Palestinian Freedom Alliance rally.

She had watched glassy-eyed as Hamid Tawfuk railed about the injustice in Palestine and Zionist evils. As typical of females in her native land, she had been raised strictly apolitical. But since coming to America, Nesti had taken a keen interest in the Palestinian cause.

After the rally, she went with Hamid to a nearby coffee shop. They sat in the back, near the folk singer who wailed, *"Where have all the soldiers gone..."*

Making sure nobody could hear, Hamid said in Arabic, "It's finally time for us to act. We must make Israelis take notice that alliance with the PLO cannot lead to peace on their terms. We must kill a prominent Israeli."

Nesti could still hear Hamid's words, punctuated by the singer's: *"Gone to graveyards, every one..."*

Frightened, Nesti asked, "How are you going to do that?"

"It is time for *you* to avenge your brother's death," he responded arrogantly. "*You* must be the one."

For thirty seconds Nesti was speechless. Finally, she mouthed her panicky reply. “I? How can I kill an Israeli? I’ve never even held a gun.”

She could still see the image of Hamid, glaring with an icy stare. “You can be much more effective. You have access to every poison known to man.”

Nesti again experienced feeling like a trapped animal and recalled her words, as she whispered desperately, “I could never poison another human. I’m dedicated to helping preserve life.”

She heard again Hamid’s harsh admonishment. “Nesti! Enough! Jews are subhuman! *Humans* did not kill your brother.”

Gasping for breath, she said desperately, “I can’t. I can’t do it.”

That Hamid was a magician. Nesti was still in awe of his quick change to a more persuasive tone. “Yes, you can. You must. I have selected your target.”

“Who is it?” Nesti remembered asking, not really wanting to know.

“He’s the Zionist molecular biologist, Professor Itzak Friedman,” said Hamid forcefully.

“You want me to kill a professor?” Nesti remembered saying next as she began sobbing softly in disbelief.

She could still hear Hamid speak stridently, as if he himself were going to be the martyr. “Killing him will drive a spike into their hearts. Jews worship scientists. Losing him will be like amputating the right arm of their god.”

“But I will surely be caught,” Nesti had pleaded in a vain attempt at dissuasion.

“No, you won’t,” Hamid said confidently. “I have a way for you to elude suspicion. We’ll plant evidence blaming someone else.”

“Then what good will it do?” Nesti asked. She was ashamed of how she began to feel warm from Hamid’s infectious fire.

Hamid had woven his words like a spider making his web. “Hurting the Zionists would be good enough. But the PPFA can still take credit for your act.”

The memories aroused Nesti’s long-suppressed feelings about her brother’s death. They flared up her until-now buried, simmering hatred of Israel and clouded her judgment.

Hamid had evoked echoes of her long-suppressed hatred. But Nesti now hated herself for succumbing to his lure and asking, "And will I be safe?"

Nesti could still hear Hamid's words of reassurance. "Of course. Regardless of what American police think, Israelis will know why he was assassinated."

Nesti wondered why she had suppressed her fear of being caught. She no longer believed her deed compensated for losing her brother. Remorseful for helping the cause, Nesti no longer felt proud. Now guilt and regret were added to her sorrow. Most of all, she mourned over her breach of contract with humanity.

Nesti responded to the doorbell, opening the door just a crack.

"It's Bill Thomlinson," the complex manager called from the hallway.

Nesti opened the door. The blood drained from her face when she saw Adam Boatwright standing next to Thomlinson.

"Nesti, I have to talk to you about an emergency at the hospital," Adam announced as he warily walked in uninvited. "Thanks, Mr. Thomlinson."

Adam was struck by the starkness of her studio apartment. There was no decoration except for one wall containing a black and white 8" by 10" photo of a young man. Beneath the picture was a small shelf holding two burning candles.

Pulling the door shut, Adam stared at Nesti. She was an attractive dark-haired woman, quite thin, with a faded olive complexion. She wore no makeup, and she had on jeans and a blue blouse, presenting an appearance as dull as her place. But her face was indelibly etched with grief and fear.

Adam wasted no words. He coldly announced, "I know about the Actifin and amoxicillin. I know you probably murdered Itzak Friedman and more or less how you did it."

Nesti could hardly speak.

"Tell me," Adam continued, imitating a steely film detective, "did you stab him first with a syringe full of amoxicillin?"

Appearing resigned to her fate and looking severely remorseful, Nesti decided to be honest—perhaps she could no longer bear the guilt.

She started to give the details. Adam recorded it all. "My friend, Hamid, and I picked the lock and were waiting inside Friedman's study when he arrived at 7:30. At gunpoint, we forced Friedman to write you a note to come. We waited in his office until 8:15, when I administered the first injection, amoxicillin. Then I gave him the injection of Actifin. Within minutes he was nearly comatose. When my friend signaled that you were walking from the parking lot, I gave Friedman a shot of antidote to partially revive him. I left the door ajar and quickly walked to the ladies' room. Later, when you ran to the main office, I went back to make sure that Friedman was dead. I left the building and took the shuttle bus to the med center."

"Why did you select me as your cover?"

"Hamid already had several candidates. After hearing you arguing with Friedman in the cafeteria, he chose you. He bragged how it was so perfect, since Friedman had shouted that you were a murderer."

"That's plausible. How did you know I would perform a tracheotomy?"

"We didn't. It was a good guess. But regardless, he was doomed. The Actifin would have caused massive internal hemorrhage, followed by death. Any open wound would also have bled profusely, and a tracheotomy would make it look like you had murdered Friedman. We had an extra syringe full of amoxicillin to plant in your office, just in case you didn't do that procedure. Your fingerprints were all over it. We knew that the Jews would make autopsy impossible, and the Actifin would not be found."

"So why did you do it?" Adam finally asked.

"It was political. I was mesmerized by PPFA rhetoric and mad at the Israelis for killing my brother. But you must believe me, Dr. Boatwright, I've never stopped regretting my crime."

Adam asked her to come with him to the police station and tell her story. She agreed, telling him she was so sorry for listening to

Hamid. She felt she had been given no real choice about killing Friedman, and she was willing to make a deal.

As they were leaving the building, Adam heard a shot and saw Nesti drop to the ground. He caught a glimpse of the man from the elevator, his arm extended toward Adam. Instinctively, Adam went prone, rolling toward a nearby stairway. Adam quickly crawled down the stairs, which led to a basement apartment. Fortunately, the door was unlocked, and he entered the empty apartment, locking the door. Adam dug out his cell phone, dialed 911, and reported the shooting. Not ready for a police explanation, he kept it anonymous.

Adam waited in the basement until hearing sirens. He left his hiding place and joined the crowd gathered around Nesti. He didn't touch her, fearing the attention. One of the ambulance attendants pronounced that she was dead.

The police would soon learn Adam had roused Nesti's apartment manager. They would begin looking for him, and he would be a suspect in *two* murders.

Adam deduced that the PPFA would be after him as well—to kill him before the police could ask questions. He took full advantage of the confusion to flee from the scene in his Porsche and call his lawyer as he drove.

Adam was driving to Essinger's when he noticed a gray Volkswagen following close behind. To determine if he was being tailed, Adam turned onto a country lane and pulled into the first driveway. He waited until the Volkswagen roared past, then backed onto the road and headed after his pursuer. The gray car disappeared within minutes.

Adam had resumed driving to his attorney's house when he glanced in his rearview mirror and saw the Volkswagen back on his tail. He was indeed being followed! It was probably Nesti's killer.

Adam wound through country roads for several minutes, not really trying to shake the tail. All the while, his mind was occupied exploring the various possibilities. Since he had the recording of

Nesti's confession, he could clear himself of Itzak's murder. If he could only reach safety, everything would be okay. His Porsche could easily outrun the Volkswagen, and then it would be over.

But would it really end? There would be time-consuming investigations. Although he would eventually be exonerated, Adam had seen how slowly the wheels of justice turned. Meanwhile, he would be vulnerable to Nesti's killer. Not only would he be in danger, but Vera and his entire research team might also be targeted. Could he count on the police for protection?

In his usual fashion, Adam decided to take immediate action himself. He would drive just fast enough to stay out of gunshot range and let the Volkswagen follow. Then he would trick his pursuer.

Adam searched the forested hillsides for the right spot. It took only minutes to find suitable stopping place, alongside a small creek running between two wooded hills. There he pulled to the side, cut the engine, and jumped out of the car.

He ran toward a large clump of trees at the edge of a pine thicket, where he took cover, making sure the pursuer had followed. Then Adam resumed his run, not trying to hide his tracks as he sped through the dense forest. He stopped at a small clearing. Using only his belt, Adam quickly made a booby trap like those used by the Viet Cong. Then he hid and waited.

There was no reaction from the running man when the swishing tree hit his face with enough force to knock him to the ground. The fall jarred loose the assailant's gun, which tumbled out of reach. Before the killer could move, Adam had pounced on his chest and pushed his knee on the man's neck. The man was very strong and managed to struggle toward the fallen weapon, causing Adam to lose balance.

Both reached for the gun, wrestling for control. During the melee the pistol fired, its bullet grazing Adam's shirtsleeve. A second round blasted loud enough to send Adam's ear ringing. That shot hit the killer, causing him to go limp. The bullet had pierced the man's skull.

Adam looked at the man's shattered face. It was the stranger from the Falcon Tower elevator. He guessed it was Hamid.

Adam carried Hamid's still warm corpse back to the road, where the Volkswagen's door was wide open. Adam seated the body behind the steering wheel, laid the gun on the floor by the dead man's feet, and locked the car.

22

Methuselah

Tom Essinger listened incredulously to Adam's story. The attorney then said: "But, none of your evidence could stand up in court. It's tainted fruit from an illegally obtained blood sample. Fortunately, there's no one to convict, and admissibility of evidence is totally moot. It's more than ample for getting all charges against you dropped. Since you have the taped confession, and forensics will tie the assailant's gun to Nesti's death, we won't worry about an indictment for killing the terrorist. That was strictly a case of self-defense."

Essinger called the DA. After a half-hour of conversation, he then placed a call to Judge Wheeler. They talked for only five minutes.

"Both the DA and the judge are angry that you took the law into your own hands," Essinger reported.

"I didn't have a choice," Adam replied, too spent to be angry.

"I'm sure they know that. I think they have great admiration for what you did. You'd better stay with me until things calm down. Though your charges have been dropped, the police will still be looking for you until they get the official word."

Astonishingly, Adam's professional life continued without missing a beat during the hectic days after solving the crime. He accepted at face value Nesti Aziz's story and involvement with the Pan Palestinian Freedom Alliance, a fact later confirmed by follow-up police investigations.

Vera believed there was more to the story. It was a strange coincidence for Itzak to die violently, just when his project was coming to fruition. It was odd for Adam to be implicated in Itzak's murder while taking over the man's work. She didn't share Adam's enthusiasm for the super-virus project and couldn't explain a sense of dread about its direction.

During the two months since its launch, the super-virus task force had engineered a promising mouse virus. That strain caused small skin eruptions, much like human chicken pox. Coded B-13, the mouse-pox virus was similar to human *herpes simplex* and not lethal.

Now the mouse pox had to be modified so that it would continually infect its host. Each engineered mutation would give unpredictable symptoms, some of which might be dangerous.

Adam enjoyed the warmth of the LSB after the chilling wintry walk from his car. He climbed the stairs, wondering about the new task force. The mouse super-virus project had progressed quite rapidly. But something was not right. There were kinks in the flow of ideas and work.

He entered the mouse laboratory just as Rita was reaching into a cage. She grabbed one mouse in her left hand, forcing open its mouth with her right. "Don't bite," she gently warned.

"Hello, Rita. How're you doing today?"

"We have seven male mice ready to receive new viruses," she said. Then she frowned.

"What's wrong?"

"I'm wondering about our breeding stock. Do these mice look like near-twins?"

The mice varied considerably in size. Two of them were very active and the remainder were in a lethargic state. Some had shorter tails, and most had rounded ears, but noticeable points were present on the ears of the rest.

"No Rita, they don't even look related."

"That's what I think. There must be a mix-up in the breeding book. We can only use mice of the same strain."

Standard protocols aimed at maximizing experimental information and avoiding bias. But none of those were necessary for Adam's hidden agenda.

"That won't be a problem for now, Rita. When we have something concrete, we'll carefully redo all testing."

"Aren't you bothered by contaminated mice strains?"

"Yes Rita, I'm bothered. But purity of mice strains will be imperative only when we go public. For now, these mice will tell us what we need to know."

"I see. At least we won't lose time replacing these host mice."

"Rita, do you think somebody's trying to sabotage our work?"

"Either that or someone carelessly mixed the breeders, resulting in these mongrel offspring."

Sandra modified the Crunchers' DNA mapping software to accommodate the mouse-pox virus. Her computer program detailed several mutations, all expected to make the skin eruptions disappear without allowing any mouse's immune system to kill its new virus. In a few hours, Jack had engineered each change. Rita then introduced each new pox into a different host mouse.

Strains A through E had no noticeable effect. As a precaution, the researchers injected the latest stopper vaccine into the host mice, completely destroying the mutant viruses. Strain F caused massive lesions, and its host mouse was put to sleep and incinerated.

Strain G worked as intended, its host mouse clearly infected. Its body temperature was elevated and was steadily generating I-complex-type chemicals. There were no surface blemishes. But the animal's temperature soon dropped to normal.

After a two-day rest, the mouse was stressed by placing it in a chilly environment. Its fever reoccurred, proving that the B-13G virus had not been destroyed by the mouse's immune system. The mutated virus had come back and caused I-complex production to resume. That mutant mouse-pox was permanent and its virus appeared to have a place to hide in the mouse's body.

Jack was excited as he entered Adam's study. "We have our first new candidate for the super virus," he announced with a wide grin.

"What have you found?"

"We have a mutant strain meeting most of your specifications. It induces no harmful symptoms, except a mild fever. Otherwise, it hibernates and recurs, just like human herpes. Especially good news is that other mice cannot catch it through casual contact."

"That's better than a human herpetic infection—no contagion and no fever blisters! Well done!"

Like a general who has just won one battle, Adam quickly shifted gears to the next challenge.

"Now, Jack, you'll have to engineer a way to keep the new virus from going dormant. We'll have a cancer-preventing mouse virus only if the I-complex-type chemical production can be maintained continuously."

This had been an enormous step. But the longest leap was yet to be taken.

Sandra's computer program selected two dozen likely segments within the DNA helixes of the new mouse-pox virus. Sandra and Jack narrowed the choices to six candidates for modification.

Using a new set of host mice, the latest mutations were tried. Variations 1, 2, and 6 disappeared completely. Those viruses were killed by the body's I-complex, and stress did not bring them back. Variation 3 killed its host mouse. Variation 5 had never even infected its mouse. Fortunately, for two weeks, variation 4 had the desired effect, its host mouse having only a slight fever, while its body continuously generated the miracle chemicals.

Designated by the code B-13G.4, the mouse super virus had been found.

It had taken less than three months for the task force to engineer the mouse super virus. They hoped it would prevent mice from ever getting cancer. The host mouse would be monitored throughout its expected long life. Believing the mouse prophetic, the task force named it Methuselah.

Adam ordered the team to infect a dozen other mice with the new mouse super virus. Those animals would be exposed to a variety of known carcinogens in an attempt to induce cancers. They would also be subjected to normally lethal virus cocktails.

As he launched that new round of research, Adam was amazed at how fast and easy it had been to find the super virus. He would wait and see what happened to the twelve experimental mice before engineering a *human* super virus.

23

The Dirty Dozen and the Snowman

Taking advantage of a February warm spell, Adam walked to the main campus from the med center, where he had just lectured on immunology. It had been two days since the "Dirty Dozen" mice had been given the candidate super virus and later treated with a highly lethal collection of pestilence. Adam had high hopes all of them would survive.

As he walked by the Elm Street Park, he watched three preschool-age children building a snowman. Their creation looked more like a sleeping polar bear. That white scene brought his mind back on track, back to mice, and from them to the next task.

Adam was anxious to get started with a human super virus. Although the DNA for humans is more complex than for a mouse, the same didn't hold for their *viruses*. Virus DNA is extremely simple, regardless of host. Some influenza viruses even reside in bird gullets, where new strains evolve. Some of those flu strains have been brought to man by migrating ducks.

A human super virus might someday be a cancer preventive. But only after many years of duplicated research, each step to be governed by protocols, trials, and approvals. For now, Adam needed to prevent Vera from getting cancer, and he would speed the process by testing on himself. He needed no approvals and wanted no scrutiny whatsoever.

This had to be secret to everybody, including his staff. It was taboo for scientists to experiment on themselves, nearly as bad as plagiarism or faking experiments. Discovery could lead to dismissal and banishment from funded research. Although his staff would maintain silence out of loyalty, the essence of the research would be Adam's own powerful secret, and he couldn't take chances. He wouldn't endanger his team's careers by letting them help with research they knew to be forbidden.

Although Adam would be doing it for Vera, humankind would benefit. He planned to share the human super virus and remained unmoved by Vera's arguments otherwise.

Adam now believed that the technology for engineering the mouse super virus should directly transfer to mutating the *herpes simplex*. He would have to work fast, minimizing false starts. There were no mice to sacrifice because of wrong turns. Only himself!

Adam was excited as he entered the LSB and bounded up the stairs to the third floor.

But his hopes and plans were about to be dashed.

Adam was just sitting down, when Rita Morales burst into his study.

"All of the Dirty Dozen are dead! Only Methuselah is still alive."

"I don't understand," said Adam, in shock.

"At first I thought they were poisoned."

"Autopsies should identify the cause," Adam said angrily.

Rita had already started. Adam handled the dead mouse splayed open on the examining table.

Rita watched, perplexed. "I've done all the preliminaries on this mouse, but I don't understand. There's no sign of poison. It appears it died of some natural cause."

"It'd be better if they were poisoned."

"Look at the pancreas of this mouse. See the discoloration."

"Yes, so what?" Adam asked nervously.

"It indicates that the body was fighting an *infection*, likely a viral one."

"I wonder how that could be? The defensive chemicals should've prevented that."

As he rolled one of the uncut mice onto its back, the scene in the park flashed in Adam's mind. The children had used pinecones to make buttons for their prone snowman. The mouse had spots of black fur on its stomach.

"Rita, the super-virus test mice were albinos, right?"

"Yes—so what does that mean?"

"Look!" Adam pointed to the mouse's belly.

"I was too busy to notice that," she said, looking carefully at the dead mouse. Suddenly Rita shrieked, "These are not our mice! Somebody has *stolen* our mice and switched them."

"Who could've done that?"

"Almost anybody. We keep our doors locked, but this isn't Fort Knox."

Adam thought again about the animal rightsists. Distracted by Itzak's murder, he had never followed through with his plan to duplicate all animal experiments at the Beckwith ranch. The super-virus research was too complex for that. Furthermore, he couldn't tolerate the disruption and delays that would cause.

"It wasn't animal terrorists," Adam said. "They would've spilled red paint and released all the animals in the building. They wouldn't bother to substitute mice. And they certainly wouldn't have *killed* these twelve mice. Where would these critters have come from?"

"Just on this LSB floor, there are three possible sources. These look like they might have come from the immunology lab. Those mice have black spots on their undersides."

Saul walked into the laboratory, staring bug-eyed at the gory scene. "Wha—" he gasped, unable to form a sentence.

"Don't worry, Saul, these are not your mice," Rita said in a reassuring tone. "Someone has replaced our mice with these. Do you know anything about this?"

"No, oh, no!" were Saul's only words.

"Then where are our mice and who switched them?" Adam asked.

"Gone? Our mice are gone?" was all Saul could say as he picked up one of the uncut mice. He wiggled the legs, paws, and tail. He smelled all around the animals. "Been dead about six to ten hours," he said sadly. "Rigor mortis is just starting."

Saul appeared extremely agitated as he left the room, a mournful look on his face.

A chill went down Adam's spine. The perpetrator had put hard-to-recognize, unprotected animals into the cages; they were slated to be killed by Rita's virus cocktails. Obviously, they were hoping to fool the super-virus team.

Why? Was this switch related to the earlier mouse sabotage?

"We'd better clean up this mess," Adam said. "We don't need further autopsies. Please call immunology and have them pick up their animals."

Downtrodden, Adam retired to his study. They would have to begin again with another dozen male mice. He resented the delay because it would slow his start with the human super virus.

Someone on the task force might the saboteur. Everyone on that team had worked together before without hitches. Everyone—except Saul Lowenstein!

Adam was laying detailed plans for the human super virus, when he was interrupted by Jill Yamamoto summoning him immediately to Dave Wiley's office.

"What the hell is going on?" Wiley demanded before Adam had a chance to close the door.

"You mean the dead mice?" Adam answered.

"Yes," Wiley raged. "Immunology is all upset. They claim that someone stole their mice and you returned them dead."

"You mean those mice didn't die of immunology's test disease?" Adam asked.

"No. Those mice hadn't even been used yet. They died from a variety of common mice ailments—all viral in nature. Immunology says you killed them. What in the hell is going on?

"Somebody stole our mice and substituted immunology's for ours."

"Musical mice," Wiley said sarcastically. "Now I've heard everything. Why would anybody want to steal your mice?"

Adam had no answer.

He took the opportunity to report the latest round of experiments. Wiley perked up when he heard they'd engineered the mouse super virus. "The stolen mice were to help prove whether or not the super virus worked," Adam concluded.

"Well, you'll just have to start again with fresh mice. Make sure they're watched around the clock."

"Hi, Beautiful," Adam said as he entered the stockroom where Mandy Rogers was checking in a box of supplies.

"Hi, stranger," she replied. "We've hardly seen you since you took over Dr. Friedman's project."

"It's keeping me extremely busy. Have you met the new team members from Itzak's group?"

"I've seen them and know their names. I don't have speaking acquaintances yet."

"My fault," Adam apologized, yet grateful for that news. "I want you to help me with some more cloak-and-dagger stuff."

"I'd love to. What's up?"

Adam told about the switched mice and suspicions. He then gave instructions.

24

The Formal Deception Begins

One person was placed in charge of monitoring the mouse laboratory. Everybody entering or leaving had to sign onto Rita Morales' log sheet.

Adam didn't relish playing detective. Although sabotaging a mouse experiment was too trivial to involve the police—at worst, a misdemeanor—he took it upon himself to find the culprit. He didn't care whether evidence would be inadmissible in court. He didn't need a trial—he simply wanted the perpetrator off his projects. Saul Lowenstein was suspected, and hoping to catch him red-handed, Adam directed Mandy Rogers to follow the assistant and note all his activities.

Excited by her new assignment, Mandy fantasized herself as a modern Mata Hari on an important spy mission. The night before, she'd followed Saul home from the LSB and sat in her car watching his apartment for hours, leaving only after she was sure he was asleep. She returned to the same spot an hour before Saul would normally leave for work.

That morning, Saul left in a beat-up blue four-door Volvo sedan. It sported a peeling old bumper sticker proclaiming "Save the

Whales!" and a Greenpeace decal on the left rear window. She followed his car to a local pet shop, where they both parked in back. Saul entered the store, with Mandy close behind. There he bought wood shavings, several sacks of hamster food, and a bottle of vitamin chews. Mandy followed discreetly as Saul walked back to his car, placing his purchases in the back seat.

Mandy was startled to see a big man accost Saul in the parking lot. Within moments, they were throwing punches. Saul was the decided loser. At first, Mandy thought the lab assistant had been mugged, but the attacker took nothing and left his victim to nurse a cut lip. Saul dabbed at his wound with the tail of his shirt, then drove away as if nothing had happened.

Mandy followed Saul to the LSB parking lot. She trailed behind as he walked all the way to the fourth floor. Panting heavily, Mandy tried to keep quiet as she followed down the long hallway. Saul stopped at a vacant lab, opened the unlocked door, and went inside. He appeared to have no idea he was being shadowed.

Rather than dwell in the unfamiliar place, Mandy went down into a third-floor hallway closet, waiting where she knew she would eventually see Saul pass by. She waited less than five minutes when, through the slightly ajar door, she saw him leave the vacant lab and enter the Genetics mouse laboratory. She then quickly climbed up one flight of stairs and entered the vacant lab. She opened the unlocked door, turned on the light, and spotted several cages with white mice inside.

"The Dirty Dozen," she gasped.

Later, Saul nervously entered Adam's study.

"What happened to you?" Adam asked, looking at the wound on Saul's lip.

"I banged into a door," Saul answered nonchalantly.

"I know about your mouse sabotage," Adam said, his voice cutting the air like a razor. "Can you explain yourself?"

"I just couldn't bear to have my babies harmed."

"You're worse than the animal rights people," Adam barked. "At least they're open about their activities. Why did you plant the mice from immunology?"

"I knew you needed mice for the experiment," he answered, as if ignorant of what the original mice represented. "I felt no kinship to those substitute animals from Immunology."

"You ruined the experiment. If all had gone to plan, your Dirty Dozen would have been okay."

"I just couldn't take that chance."

"Did you substitute mice in the earlier virus experiments?" Adam asked.

"Yes," Saul said, registering surprise. "How did you know?"

"They were a mongrel batch. Why did you do that?"

"Because I was mad. I suspected that you and Rita killed Little Oscar. I wanted to give you trouble. Only later did I learn the truth. That made me feel real good."

"You don't belong in a laboratory," Adam said grimly. "What you did was criminal. I don't have the time and energy to pursue this. Gather your things. I want you out of here within the hour. Jill Yamamoto will have your termination papers. You'll be followed until you leave the LSB. You'll be arrested if you ever step into this building again."

Seemingly without remorse, Saul left Adam's office. Meanwhile, Adam bumped into Rita Morales on her way out.

"I've just fired him," Adam told her. "Saul confessed. He claims he did it for revenge."

"I don't believe that crap. There's got to be more, but I can't put my finger on it. I've never liked Lowenstein. He's a phony."

"Why is that, Rita?"

"He's supposed to be a college dropout. Right?"

"Yes."

Rita's dark eyes reflected the intensity of her feelings. "Well, I've seen him reading various journals on chemistry. These manuals are technical and far too challenging for a nonscientist. He was one hell of a busybody, always snooping around when nobody was looking."

Although curious about Rita's intuitions, Adam hoped never to see Lowenstein again. But he had a premonition their paths would cross again at some inopportune time.

Back in their home cages, the original Dirty Dozen mice passed the first test. None caught diseases from the Rita's concoction. The super virus had protected them. They were tumor free, but it would take months of waiting to be sure about the super virus's capability to ward off cancer.

Adam refused to wait for those results and would soon begin experimenting with the human super virus.

Only Sandra Wickham was present when Adam entered the computer lab. She was gazing at her workstation monitor.

"How are we coming on the mouse-human correlation?" he asked anxiously.

"I know how to engineer the human super virus from *herpes simplex,*" she answered triumphantly.

"Great. Now we can lay plans for human studies. Unfortunately, we're forbidden from any *human* experimenting before completing workup on the mouse studies," Adam said with emphasis, hoping to obscure his real intentions.

"Does this mean I'm done with super viruses?"

"Sort of," said Adam, hating the deception. "The FDA will have to approve our research plan for humans. Actual experimentation will be several years downstream. This is just a computer simulation to help with the human DNA mapping exercise.

"There's one more thing, Sandra. Tell me about the human stopper gene-vaccine."

Sandra smiled as she reported the good news. "The computer analysis indicates nearly identical chemistry to the mouse's. I've found the coordinates for attaching the stopper gene to a human herpes virus."

"Wonderful. Download the complete report and e-mail it to me. Then you can go back to baby-sitting Dutch and Timothy and helping Jude."

"I never stopped."

Back in his study, Adam booted his computer and opened his e-mail program. He downloaded Sandra's MS Word report file and did a global search and replace, so that every reference to "human" was automatically changed to "mouse" or "mice." He had picked the mouse virus B-17 as the cover for the human one. A second editing round of search and replace changed every mention of herpes or *herpes simplex* with "B-17."

The formal deception had begun.

"Congratulations, Jack," Adam greeted as he entered the instrumentation laboratory. "No cancer so far."

"Yeah, but we're not out of the woods yet," Jack answered, peering up from the eyepiece of his electron microscope.

Feeling a bit shaky over having to lie and concerned about showing it, Adam slid his hands into his pants pockets. "While we're waiting, help me push forward with mouse virus B-17."

"But B-13G.4 appears to fill all of our requirements."

Adam hated bending the truth. "This is just for insurance. We need to do the DNA chemistry so it'll be ready if one of the Dirty Dozen shows a carcinoma and proves our original super virus doesn't work. Besides, a second virus will be needed in mouse wrap-up studies, prior to human experiments."

Adam handed Jack a copy of the altered B-17 DNA analysis. To minimize the chance of discovery, Adam wanted to keep Jack from talking to Rita and Sandra about B-17.

"I'll wait until the B-13G.4 finals before we do the mice with B-17. I'm releasing Rita back to germ-line intervention and black-eared mice. Sandra is rejoining the Crunchers full time."

"I've never stopped germ-line work," Jack replied. "I'll be glad to get back to it 100 percent. The backlog is piling up."

"This should just take a few days. After you've worked out the proper chemistry, I want you to grow a clone culture having the B-17 with its stopper gene and the other modifications. Then you'll be done with the super virus for a while."

Adam hoped his secret would hold. In place of actual mouse B-17, Jack would be engineering Adam's own herpes virus retrieved from a fever blister. Under the guise of B-17, he hoped Jack would actually create a *human* super virus.

Adam would eventually give himself an injection of that modified virus. It had to take—to work—the first time.

25

In the Mood

Adam arrived home from a rough day. It began with misplaced lecture notes for that morning's physiology class, for which he had to extemporaneously discourse on bladder and kidney function. That was followed by a row with Dave Wiley regarding funding. Adam was just leaving the departmental office when a young squirt slapped a subpoena in his hand, requiring him to appear for a wrongful termination suit filed by Saul Lowenstein. The *coup de grace* was Jack Chin's flu, which delayed the B-17 culture to be engineered from Adam's fever blister virus.

Adam remembered Vera would be in San Francisco that evening. He missed having her as his confidante and alter ego. She hadn't wanted him to self-experiment with the super virus, and they had fought over that. He craved the intellectual stimulation she provided before their cold war. That conflict now crimped their love life as well. Sex became a dutiful mechanical exercise just to maintain some semblance of marriage.

Maybe she was right after all. Maybe he had no right to play god

Needing cheering, Adam went to O'Connor's Tavern, a favorite hangout of medical students and staff. It was still early as he sat in an empty booth and ordered a pint of bitters. He was sipping on the ale when he heard a familiar voice.

"Hello, Dr. Boatwright," Bonnie Burton said cheerfully. "I've never seen you here before."

"Hi Bonnie," Adam replied, grateful for some intellectual conversation. "Why don't you sit? Let me order you something."

"Thanks. I'll have whatever you're drinking."

They nursed their Irish brews. Adam couldn't help noticing how beautiful Bonnie was, looking vulnerable in the lab coat that she still wore over the standard med student garb—jeans and T-shirt. Cold uniform for March.

She gave Adam a penetrating look with her large brown eyes. "I really enjoyed your lecture today," she said, breaking the spell.

"I was so embarrassed," Adam confessed. "I lost my notes. It was all off the cuff."

"You should leave your notes at home more often."

"Well, thank you for the compliment. We haven't talked since we solved Itzak's murder."

"I was glad to help. I'm sorry about your trouble with Saul. He got what he deserved."

They continued with shoptalk through another round of ales. "I'm hungry," Bonnie finally announced. "Why don't you join me for dinner?"

Taken by complete surprise, Adam agreed.

"Let me call home first. My son was going to his friend's for the night."

Adam admired her as she walked to the phone. She smiled at him all the way back to the table. "Okay, let's do Chinese. My treat!"

Bonnie was only in her late twenties, but so much more mature than the younger medical students. Adam found her to be a great sounding board. Throughout dinner, he talked about long-range plans for the three research projects. Bonnie listened with absolute fascination.

Bonnie then told Adam of her plans to be a pediatrician.

"So there's no man in your life?" Adam asked.

Bonnie looked shyly into Adam's eyes. "There *were* several. The father of my son died before we could be married. I've had a couple of relationships since. But you and your colleagues are keeping me very busy. I hardly have time for a quick date."

Adam couldn't tear his eyes from her full lips as she spoke.

"Let's have dessert," Bonnie announced. "Apple pie!"

"I think they only have fortune cookies," Adam said, a bit puzzled.

"No, I mean *my* apple pie. Let's go to my place; it's only two blocks."

"Okay," Adam replied, not quite ready to end the evening.

Bonnie had a one-bedroom apartment, with the kitchen melding into the living room. "Nice place," said Adam, remembering the dumps he had lived in while in medical school.

"It could be bigger," she apologized. "My son has the bedroom. Since I have such odd hours, to sleep I use the hide-a-bed in the couch."

After pie, they were having coffee, sitting on the couch. As they talked more about hopes and aspirations, Adam started to unwind, his cares sliding away.

"I have an early Led Zeppelin CD," she said. "Would you like to hear it?"

"Okay," Adam said, thoroughly enjoying Bonnie's companionship.

The music was familiar, bringing to mind Adam's med school days. As they sat on the couch, Adam was not even aware that his arm was resting on Bonnie's shoulders. She planted a kiss on his cheek. He turned to look at her, and she kissed him full on the lips. A tingle ran up Adam's spine as Bonnie's tongue forced his lips apart, and he began to breathe heavily.

Adam turned away. "Wow!" he exclaimed, automatically responding to the passion of her kiss.

"Is everything okay?" Bonnie asked, still caught up in the spontaneity.

"You're my *student*. I'm married. We shouldn't be doing this."

"This is definitely not harassment. I feel very comfortable with you. I've been wanting for months to give you a passionate kiss."

Adam's head started spinning. The professor–student thing bothered him and he felt very guilty. He looked at Bonnie, who was so beautiful, so vulnerable. He told himself to stop. But Bonnie gave him another passionate kiss and Adam felt as though he was going to explode.

"Not with that loud rock," he managed to say, coming out for air.

Bonnie jumped up from the couch and switched disks on the CD player. Glenn Miller's "In the Mood," began to play. "Oh, God," Adam whispered, as Bonnie headed for the bedroom. Adam's heart thumped loudly, almost drowning out the music.

Bonnie came out of the bedroom wearing the sexiest teddy Adam had ever seen. He stood as she walked toward him and grasped him in a hard embrace, smothering him with another deep kiss.

That was when the music changed. Her CD player had been set on the scramble mode and was now giving the third movement of the Brahms violin concerto! A vision of Vera playing the violin in front of the orchestra sobered Adam quickly and blocked out all other thoughts and feelings.

"Bonnie," he said, pulling away. "You're a beautiful, desirable woman. But you know I'm a married man. I need to keep the faith with my wife."

"I don't mind," Bonnie said, seeming to sense an impending end to their passion.

"I just can't continue this," Adam said with finality. "Please. I'm very sorry."

"I understand," Bonnie said with obvious disappointment. "I love you, Dr. Boatwright. I'll still love you, no matter what."

"I'm sorry, Bonnie. I must leave right now, before something is said or done we'll both regret." Adam walked to the door. "Good night, Bonnie."

Bonnie's eyes were mournful but she appeared stoic. She gave him a big smile and waved goodbye with the fingers of her right hand.

Adam left in total ambivalence. His body ached for satisfaction. But he felt terribly guilty. Although he felt incredibly tender toward Bonnie, his soul was aching for Vera.

26

Reconciliation and Resignation

Adam gasped when he saw Bonnie in the third row of the lecture hall, smiling down at him. She was striking in her red dress, her appearance contrasting sharply with the rest of the grubbily attired medical students. It had been nearly a week since that night in her apartment, and he hadn't seen her since leaving there in a fluster.

Adam took a deep breath. He had been the target of numerous infatuations by female students and several co-workers, surviving all of them gracefully. But he was not married then, nor did he have feelings for any of those women. He gritted his teeth and began his lecture on the vascular system.

After class, Adam gathered his notes. As the room emptied, he glanced up. Bonnie was walking down the stairs to the podium, her black high heels clattering in the same rhythm as her gentle sway, exaggerated by the back-and-forth movement of the dress. Adam found it hard to breathe and could feel himself blushing outrageously.

"Hi, Doctor Boatwright," Bonnie said as she reached the floor level.

"Hello, Bonnie," he replied struggling to form his words and not look sappy. "Sorry about today, but I found my notes."

"We noticed. I'll give you a B+," she teased. "Please excuse my outfit. I'm going to a luncheon with the hospital auxiliary. They sponsor one of my scholarships."

Adam's equilibrium slowly returned as he waited for the shuttle bus, trying to figure out why he felt this way. He had not blushed so hard since those early days when he and Amy met during their paper routes, holding hands and looking at the stars. At least then it was dark, and the poor light obscured his embarrassment.

Adam must have been working too hard.

Adam thought about Vera, his heart leaping because she would be returning today. Maybe the problem was his taking her for granted. He vowed to try extra hard to restore the camaraderie they had before Itzak's death and the bad news about her sister Nora.

On the bus, Adam's mind shifted to the super virus. Jack had returned several days back and promised something definitive today. The test mice were still alive and well, with no visible signs of cancer.

As Adam entered the instrumentation lab, Jack was thumbing through a stack of photos.

"Hello boss. Sandra's DNA changes were a challenge. It took several vats of mutations before I was able to get it right. There are two ampoules of converted B-17 mouse virus in cold storage."

"I knew I could count on you," Adam said happily. Then he *lied*. "We'll use that as backup if the original mouse super virus doesn't prevent cancer in the Dirty Dozen. A scaled-down mouse experiment is coming soon."

Jack interjected some rare humor. "It guess the Dirty Dozen and Methuselah are the last of the Mohicans, so it's back to big DNA molecules. We've done black ears. What's next—black feet?"

"We'll have a pow-wow on that soon," Adam replied with a feigned chuckle.

Adam had been waiting until Jack left for the day. He then entered the instrumentation lab and removed one of the ampoules labeled B-17, replacing it with a dummy container. He hoped that was the workable human super virus. Although a tube of mouse virus was sufficient to infect such a small animal, a far greater volume of human virus would be needed to guarantee infection in a person. That quantity would be cloned at Millner from Jack's vial, to be personally delivered there in the morning.

It was 7:55 p.m. when Adam pulled into the airport parking lot and rushed to meet Vera's eight o'clock flight. He hated to be early for anything, even picking up his wife after a two-week trip. Fortunately, she was just walking into the baggage area as he arrived. "Hello, gorgeous," Adam greeted, just before smothering Vera with a huge kiss.

"Hi, honey," Vera said with a smile, as they finally pulled apart. "Wow, I should travel farther and more often."

"You can't possibly imagine how much I've missed you," Adam said as they walked down the long ramp toward the parking garage. They chatted about the concerts and tour social gatherings while waiting for the elevator. They continued talking all the way down. When they left the elevator, Vera was the first to break out of the cold.

"Adam, I'm sorry. I've been such a witch these past months. I really love you and admire you for the terrible risks you're taking on my behalf."

"You beat me to the punch. I've been thinking about your arguments. I'm persuaded the world isn't ready for virtual immortality."

"Oh, Adam," Vera said emotionally. "I've been such a fool."

"I was the fool. We've just been conjecturing. We had something to disagree about only if the experiment works. But that's still a very big *if*. While you were away, we engineered a *human* super virus. Totally untested, of course."

That left Vera momentarily speechless, but she soon blurted a response. "Before I was angry. Now I'm frightened."

"So am I, my love," Adam replied. "So am I."

At last they were back at the car. Adam nervously fumbled for the car keys. It took two attempts to insert the proper key into the trunk. After a few more clumsy minutes, they were finally underway.

Adam unleashed another bombshell. "Tomorrow, I'll be ordering enough of the new virus to infect myself. The day after tomorrow, I'll inject it."

"Oh, Adam," Vera cried out, starting to panic. "What if there is some sort of horrible infection?"

"I guess we haven't talked much about this. We've developed a stopper vaccine. Injecting it activates a gene that eventually kills the virus."

"How do you know it works?" she asked.

"The stopper vaccine worked on the mouse virus. In all but one case, we were able to destroy any virus mutation that didn't have the desired effect."

"What happened to that mouse?" Vera asked, her concern mounting.

"It was riddled with lesions and died before we had a chance to make the injection."

"Adam! Please don't be in such a hurry," Vera pleaded in desperation.

"I have to, Vera. There isn't much time left."

27

I've Never Had Fever Blisters

Adam enjoyed the pretty drive to Millner Laboratories, especially since Vera had no rehearsals that day and was accompanying him.

But Adam was so anxious to begin testing the super virus on himself that he had neglected an important step. The stopper vaccine had never been tested. There just wasn't enough time to test for everything, and he would be taking a chance that he would be injecting himself with a potentially deadly virus. In the worst case, such an infection might be unstoppable. Adam took comfort in knowing that the analogous vaccine had worked with the mouse viruses. But he still felt guilty, even a bit fearful.

While Vera strolled around the Millner campus, Adam met briefly with the company representative for Central University. Adam left the human super-virus ampoule, ordering 500 milliliters of virus clones in a 50 percent inert solution, to be delivered to his office at the medical school.

The return trip was a somber one. Their lives were about to change substantially, and neither wanted to dwell on the various possibilities.

"You know, Adam, I've never had fever blisters. We've kissed hundreds of times while you've been infected, but I've never gotten the disease."

Adam cursed himself as he realized that his super virus might not infect Vera.

The super virus was derived from a herpes virus that she'd never caught. Adam took comfort in knowing that not having herpes and being immune are two different things, and it was unlikely that Vera was immune. During all those years, her mouth had likely provided a poor conduit for natural infection. An intravenous injection would overcome such a superficial defense and should bring on infection. But that was not absolutely certain.

If Vera did not react to the super virus, Adam would have to begin all over again.

That could take months, even years, perhaps!

It was Vera's disease he was trying to prevent, not his own. Had Adam been foolishly using his own physiology as inspiration for that? Adam was aghast and ashamed of playing god without competently planning the most basic element.

But he wouldn't to dwell on the negative. The probability was high that if the super virus worked on him, it would also work on her.

The super virus had to work on Vera.

28

The Self-Experiment

Today was the day. Adam would be taking the human super virus.

He breezed through a lecture on the nervous system, talking almost mechanically, his mind on autopilot. Just once he looked up at Bonnie Burton, who sat in her usual place, wearing her usual smile, and he gave her an obligatory smile back. But today she had no effect on him whatsoever.

Instead of shuttling back to the LSB, Adam bounded into the Physiology Department office. He grabbed the FedEx package, barely acknowledging the staff, and headed directly to his little-used med school office. Nervous as a cat, Adam assembled the portable IV apparatus. He then positioned the syringe for injecting the stopper vaccine, if it was needed, and tore open the package from Millner Laboratories. His hands shook as he connected the container to the IV tube. He quickly rubbed himself with a dab of alcohol, aimed the IV needle at the main artery in the crook of his left arm, and made a quick jab.

The liquid drained into Adam's arm for half an hour, after which there was nothing to do but wait. He busied himself disassembling the IV stand and disposed of the bottle and tubing.

Adam felt nothing unusual except for extreme agitation and apprehension. Soon, his body would become infected with the super virus and show unknown symptoms. It would begin generating chemical substances to combat the infection—continuously he hoped, for the rest of his life.

Adam rested prone on the couch and began piling through a thick stack of unread medical journals. After about two hours, he started pacing the hallway. His ears were starting to ring from hunger, so he headed to the med center cafeteria. He treated himself to a Reuben sandwich—the two pieces of toasted rye bread thick with hot corned beef, melted Swiss cheese, and sauerkraut. Adam took a table in the far corner, away from the noisy activity. He sipped a large cup of black coffee, knowing that it would soon stop the ringing in his ears.

Adam was still anxious and feeling a little out of sorts, but the anxiety rush from before had subsided. The sensation was similar to what he felt awaiting the birth of his first child, Anne. Navy doctors did not let expectant fathers participate in the birthing process, and he'd had to spend Judy's entire labor in the hospital waiting room.

The ringing in his ears did not stop with the meal. Even though three hours had passed since the injection, there were no symptoms. Adam walked back to his med center office and phoned Vera. "I'm still alive. There are no symptoms yet."

"Isn't that a good sign?" Vera asked.

"Yes and no. It looks like I'll survive. But I'm beginning to wonder if the virus is taking. The mice only showed slightly elevated body temperature, but mine hasn't moved all day. We'll just have to wait it out. I'll call you again when something changes. I love you."

Hating the waiting, Adam continued pacing around the hospital, taking care to avoid close contact with anybody. Not concerned about the virus spreading, he just didn't want conversations. His ears rang too much.

Six hours had passed since the injection and Adam still had no recognizable symptoms. But the high-pitched squeal hadn't gone away. Ringing ears are sometimes caused by pressure from fever, which he didn't have.

The critical time finally passed, and Adam drove home, the trip seeming to take an eternity. It looked as though the virus had not taken.

Vera was waiting at the door. "How are you feeling, honey?"

"There are still no symptoms," he answered. "I'm just beat. I wish my ears would stop ringing."

"Adam, in all the time we've been married, I've never heard you complain about ringing ears."

"My ears only ring when I'm hung-over or have the flu."

"That must be it, Adam! You're hearing a symptom from the super virus."

"God, I hope you're right."

"Don't you have tests for this sort of thing?"

Adam took a minute to collect his thoughts. "I'll know when I don't get sick. I'm going to infect myself with diseases, just like we did with the mice."

Vera was stunned. "Oh my God, Adam," she protested loudly. "You said nothing about this."

"I know," he said sheepishly. "Everything is backward. Doctors don't go infecting patients to see if they can ward off a disease. Immunologists are a passive bunch who vaccinate large groups and then wait and see what happens. Medical scientists never knowingly expose a person to the disease."

"And now you're going to expose yourself!"

"There's no other way."

They were interrupted by the shrill whistle of the tea kettle. Vera poured them each a cup of tea and resumed the conversation. "There is a better way to solve this dilemma. Tell me Adam, why do you have to know whether or not you're being protected by the super virus?"

Adam guessed where they were heading. "If I know the super virus works, then *you* can take it."

Vera continued. "I don't think we need to know that. I'm willing to take it now. We already know it won't kill me. You're still alive."

Adam lectured. "We only know that the super virus doesn't cause harm. We don't know that it does any good."

"You must treat me *now*, if you're ever going to do it. There won't be time to improve your super virus. This will be your last shot, if preventing my getting cancer is your goal."

"That's the *only* reason I've done all this."

Adam methodically thought it through.

"You're absolutely right, as usual," Adam finally said. "Either the super virus will work or it won't, and knowing that will make no difference. There's no reason to make you wait. I don't have to expose myself to diseases."

"Thank God I made you see that."

"My expectations and hopes are always one jump ahead of good common sense and logic. I'll send Millner the second B-17 ampoule tomorrow and order a batch of super virus for you."

29

The Greatest Financial Venture ever Undertaken

It had been less than two weeks since Adam infused the super virus and seven days since Vera injected the same substance. Adam's ears never stopped ringing and Vera's never started. She showed no symptoms whatsoever. All they could do now was wait and see what happened.

Life had returned to normal for the Boatwrights. With the medical school year winding down, they were preparing to take their vacation in New Mexico, exploring the Lechuguilla Cave. Vera would give up the violin for two whole weeks—a real sacrifice, since from age four she had hardly ever taken more than a few hours off without playing.

Adam had bad vibes as he climbed to the third floor of the LSB and entered the Genetics Department office to see Dave Wiley. Unannounced, he knocked on Wiley's door, wondering why he had been summoned. "Come in," Wiley ordered in an icy voice.

"Hello, Dave," Adam greeted.

"Please close the door and sit down."

"What's up?" Adam asked, more worried than before.

"First the good news. National Cancer is very happy with preliminary results from your mouse studies. They'll fully fund the next round."

"Great. But this is not unexpected. We've already planned the experiments. You have my staffing recommendations and budget."

"And I see no problems there."

"And the bad news?" Adam asked, waiting for the ax to fall.

Wiley looked sternly at Adam. "Millner tells me you ordered a huge batch of modified mouse B-17 clone. Your reports show no record of that."

"I guess I'm a little behind in my paperwork," Adam replied uneasily. He struggled for calmness as he wondered what this was leading to. Wiley ordinarily couldn't be bothered with such details.

Wiley glared at Adam. "I've done some checking. Jack Chin said you engineered the B-17 several weeks back."

"True," Adam replied, extremely worried now. "What's the point? Surely, you don't care about these details!"

"Wrong! Chin told me you already had two ampoules in cold storage."

"That's true," Adam replied, swallowing hard.

"How come you didn't use Millner with the mouse super virus strains?"

Adam had no control over the conversation and could barely get his sentences out. "We could generate sufficient quantities for mice ourselves. We didn't need a big lab's assistance."

Adam knew what was coming next. How stupid to use Millner and to take Wiley for granted.

"So, then, tell me," Wiley said smugly, "why did you need two 500 milliliter containers of transfusable B-17 clones?"

Adam saw no way out. "For *me*, and my wife."

"Why do you need *mouse* viruses? Are you going into the pest eradication business?"

"The shipments contained *human* super virus," Adam confessed, feeling a tremendous pressure release.

Dave Wiley's jaw dropped, and after a moment he broke out in a smile. "You've engineered a human super virus?"

"Maybe," Adam replied, emotionally spent. "I don't know yet if it works."

"You must feel good about it," Wiley said smiling. "But how will you find out if it works?"

"Vera and I have infused it," Adam answered, his composure regained. "If we don't get any viral infections, and if the mouse and rat experience applies to us, we'll never get cancer either."

Wiley grinned like a Cheshire cat. He seemed to envision fame and research funding rolling in.

They were interrupted by the intercom. President Wentworth was on the phone. "We'll talk more about this later," Wiley said. "It's almost lunch time."

Adam left Wiley's office in a daze, skipping his usual chat with Jill. He knew about Wiley's connection with Millner, but never imagined that Wiley would be watching. Adam regretted not choosing another lab and paying from his own pocket. He took some comfort that Wiley was unlikely to discipline him. The chairman seemed too interested in the human super virus and would want it despite the clandestine origin.

Except for those discussions with Itzak and Vera on the cessation of aging, Adam thought little beyond getting a cancer cure. Adam presumed Wiley's interests were just a cancer cure and the research dollars that would bring.

All the while he gobbled down the takeout lunch he was eating in his office, Dave Wiley thought about Adam Boatwright. He wondered why Boatwright had been so desperate to self-experiment—and with his wife! He guessed that Boatwright was trying to head off his wife's getting cancer and that he must have been close to finding a workable super virus; otherwise, he wouldn't be taking such a risk.

Wiley recalled some of the earlier discussions he and Boatwright had regarding the I-complex therapy. That procedure led to faithful cell replication, which in turn stopped aging. Although there would be power and prestige from curing cancer, that was small potatoes.

Wiley's real motivation for mouse super-virus experiments was finding a way to stop *aging*, and that's precisely why he allowed Boatwright to take his research wherever he wanted. And now, Boatwright was giving him virtual immortality on a silver platter. Better yet, Wiley now had a lever to force Boatwright to join him in the greatest financial venture ever undertaken. What a "goody-two-shoes" that workaholic was.

"Jill," Wiley hollered through the door to his inner office. "Get Dr. Boatwright back over here ASAP."

Within minutes Adam had returned to Wiley's office. The chairman sternly resumed the earlier conversation where it had been interrupted. "You know that human infusions of untested substances are forbidden until FDA authorization. Furthermore, that's granted only after extensive animal studies."

"Of course," Adam answered, still hoping to avoid sanctions. "We're desperate to head off hereditary breast cancer."

"I'm sorry for your personal problem, but you've violated medical restrictions, too. My immediate concern is self-experimentation. You know that's strictly forbidden. You could have your career ended over this."

"I know. Believe me, I know," Adam said stoically, waiting for the other shoe to drop.

"Boatwright, listen to me. I'll never tell," Wiley said softly, beginning to disclose his hand. "But you'll have to cooperate."

"What did you have in mind?" said Adam, relieved.

"I want us to form a company and patent your super virus."

"But how would that affect my problems with the FDA, the university, and the medical boards?" Adam felt as if he were sliding into a quicksand of greed, deceit, and unlawfulness.

Wiley grinned. "We'll cover our asses with documentation of all the proper studies to verify everything. As far as they're concerned, it'll all be above board."

"And what about the university and National Cancer? They'll want participation and royalties."

"I can handle them. No problem."

"I'll have to think it over."

Wiley concluded the discussion. "Call me tomorrow. God, this is exciting."

Adam had never expected to be caught. But he had just experienced a scenario never even imagined. Fear of punishment now evaporated, but it was replaced by greater worries, as Adam was being pushed under a darker cloud. He had never wanted to lie, cheat, or steal from the university or the cancer institute. All he wanted was to find a cure for Vera's impending cancer.

Adam went directly to Jack Chin, who, as usual, was busily scanning films. "Hi, Jack. We need to talk about your meeting with Dave Wiley."

"Oh, that! He just wanted to know about the B-17. I told him it was insurance, in case there was a problem with the first mouse super virus—exactly what you told me."

"Did he tell you about the *spying*?" Adam lied, starting a new web of deception that might detour Wiley.

"No, boss. What spying?"

"There's some industrial espionage going on around here—we're not sure who the perpetrators are. We need to take some security precautions. I want you to give me your B-17 vials. I'll remove them to the med center where they'll be safe."

"No problem."

Adam continued with his fabrication. "We must secure the B-17 documentation. I need Sandra's report and all of your records on that virus."

Jack pulled two ampoules out of the refrigerator. He then pulled a fat folder from his filing cabinet. These he placed on the table in front of Adam. "It's all in here."

"What about computer records?"

Jack gave a reassuring answer. "I'm old-fashioned. I don't care much for electronic storage. I erase daily what I don't need. There's nothing about B-17 in my hard drive."

"Thanks, Jack. I'll keep everything out of harm's way."

Adam next went to Sandra Wickham, telling a version of the same story. In seconds, she electronically destroyed all herpes computer files, as Adam watched. "Do you have any other records?"

"I never use paper," Sandra said, "except for paper airplanes or letters to Mom."

"Thanks, Sandra."

Adam tossed the ampoules in the recycling bin. Both were dummies of the originals already used to seed the Millner clonings. He took Jack's file folder and left for home, worrying all the way about Millner. It was standard procedure with such jobs to destroy all leftovers. But if that was not done, Wiley could access the super virus and proceed without him.

30

Keeping the Genie in the Bottle

At first, Adam regretted telling Wiley the truth about the human super virus, disguised as mouse B-17. But after some thought about the man's deviousness, Adam came to realize that lying would have been worse. It was right to conceal from Wiley details for changing *herpes simplex* DNA. But the smart man might easily assemble the puzzle, especially if he connected with Sandra Wickham. Adam had to prevent that.

Vera was marinating lamb chops when Adam walked in the door and gave her a quick kiss. He watched her pained expression as he described the meeting with Wiley and the steps taken to prevent the man's access to the super virus.

"You did good," Vera finally said.

"Yeah, but we don't want to cooperate with Wiley. Boy, have I learned from you! The man's a monster. He could end up controlling a substance for prolonging life. Billions of people would pay thousands each to have it. He'd have the greatest monopoly ever conceived by man."

"I agree, Adam, but Wiley's only the mist on the iceberg." Vera went on to say that if others—especially powerful corporate types—discovered the secret of virtual immortality, they could launch the greatest treasure hunt ever seen. Control of the super virus would bring *trillions*, not mere billions. The pair would be helpless to stop the juggernaut. The traffickers would run right over Wiley. Adam had made a substance infinitely more attractive than cocaine or any other psychotropic drugs.

"And look at those substances' negative impacts."

"Pandora's box was a trivial matter compared to the hell I've unleashed," said Adam, shaking his head.

"This is where your mouse research would have inevitably led. Once human testing begins, the race will be on for the Wileys of the world."

"I need your help through this mess," said Adam, almost in a whisper.

As usual, Vera had a good grasp of the total picture. "As I see it, we have an immediate problem and a long-range problem. Let's try to resolve the immediate one—Wiley. I think you have to play with him indefinitely, stringing him along. Wiley's your enemy, but he'll also be a powerful ally against other—potentially more sinister—enemies."

"But he already knows about the *human* super virus."

"Wrong!" Vera almost shouted. "*We* don't know ourselves the effects from the virus we've infused. How can Wiley know?"

"Let me rephrase that. He knows about the *potential* for the human super virus."

Vera continued. "Potential or not, you must let Wiley actively participate in developing what he thinks is a workable human super virus."

"As usual, you're leaving me behind."

Vera laid it all out for Adam. "If Wiley's a passive observer, he'll always be a thorn in your side. He has to know you're doing the best possible job. That way you'll keep control. By making Wiley believe in you, he'll be less likely to allow someone else to foster super-virus development."

"And how do we keep up the ruse?" Adam asked, admiring Vera's mental feat.

"Just continue what you've been doing with the mice. Let that project unfold in its natural progression."

Adam admired his smart wife.

Vera was on a role. "Keep the fire warm by throwing in an occasional decoy virus that Wiley thinks might work, but which *you* know never will. Get *him* to be the Guinea pig. He'll never be able to nail you on self-experimentation without compromising himself. He'll die of old age before you ever get another super virus."

"Beautiful! But that'll only take care of Wiley. We have the super virus now, and I still want to put it to good use."

Now was the time for Vera to use all of her logical ammunition. She would take a Socratic approach, letting Adam see, through his own answers to her questions, what she felt to be the crux of the matter.

"Do you want to live forever, Adam?"

"No," Adam replied in surprise. "I only want to prevent your cancer."

She quickly made her next point. "Either you've done just that, or it's too late. You no longer need the super virus for your stated purpose." Her logic was cold and as sharp as an ice pick.

"And do you want the world to have virtual immortality?"

"No. It'd be the ruination of humankind and the world. I'm sorry I didn't see that sooner. But we've promised a cure for cancer. That's where the mouse studies are headed."

"Then *do* it," Vera said. "Find a way to cure cancer that doesn't stop people aging. That'll solve the long-term problem."

"You never said what the long-term problem was."

Again, Vera filled in the holes. She noted that the long-term problem was the deleterious impact of non-aging humans on themselves and the planet. Earth clearly couldn't support an endless stream of humans who never age. They wanted to avoid that nightmare with all their hearts. They also had to prevent the incredible treasure hunt only hinted by Wiley's avarice. Greedy cartels shouldn't parcel out virtual immortality to highest bidders. Those evildoers couldn't be allowed to corrupting institutions, as cocaine traffickers had done in Latin American countries.

"And how do we stop it?" Adam asked.

"You are the one person who can unleash the immortality genie. Only people tied to you have made the connection."

"That's true," Adam confessed. "Now I have to figure out how to re-cork the genie."

Nodding in agreement, Vera answered Adam with a big smile.

31

Rhinovirus Ruse

Adam paused at the door to the Genetics Department, getting ready for the next few minutes. He wished himself success, as he opened the door.

"Hi, good-looking," Adam greeted Jill Yamamoto, coughing and wheezing.

"Hi, Dr. Boatwright. Sounds like a pretty bad cold."

Adam reached for his handkerchief and blew hard. "I need to see the boss," he said, going directly into Dave Wiley's office.

"Adam, I've been waiting anxiously for you."

Wiley's smile vanished as Adam spontaneously coughed loudly. "You have a cold!"

"I'm afraid so." Adam rubbed his nose with the cloth and sneezing violently. "Vera's really got it bad, coughing and sneezing all night."

"Does this mean your super virus isn't working?"

"Yes. I guess it's back to the drawing board," Adam said with resignation.

"But your mice!"

Adam embellished his story. "They'll probably end up catching something. Our engineered viruses may have some effects, but apparently long life isn't among them. They aren't even good enough to ward off disease or cancer, except temporarily."

"What about our new company?" Wiley asked, his voice wavering.

"I'll work with you," Adam promised, mentally crossing his fingers. "Don't give up hope. We'll keep looking and keep experimenting. We're on the verge of a cancer cure, no doubt about it. But a cure for aging is apparently not within our grasp at this time."

As Adam left his office, Dave Wiley was staring expressionlessly out the window.

Adam threw away the handkerchief that he and Vera had laced with pepper paste and cinnamon oil. They didn't have colds.

Vera joined Adam in her first meeting of the Central Cavers, a group of professors, staff, students, and their family members with an interest in spelunking—the technical term for people who explore caves and caverns.

The meeting began with a technical lecture and demonstration of equipment. Vera was fascinated with new apparatus for dropping and ascending with rope. Next, a slide show accompanied one member's description of a trip to Lascaux in southwestern France, famous for its Upper Paleolithic and Neanderthal cave drawings.

After the meeting ended, Adam introduced Vera to his old friends, Ernie and Jayne Dickson, with whom they would be exploring the Lechuguilla Cave. The Dicksons were as handsome as models for athletic wear. Ernie was a big man, well built and perfectly proportioned. A dark tan hid his light complexion and contrasted with his shortly cropped blonde hair framing his long bald streak. Jayne Dickson was tall, like her husband, and had similar features.

"I can't wait until Saturday," Ernie said with enthusiasm. "Lechuguilla, here we come!"

"I understand parts of that cavern system are still unexplored," Vera said.

"Yes, and pristine. Unspoiled by human activity," replied Ernie, full of excitement. "Until recently, the National Park Service has only allowed mapping teams into Lechuguilla. The mineral formations are said to be spectacular."

"I thought the Carlsbad Caverns were the greatest complex," said Jayne.

"That was before this new limestone hollow was discovered," Adam said. "It's in the same national park as Carlsbad, but totally independent."

The two cavern complexes lay within five miles of each other, though Lechuguilla was much deeper. Over fifty miles of passages had already been explored in that recently discovered complex's partially mapped caverns.

"I've never been caving before," Vera said, a bit intimidated at the prospect. "But I've done lots of rock climbing and short mountain trips. I've never been able to leave my violin for more than a day."

"We'll be gone over a week," Jayne said.

"I'll take my traveling violin so I can practice at our campground," Vera said. "I'll leave my Stradivarius safe with a friend."

"You have a Strad?" asked Ernie, incredulous.

"I guess we've never told you," Adam said. "Vera is a concert violinist. She has soloed with many great symphonies."

"I'm not that good, really," Vera said, blushing.

"I'm leaving my work behind, too," Jayne said. "I'll be glad to get away from students for a while. Unlike Lascaux, these caves have never been inhabited. I won't have to take pictures and notes for a paleontology paper."

"Two professors and a violinist," Vera said. "And what do you do, Ernie?"

"I'm a veterinarian. I'm sort of a general practitioner. I work for the Central City Zoo."

"He's being modest," Adam said. "Ernie leads an International Wildlife Fund team. They're trying to save endangered species."

"Fabulous," Vera said. "That's one of my main interests. It's too bad about the black rhinoceros. What are your thoughts, Ernie?"

Ernie sadly reported that—except for a few on ranches outside of Africa—the black rhinos would all be gone within ten years.

Pressures from human population growth were squeezing rhino habitat, though poaching was the main cause. He noted that twenty million years of evolutionary development had almost been wiped out—just for dagger handles and non-functional aphrodisiacs made from the animals' horns.

"Is there any hope for them and other animals on the brink of extinction?"

"That depends." Ernie replied.

He said that it was becoming too expensive to gather individual animals in zoos. That made genetic diversity is harder to maintain. The Fund was working on collections of embryos, which could be stored indefinitely with little expense. Zoos were planning to propagate animals in their collections using embryo implants. The Fund's goal was viable world populations with sufficient diversity for eventual reintroduction into the wild.

"This goes beyond the black rhino," Adam added. "The Fund wants me to help control this effort. Hundreds of animal species are involved, from elephants to orangutans and from tree frogs to marmosets."

"As if you didn't have enough to do!" Vera said. "But this seems like a natural extension of your talents."

The conversation returned to the caving expedition.

"Okay," Adam said. "Here is an inventory of equipment we'll be needing."

They spent the remainder of the evening planning the trip.

32

Cavers' Delight, Cavers' Fright

Flight 466 left Central City for El Paso at sunrise on a beautiful May Saturday morning. Shortly after takeoff, the plane pierced a layer of light clouds, rising above a panorama resembling wads of cotton for as far as the eye could see. Above the morning clouds, the sky was a brilliant golden spread of morning sun's rays, splaying across the new clouds. A sight rarely seen on any flight.

The flight attendant served mushroom burritos and juice. "Enjoy!" Adam said, breaking the spell. "This will be your last hot breakfast for several days. You also won't be seeing any sun."

"No campfires?" Vera asked.

"Definitely not. Smoke would pollute the caverns and stain the walls. It won't be very cold, a constant 68 degrees, but with high humidity. We'll be sweating while we move. But we'll chill during sleep, so we're bringing light sleeping bags. There are small lakes to cross. We'll swim those *au natural*."

"Skinny-dipping! How wonderful."

"Yes," Adam said with a big smile. "But we'll make several trips each time, holding our paraphernalia out of the water. It'd take forever for stuff to dry."

"I can't wait," Vera said.

Carlsbad National Park was a three-hour drive. Ernie drove the rental van, Adam at his side.

"Jayne, how much caving have you done?" asked Vera as they were leaving the airport.

"I've spent a great deal of time in caves, but primarily on explorations to study prehistoric man. Those caves were not very long or deep. I've been on three limestone cavern expeditions, once to Carlsbad."

"I'm a bit intimidated by it all," Vera admitted.

"At the beginning so was I. For me, caving is the ultimate high. All your senses are involved, and immediate concerns wipe out all other thoughts. In that sense, it's kind of like being reborn."

"I'm guessing I know what you mean. And how about Ernie?"

"He's the real caver in the family. He's discovered some new passages in several limestone complexes. But he's never seen Lechuguilla. It was discovered after we went to Carlsbad."

"Adam's never been there either, although he's been inside lots of caverns."

Vera could only imagine what the excursion would be like. She had a good feel for intense physical experience, based on her own climbing and skiing. Those activities also demanded complete attention and fully occupied the mind.

They arrived at park headquarters in the early afternoon and proceeded directly to a campground, where they assembled their gear. While the others worked, Vera took some time to play Ravel's "Tzigane," a haunting composition inspired by a Gypsy tune; the violin portion of a Shostakovich string quartet; and several Fritz Kreisler pieces. The others gave a long applause at the end of the improbable recital.

After a hearty supper, the explorers drove up a dirt road to the entrance to Lechuguilla. It was a nearly ninety-foot drop to the sealed entrance of the pitch-dark cavern complex. All illumination would be from battery-powered lanterns attached to hard hats, snugly strapped at their chins. They would also wear gloves and knee and elbow pads to minimize injury from sharp rocks.

The spelunkers rigged up the ropes for the descent. Altogether, they would be leaving over five thousand feet of rope in place for their ascent out of the caverns. There was just one way in and out.

After readying themselves and their equipment, Adam and Ernie lifted the grate covering the cavern entrance. A strong wind nearly blew them over. That hole was the only known air source for the complex, and the air moved in or out with considerable force, depending on atmospheric pressure.

"It's like a gigantic breathing creature," Vera said in awe.

Their plan was to traverse the eastern complex, all the way to a place called Firefall Hall. Because of the huge vertical rises and drops, plus lakes to cross, that journey would take three days. The first "night's" rest would be taken at the Ocean Wave Room. Of course, night or day on the surface, it was always dark down there.

"A claustrophobic person could never do this," Vera remarked after a half hour of crawling on her belly along a shallow tube connecting the entrance to Boulder Falls, the first open space.

Vera's calm was restored when they emerged into a large room. "Look up," Adam spoke softly to minimize echoing. He shone his light up, but nothing could be seen. "The ceiling's too high to be illuminated by our lamps."

Vera moved her light along the walls, awestruck by the formations and colors, ranging from snow white to blood red. She was fascinated by the incredible variety of textures and patterns formed over eons by slowly evaporating mineral waters. The place reminded her of the Grand Canyon, except all underground and eerily quiet.

Vera broke the silence as Jayne and Ernie entered the room. "I've never seen such beauty in a confined space." Her words echoed loudly several times.

"Hi, gang," Ernie nearly whispered. "It's best to speak in soft tones. Loud noises might dislodge material from the walls or ceiling."

They continued their trek, traversing through a narrow passageway leading to the first lake, Glacier Bay, reached after two hours of crawling. The large pond was in the center of a great hall that looked like a surrealistic Sistine Chapel. To the left and right were tall flowstone columns. In many spots the lake lapped vertical walls. In some places the pond was bordered by sprays of gypsum crystals resembling white-lace filigrees on a glass tabletop, underneath which sat rocks colored blue by the water.

Vera gasped at the jewel-like beauty. "This was definitely worth the price of admission." The explorers took off their helmets and beamed each lantern in a different direction, resting for several minutes in silence, absorbing the spectacle.

It was time to cross to the other side—via the water. As Adam had warned, they would now have to strip naked. Vera was a little shy at first, but the necessity of moving all their food, ropes, climbing instruments, lanterns, and supplies absorbed her mind—almost. She felt a little tingle when she saw Ernie sneaking a long look at her. It happened again as she watched him and Adam gracefully walk to the edge and slip into the water. But after hitting the frigid water herself, she had to concentrate on swimming to the other side without spilling her load. Vera was surprised at the difficulty of swimming in cold water without using both hands.

After the first trip, everybody was too cold to care about being naked or to even take an interest in looking at the others. Altogether, it took four round trips to carry everything across the lake.

They quickly dressed and ate several ounces of a special trail mix, laced with lomotil. Rules of the cave were that spelunkers bring out everything brought in, including their own body wastes, which had to be bagged and retrieved on the return trip. There would be very little urine, since they sweated profusely from heavy exercise in the high humidity.

They continued along the Rift, through Freakout Traverse, and made camp at the Ocean Wave Room, so named because of the shape of the rock formations. There they witnessed rounded calcite stalagmites, some resembling ostrich eggs. In one corner there were columns of white helictites, reminiscent of knotted and twisted popcorn strings, hanging from floor to ceiling. In another portion of the room was a forest of stalactites, deposits of calcium carbonate and other minerals that formed spiked formations pointing downward. Vera thought they resembled icicles made from coffee rich in cream.

Setting up the camp was little more than rolling out the sleeping bags and padding the underneath with clothing and packets of food. Until then there had been little opportunity for conversation.

"I can't get over the stillness here," Vera said. "Is there any life?"

"There's lots of life," Adam answered. "The ecosystem is based on bacteria that eat metallic chemicals in the rocks. These bacteria, in turn, feed fungal molds. Life down here is strictly primitive. In some caverns, the food chain extends all the way up to small fish. Many caverns have bats, but they feed outside. Bat waste supplies a host of worms and insects, and there's even a food chain among them. We won't see any here, however. There are no known bats in Lechuguilla."

"I wonder if man could ever colonize a cavern like this," Jayne mused.

Adam took a turn at that. "It might be possible to develop an ecosystem based on rock-eating bacteria, molds, and so forth, up to man. But those bacteria tend to be poisonous to vertebrates."

Ernie added more. "Vertebrates would have to bring their food with them. All of our sustenance comes from sunlight. That's obtained indirectly through plant photosynthesis and from animals who consume those plants or fungi. Nearly all animal food chains start with plants."

"Yes," Jayne said, "but I wonder how long humans could survive with whatever they brought. I mean, with recycling, they could grow a lot of their food."

"True," Adam said. "Our own wastes could nourish mushrooms, which would have some food value for us. But that'd only prolong the inevitable need to surface and forage, just like the bats."

"Okay, Batman, I'm really sleepy now." Vera said, signaling her desire to end their conversation.

Seemingly minutes after their goodnights, Ernie's watch alarm squawked, signaling 6:00 a.m. They had slept seven hours!

Ocean View ground water had been tested before and was safe to drink. That liquid washed down a breakfast of energy bars. Vera's adrenaline rushed strongly as she contemplated the adventures ahead. She hardly noticed being covered with small cuts and bruises.

A series of shallow seams, drops, and climbs would bring them to the Lake of the Blue Giants. Adam and Ernie had an argument about the route. Although Adam thought it would be dangerous, he finally agreed splitting into two groups. Vera and Adam would take the direct path, while Ernie and Jayne would traverse through the deeper parallel channels. They would meet again on the other side of the Blue Giants.

After two hours of climbing and crawling, Adam and Vera stopped at a small lake. The waters were placid and clear, except for a deep spot, where there appeared to be some turbulence. They stripped and swam to the other side, carrying their loads of food and sleeping bags. For the second trip they packed rope and climbing equipment.

As they were traversing the lake again, Vera's hand slipped, spilling all of her equipment into the lake's deepest part. Hoping to retrieve the gear, she did a quick surface dive. She felt the tug of a strong current, which pulled her down into the dark. It was impossible to return to the surface.

Adam was terrified as he realized Vera was caught in an underwater stream of strongly moving water. He had no choice but to quickly follow, first lashing the equipment and his lantern hat around his waist. Now in the dark, he swam underwater toward the turbulence. The undertow sucked him down, tumbling and bashing him into rocks and pulling with tons of force. He felt his life was ending as he crashed into a wall, pinned by the current moving through holes too small for him to follow.

But miraculously, the gyrations and buffeting suddenly stopped and the water movement gradually ebbed. Adam sensed that he was in a large body of water, but it was impossible for him to tell up from down. He groped along the wall and picked a random direction, and, just when his lungs seemed ready to burst, his head broke the surface and he breathed in spastic gasps.

It took a few seconds to reposition the lantern hat and switch on the lamp. Adam slowly turned his head until Vera was illuminated. She was face down and floating motionless, only twenty feet away. Adam quickly swam to her, grabbed her seemingly lifeless body and twisted her face-up. He towed her toward a rocky ledge, which he climbed while holding onto her hair, trying to keep her head upright. He pulled her completely out of the water onto the sharp rocks, squeezed her chest to clear the lungs, and began CPR.

Within minutes, Vera regained consciousness and was breathing again. Groggy and disoriented, she finally spoke, "What happened?"

"Oh, my darling, you nearly drowned. We're both very lucky to still be alive. We were caught in an incredibly strong undertow and sucked into this place. *Another* lake."

"It looks the same."

"No, it's a different place. We've lost most of our equipment, our food, clothes, and sleeping bags. I think we're in an unexplored complex."

"Can't you go back and find our things and find Jayne and Ernie?"

"No," he said. "The current's too strong. We'll have to find our way out of here."

"But Adam, there's only one way out of this place!"

"One way out that we *know* about, but we can't reach it."

"And how do we find the way out of here?"

"We'll have to walk around until we feel a breeze. If we're lucky, we'll hear bats, and we can follow them out."

"But you said there were no bats in Lechuguilla."

"We're in a separate place from the explored portion of Lechuguilla. There may likely be bats here."

"What about food?"

"We can survive a long time without food," Adam reassured her. "We have plenty of water. But our greatest problem will be our light source. We'll have to conserve the battery in our one lantern. It'll be impossible to find our way in the dark."

"What about rescue? Can't Ernie and Jayne go and get help?"

"No, dear. How can they know we're lost, much less where we are? Even when they realize we're missing, they might never find us. This complex is not on the map. It must be independent of the rest of Lechuguilla."

Vera and Adam walked for several hours, through thin channels, up and down crevices, swimming across two lakes. To save power, they would switch on the lantern, pick a landmark several feet away, and then turn off the light and feel their way along in the dark. The battery would last about a hundred hours under that limited use. Both of them were completely naked and covered with scratches and bruises. Vera was still winded from her unconscious state. Their feet were stinging messes of cuts and open flesh. They collapsed every so often out of sheer exhaustion and hunger, clinging tightly to each other and grabbing a few minutes of restless sleep.

"I don't think we're going to make it," Vera despaired.

"We have to keep hoping," Adam said, not wanting to admit he was reaching the same conclusion.

"What a way to go," Vera said. "We have the biggest and prettiest tomb in human experience."

"Stop it! We're not dead yet."

During the next nap they experienced more terror. Adam was having one of his nightmares about hell, waking only to feel like he was actually there. It was totally dark, and they were inside a narrow tube. Adam could hear Brother Jonathan's voice. "Welcome to hell." His screams created horrendous echoes that seemed like a chorus of gargoyles.

Vera shivered as she shook Adam, her voice breaking: "Darling, wake up. It's only a dream." But Adam couldn't hear her over the screams of his imaginary "gargoyles."

Reaching out and feeling Vera, Adam screamed, "Oh God. Not you too. Vera, we're in hell."

"Stop it," she shouted.

But Adam didn't hear, as he hallucinated highlights from his nightmare of being in hell. Adam began sobbing like a baby while Vera embraced him, patting and rubbing as if he was a small child. Soon he was asleep again, restlessly.

When at last Adam awoke, his mind had returned to normal. He felt Vera, checking that she was awake.

"I just had the most awful nightmare. It was so real."

Vera told him the truth. "Darling, it was only partly a dream. You were awake most of the time, hallucinating about hell."

Adam had lost some of his tremendous psychic strength. "We couldn't be closer to hell than this. Will we ever find our way out?"

Vera gave her husband some encouragement. "I believe you can get us out."

They trudged on, losing all track of time. It seemed as though they had been staggering for a month, when Vera heard a high-pitched sound. "Do you hear that, Adam?"

"I only hear my ringing ears. What do you hear?"

Vera gave a good description. "I *feel* it as much as hear it. It is a strange sound, like a shriek."

"A bat!" Adam said, as he shone his lantern around, pleased to see that they had entered a gigantic chamber. In the middle of the chamber was a lake, about two acres in size, surrounded by a gently sloping beach of limestone. Although their lantern could only illuminate a short distance, Adam estimated that the whole place must have been as big as the Louisiana Superdome.

He turned off the lamp, listening for the sound again. There was a glow from the lake, giving off enough light for them to see the general shapes. "Bioluminescence," Adam said. "Certain types of bacteria glow in the dark. We can use that light to navigate and save some battery power."

The shriek came again, closer now and louder. It was coming from the ceiling. Adam shone his lantern up, spotting the bat, which was hanging upside down from a small rocky point. It squealed again and flew to the opposite side of the lake, disappearing into a dark crack.

"I saw where it went," he said. "We'll rest here and then follow it. I think we'll be likely to find more of them. They'll lead us out of here."

They slept for several hours, hugging tightly for warmth. Despite awaking sore, cold, and hungry, they did not hesitate to begin their swim across the lake. Only one trip was needed, with Adam ferrying all of their belongings. They climbed toward the crack that the bat had entered, crawled through, and emerged into a narrow cavity, barely thick enough for a person.

They wormed their way up, down, and around, gathering more scratches and wounds, until the passage became wider. It spilled into a small chamber where, with relief, Adam could detect a very gentle breeze. They started to climb the walls, feeling the breeze become stronger as they moved up, until they reached a ledge. Real wind was coming from another tube at the end. They entered that duct and crawled.

"Bats!" Vera said. "They sound like banshees wailing." Adam could hear them too, echoing into their cavity. Adam and Vera followed the sound, which was getting progressively louder, until they broke into another chamber. Adam shone the lantern up at the ceiling, entirely covered with a wiggling mass of bats.

Avoiding the messy floor, they slowly stepped along a clean rock ledge circling the chamber. Adam turned off the lantern as they stopped to catch their breath in the foul air. Vera retched, but her stomach was too empty to vomit, and she just coughed and gagged.

As they made a sharp turn, Vera shouted loudly, "Light!" causing a raucous echo lasting several seconds. The weak glow was coming from directly above them, from the top of the chamber.

Using plenty of rough edges to gain footing and handholds, they began climbing toward the light. After climbing through the tube leading to the light source, they discovered it was just a reflection from the white ceiling of a new chamber. Then their eyes caught a stronger light from yellowed walls at a distance.

It took them five minutes to navigate horizontally to the yellow area, where they looked up and saw a bright blue sky, about a hundred feet up the wide yellow tube.

Using climbing pitons and rope, they inched their way up the smooth walls. Those last two hours seemed to Adam like five minutes, when they finally reached the top. By then the light was fading. In the setting sun, they found themselves on a chimney formation poking from a rocky hillside, sprinkled with small pines. It was one of the most beautiful sights Adam had ever seen.

Vera gratefully sucked in the fresh air and stared at the vista in disbelief. "Oh Adam, I thought we were done for. Where are we?"

"I'm guessing we've traveled about ten miles, over a period of thirty-six hours, and we're several miles south of Lechuguilla's eastern complex. I think we're outside the park boundary, to the south."

"We're so lucky to be alive. I need a shower and a big dinner."

"We're not out of the woods yet," Adam warned. "We have to reach the park as quickly as possible."

"What's the hurry? Can't we wait until morning?"

"We're naked! It's going to drop to thirty-five or forty degrees Fahrenheit tonight. Besides, by now Jayne and Ernie will have discovered we're lost. We want to get back before a rescue party is launched. We can't endanger people unnecessarily."

The rope assisted climb down the chimney took only minutes. Near the base of the yellow rock formation, Adam spotted a deer trail winding downhill toward a dry gulch. It was going to be entirely dark in minutes, and they would have to hike in the now familiar darkness. In the twilight they followed the trail for about fifteen minutes. The packed dirt felt good against Vera's bare, mutilated feet.

It was fully dark when they reach the gulch, where Adam fashioned a small rock pyramid at the edge of the rough channel, just where the trail stopped. He made a similar one inside the trench. "We'll want to come back. Ernie will be furious with me if we can't find the chimney rock again."

Suddenly a chilling scream pierced the air, sounding like a woman yelling at a cliff to hear her own echoes. "Don't worry," Adam reassured his startled wife. "It's just a coyote. She's as harmless as a cocker spaniel."

They followed the gulch as it steadily descended in a northeasterly direction. They moved quickly, fully erect and stepping into soft warm sand. At a point where the gulch crossed a dirt fire road, Adam built a larger rock pyramid. They followed the road, heading east. About five miles away, with relief they could see car lights on what Adam reckoned to be U.S. Highway 180.

They walked toward the lights at a fast clip, ignoring the pain from stepping on rocks and sharp objects. It took only an hour to reach the highway.

A few feet from the pavement Vera help Adam build another rock pyramid bigger than the rest, all the while ignoring cars whizzing by.

When they were finished, Adam said, "We'll cross to the other side and head north. Surely somebody will stop and give us a lift."

"It'll be a lot sooner than you think," Vera said. "We're buck-naked. I hope we don't attract a carload of drunken men."

As they flagged passing cars, one of the first to pass them stopped, a young couple inside. "My goodness!" the woman exclaimed as Adam and Vera entered the rear seat of their car. "We thought you were wearing bathing suits. What happened? Were you in a car wreck?"

"Worse," Adam answered. "We were lost in a cavern. We're lucky to be alive."

The good Samaritans gave Adam and Vera some basic clothes and drove them to the park. It was 11:00 p.m. when Adam wakened the duty ranger, who hadn't heard from Jayne and Ernie. The generous young couple had the rangers escort them to their van parked by the Lechuguilla entrance. Vera and Adam changed clothes and returned the borrowed togs. After the couple left, they started a campfire and began cooking a full meal.

It was around 2:00 a.m. when Jayne and Ernie showed up.

"What happened to you guys?" Ernie shouted as he ran to the fire.

"We found another Lechuguilla," Adam said.

Ernie and Jayne listened in amazement to their story. "I want to see it," said Ernie.

"You can have credit for mapping it. I'll guide you there in the morning. Vera and I are going home. We've had enough caving for a very long time."

At ten in the morning, Ernie woke everybody up to a breakfast of sausage and eggs.

"I feel like I've been in a scuffle with ten ferocious cats," Vera complained. "My feet are cut to pieces, and I feel like Mark McGwire beat me with his bat. But I feel good inside."

"Ditto, here, all the way," Adam added.

"All we need is a bath. And then, a concert. I haven't touched the violin in four days."

Ernie and Jayne would be driving Vera and Adam back to El Paso. They stopped on the way and backtracked to the yellow chimney rock, the route discernable only by Adam's small rock pyramids. The entrance was well hidden, and it was impossible to tell a cavern was nearby. Ernie sketched a detailed map, which showed Adam's guessed positioning to be very accurate. He then took notes as Adam dictated from memory the internal topography.

Ernie was especially excited about the great hall with the lake in the middle and the bioluminescence. "I may set up a camp in there for an emergency embryo stash."

"What for?" Vera asked.

"It would be in case of a disaster, such as a meteor collision, huge earthquake, flood, or nuclear war. Nothing should stop us from preserving animal species."

"Survival of humankind would also be jeopardized by those calamities," Jayne said.

"True. Our caretakers might be the only humans to survive. It's a long shot, but if we had the funds, I'd definitely do it."

"And how will your keepers get underground fast enough?" Vera asked, eagerly pushing the discussion to its limit.

Ernie had clearly thought this out. "We'll need a permanent crew on station at all times."

"The Park Service won't let you take over its caverns," Adam objected. "They'll insist on public access. You'll have people trampling all over the place. Wouldn't that make your stash impractical?"

"Yes," Ernie replied. "We can't have that. That's why I'm asking you two to keep this place a *secret*. This entrance is outside of the park boundaries, in the national forest. I could apply for a grazing permit and permanently run a small herd of cattle through here. It would all be legal."

"But what'll you do with those embryos if the planet experiences a disaster?" Vera asked. "You won't have mothers to carry them to term."

Ernie would not be deterred. "We'll have to bring some female animals into the cavern."

Adam and Vera napped the rest of the way to El Paso. They also slept most of the way on the flight home. During his waking moments, Adam daydreamed about a "Noah's Cavern," from which many animals could emerge to recolonize a planet left dead by nuclear war.

The cave experience reminded Adam how important life's small things were. The humbling events forced him to face up to not always being in control. Vera was also changed by the adventure, and she had to admit not having a solution to every problem.

33

Playing Second Fiddle to Her Fiddle

Adam and Vera spent the remainder of their vacation at home, enjoying their last Sunday afternoon walking in the park. Spring was in full force, the fruit trees brilliant with flowers. They had gone a short distance, when Vera started to sneeze convulsively.

"Pollen time," Adam said.

"I don't think so," she said with alarm, "I've never been allergic to pollen before."

The doctor in Adam replied. "As people age, their immune systems go into overdrive."

"Oh, Adam, I'm not supposed to age, remember?"

"This must be aging from before the super virus," replied Adam, now worried.

Vera sneezed all the way home.

"I feel like Sneezy from *Snow White*," she said as they arrived at Falcon Tower. Adam felt more like the Wicked Witch than Doc, hoping that she was not getting a cold. Under normal circumstances, both of them should have a strong case of pneumonia—after spending three days in the nude, followed by a fifteen-mile walk in the middle of a cold night.

Vera coughed all night. When Adam finally took her temperature, it was 102 degrees.

"Oh no, Adam. The super virus didn't take with me, did it?" she asked, knowing the answer when she saw his face.

"I'm afraid not. But everything's going to be all right."

It was an hour before Vera finally fell asleep in a feverish stupor. Adam's mind was racing too fast for sleep, as he played the scenario out. It all revolved around the strong probability that Vera soon would show signs of cancer. If they went in for tests now, they might spot the cancer early, considerably enhancing her survivability. Still, Adam feared the prognosis, and he was convinced that she eventually would need a mastectomy, ending her violin career but giving her a shot at a complete life.

As soon as her flu was over, Adam vowed to try once more to get Vera to have the preemptive surgery.

He perked up with the thought that she might be suffering from a *bacterial* infection. He would take a throat culture in the morning.

The lab test for Vera's culture was negative for bacteria, verifying that a mild viral infection caused her flu. The super virus had not done its job.

Adam went directly home from Central Hospital to confront Vera again. He found her playing her Strad.

"Sweetie, how do you feel?"

"Like a crummy case of the flu," she croaked. "What did the lab say?"

"It's viral. I'm sorry."

"I knew it! And now you're about to ask me to have the mastectomy. Right?"

"Right," was all he could say.

"The answer is *no*," Vera said firmly. "I'll continue with my violin career as long as practicable."

Vera knew a mastectomy involved the removal of muscle tissue. That would be followed by a lengthy convalescence, during which she couldn't practice the violin. Surgery removing tissue around the pectoral muscles would prevent the intense movements she needed to play the violin at a professional level. It might well ruin her career. Adam disagreed, of course, even though the odds didn't favor continuing violin concerts.

"Okay. I was just hoping," he said, totally downcast.

Vera grasped Adam in a strong embrace.

"I'm not dead yet," she finally said. "There's a lot of living to do."

"Will you go with me to oncology? We can investigate therapies that won't ruin your violin playing."

"Of course, I'll go. I don't want the cancer. But I won't let them mutilate me."

Adam was just on time for his urgent appointment with Mildred Rose.

"Hi, Mildred," he greeted.

Mildred was wearing a green blouse and a lifelike lizard pin. Her red hair was wound in a bun.

"Good to see you, Adam. It's been a while since we talked. I know you recently had a confrontation with Itzak Friedman."

Adam fidgeted as he began. "You were sure right about him. The Nazis had forced his father into biological experimentation with animals. In discussing my research with him, I must've evoked dark thoughts about Treblinka."

Mildred gazed into his eyes. "I was pretty sure it was something like that."

"I guess you heard about Itzak's death."

"Wasn't he murdered by the Pan Palestinian something or other?"

"Yes. They implicated me. It was a horrible experience. I ended up killing one of them in self-defense."

"I didn't know the extent of your involvement."

"But that's not why I've come. I want to share some very personal information. I ask you on your strongest honor to repeat none of this."

Mildred spoke professionally while unprofessionally admiring Adam's body. "This will be privileged conversation, like doctor to patient. No court could gain access."

"Acknowledge that I'm just a patient today. Here we go. My wife Vera has a high chance of getting breast cancer—a virulent form usually ending in quick death."

Adam gave a thumbnail sketch of Vera's familial breast cancer. "She won't agree to preventive mastectomy," Adam concluded.

Mildred seemed at last to find Adam's problem interesting, although Adam the man still dominated her thoughts. "From what I know about Vera, that's not for the traditional reasons. Why is she so adamant about early mastectomy?"

"It's her *violin career*. She dreads the pectoral muscle reductions and long convalescence. She's convinced she would never be able to again play professionally."

"So, you're angry and a bit jealous."

"Damned right I am! I resent playing second fiddle to her fiddle."

"An interesting play on words," Mildred said, diverting some of the sting. "But intellectually, can you accept that?"

"Of course I can. The violin is the major part of her life."

Mildred gave a clinical answer. "You're torn between losing her and having her lose a major part herself. And it's hard to accept that she would shorten her life—and time spent with you—just to prolong her career."

"Well put. I hadn't seen it that way."

"You're grieving before the event. You should stop dwelling on the future and enjoy the present more."

"You're very insightful. But there's more."

Adam kept secret his agenda. He had a need to unload, and with his guard now down, he felt compelled to tell everything. Leaving out most details and the deception with Dave Wiley, Adam confessed to self-experimentation.

Then Adam dropped the first bombshell. "If the therapy works, it should prevent all forms of cancer."

Mildred seemed to struggle maintaining her professional demeanor. "Do you actually believe you can prevent all forms of cancer?" asked the analyst.

"I think so, but—" with an anguished expression, Adam finally let go, "it definitely won't work on Vera."

"And you feel guilty?"

"Yes," Adam blurted, attempting to hold back tears.

"From what I hear, you've done this for Vera. Why should you feel guilty because it didn't work?"

"I see that now. But I feel most guilty about lying, about my unprofessional behavior, about not sharing."

"You don't yet have anything to share. You don't know if your cancer prevention even works."

"I guess I feel guilty for what might come."

"I don't see it. Please elaborate."

Adam made a second revelation. "Besides preventing cancer, my therapy will stop *aging*. If it works, I'll have discovered what I call virtual immortality. People wouldn't die from the usual causes—heart failure, viral disease, or cancer. They'd be able to live for several hundred year—maybe thousands—until they die from accident, drowning, poisoning, and so forth."

There was a long pause.

"I—I'm at a loss for words—" Mildred seemed to stage the proper confused expression and tone, perhaps to disguise thoughts that he might be delusional.

Adam continued. "But it's still to be proven. One of the laboratory rats lived over three times the typical life span. It eventually died of poisoning from one of our experiments."

Mildred was speechless.

Adam gave a quick but disjointed summary. "Itzak argued convincingly that immortality was a violation of evolution and would turn genetics into a dead science. Vera then pointed out that the world would not be a better place, with billions of extra people and few deaths. Finally, I realized that human greed would use virtual immortality to ruin society, as we know it. I couldn't share it."

Still Mildred said nothing.

"Can't you see?—I feel guilty about what I've created and about my growing reluctance to share this discovery."

"Well," Mildred finally responded, "you should wait for proof of 'virtual immortality.' I see no great moral issue about keeping this secret until then."

"And what about after?"

By now, it seemed as though Mildred had lost all of her sexual interest in Adam. Perhaps she was seeing him as just another neurotic patient with delusions.

She gave a frank reply. "The quest for immortality has been going on since humans knew about death. Your main focus should be the therapy's corrupting influence. That would be my emotional trigger on the issue, too. If you truly believe immortality will harm the human race, then you should feel positive about not sharing."

"But, how can I do that, knowing I may be immortal?" asked Adam, his anguish transparent.

Adam must have appeared totally detached from reality. Mildred continued, following the "book," as would any good analyst with a delusional patient.

"Well, you'd only be *virtually* immortal. You could still pull the plug on yourself if you could no longer stand it."

"True," Adam admitted. "That's one aspect I'd never considered. Thanks, Mildred, you've been a big help."

"I'll be here if you want to talk some more," replied Mildred, taking no lustful looks. "Next time, however, the meter will be ticking."

34

A Temporary Reprieve

Vera sat in the hallway at the med center Radiology Department, wanting to avoid the unpleasant business altogether. But she had promised Adam to allow diagnostic intervention without waiting for obvious symptoms.

Finally, Vera was called into the scanner room, where the attendant asked her to remove her blouse and bra. She positioned for a scan of the right breast, resting it on a cold plate while pressing her chest against the metal apparatus. The attendant closed the top plate onto the breast, the two plates squeezing the gland like a ball. The painful process was repeated with the left breast.

Vera was cleared to go home, even though she was experiencing a dull ache in both breasts. But she planned to force herself into a normal routine and practice the violin anyway.

Vera had tried to relax at home. But only four hours since the mammogram, Dr. Smith telephoned, requesting her to return to the hospital immediately.

Adam was already in the waiting room when Vera arrived.

"Hi Vera. They've found something. Apparently we were not a day too soon."

"Oh Adam, I've been dreading this moment."

They walked in silence as the nurse led them into the examining room. Dr. Smith greeted them and got right to business.

"Here's a picture of your left breast," he said, pointing to the X-ray mounted on the light stand. "Here's a small growth. I want to manually probe it."

Dr. Smith asked Vera to remove her top and put on a hospital smock. Ordinarily this procedure was done with a nurse chaperone. Today, Adam played that role. After a few seconds of gentle probing, the doctor gave his diagnosis: "Ms. Sokol, you have a small tumor. We need a biopsy to see whether it's malignant."

Vera gasped. "You and my husband have discussed my wishes?"

"Yes. Surgery will do a lumpectomy today, removing all of the tumor tissue. We'll send that to the lab. Only a small incision will be needed, and they'll stitch the wound shut. If the lab results are negative, you'll have soreness for a few days, but you can continue your normal routine."

"And if they're positive?"

"You'd begin daily radiation therapy to kill any remnant cancer cells. Since we found this tumor early, we'd assume the cancer—if that's what this is—hasn't metastasized elsewhere in your body. We wouldn't do chemotherapy at that time."

"And how would radiation affect my lifestyle?"

Dr. Smith's bedside manner was impressive. "Various side effects might accompany radiation therapy, including loss of appetite and headaches. They'll be very minor, since the radiation would be localized to your breast and neighboring lymphatic glands. But there should be no more tumor growth on that side—at least for a while."

"You mean we might have to do it all over again?"

"There's a high probability that tumors will grow again, in either breast."

"How long will this go on?"

"Until menopause—maybe longer. But tumor formations may stop spontaneously. Regardless of what pathology finds, you should have monthly mammograms for the rest of your life."

"What about my violin? I finger with my left hand and draw the bow with the right."

"You should be able to play immediately if you can tolerate the pain. That should subside in a couple of days."

Adam now asked the question. "John, assuming that this is cancer, what's the probability Vera can continue her violin career?"

"Her chances are better than even. And regardless, she can continue playing for a long time. We plan to aggressively search for tumors *early*. That's the key."

He concluded, "Surgery is ready for the lumpectomy now. Good luck."

It had been two hours since the fifteen-minute operation. Vera was resting on the recovery bed with Adam sitting at her side. As the anesthetic wore off she began to feel a dull ache on her left side, and certain movements sent sharp pain signals.

"This isn't nearly as bad as I'd imagined."

Adam was more relaxed than Vera had seen him in months. "I'm relieved. I thought cancer therapy would be far worse than Smith indicated. I've been too pessimistic to recognize the advantages of vigilance and early detection."

A smiling Dr. Smith announced that the pathology report was negative. Adam wanted to celebrate their temporary reprieve. But Vera was in too much pain and asked to go straight home.

On the drive, Adam's mind was on another journey—a *guilt* trip. He had gotten into the super virus mess to prevent Vera's cancer. All of that had been so unnecessary. Not only did her protective virus fail to take, but her breast-cancer threat was far less than imagined. Adam felt stupid, like a mad scientist with blinders on. How could he have been so naïve? Why had he presumed to know everything about breast cancer? Why hadn't he talked to Dr. Smith earlier, before dragging so many people into the virtual immortality quagmire?

Adam forced himself to stop dwelling on the negative. The past could not be undone. Vera would be okay—that was all that mattered now.

It was 8:00 p.m. when they arrived at Falcon Tower. Adam made soup and sandwiches while Vera played some short pieces by Sarasate, wincing occasionally, but continuing to play her violin without interruption. After a half hour of playing, Vera too began to show her release from the strain that had been building over her health.

As they ate, Vera directed the conversation to Adam's situation. "Are your ears still ringing?"

"They've never stopped, and I never got your flu bug. I guess the super virus is still active. But it looks like the whole exercise was unnecessary. The odds are that you'll do okay, even if you get the breast cancer."

"That's not the end of it. All indications are that you won't age," Vera added, biting into her BLT sandwich.

"I suppose so." Adam said after pausing to swallow. "But the super virus has never been fully tested. Not getting your flu hardly proves it's working in me."

"Maybe you should test it," she suggested.

"What for?" Adam asked, gulping a spoonful of mushroom soup. "I don't care whether or not I'm virtually immortal. It's not going to change what I'm doing. Anyway, we'll find out soon enough."

"Well, we've been skirting this issue. Suppose you are virtually immortal. That should make a vast difference in how you spend your life."

"I love my life the way it is. I don't want to change."

"There's nothing you would change?" she asked, persistent in her probing.

"Well, I'd like to get away from Dave Wiley."

"Your wish will come true. He's bound to retire in a few years, and voila!"

"Yeah, but I'm scheduled to retire shortly thereafter."

"Adam, don't you see? You don't have to retire! You can keep doing the job you love indefinitely."

Adam finished his sandwich, wanting to digest the issues Vera had just raised before continuing the discussion. At last, he gave his response.

"Of course Vera, I don't have to retire. Even before this, I've never given my future lifestyle much thought. People retire because they're slowing down or to squeeze a few years of quality time into their lives. My years probably won't have those limits."

"Yes, Adam. You won't die—you can continue your work as long as you like."

"We don't know that," Adam shot back.

"But all indications are pointing that way, right?"

"Yes, they are."

Vera stared intensely at Adam. "You can begin a new life whenever you wish. If you get bored, you can make a fresh start with something else. You won't have a sword hanging over your head. You can make mistakes, and get on with it."

"It would be like being reborn," Adam mused.

"Better! You'll get to keep all your memories, all your knowledge."

"But I'd lose things I love, too. I'd lose you."

"But you'd lose me anyway, no matter what. This way, you won't be losing yourself."

""But I might get tired of it all," Adam said sadly.

"God forbid," Vera said, shaking her head. "If your life becomes unbearable, you can always end it. But knowing you, you'll always find a purpose."

Adam wondered how he would spend his life as a virtual immortal. He had lost zeal for the cancer experiments and was almost ready to conclude his cure would be worse than the disease. He had no stomach for a prolonged game of charades with Dave Wiley.

Regardless of whether the super virus was working or not, he would have to find something else to do. Knowing now where it would lead, he didn't want to continue pursuing cell-division fidelity as a cure for cancer. He still had his DNA mapping and germ-line intervention projects and believed both worthwhile. But with the gift of time, they wouldn't be enough. He needed something bigger in his life.

Adam would have to plan a new career path.

35

A Heroic Test of Fire

Adam was driving to Central University Medical Center, where he would lecture on genetic counseling to a group of practicing physicians. He still didn't know if his super virus was working. Although getting a viral infection would prove it wasn't, the opposite would be difficult to establish. He would have an indefinite wait to find that out.

His wait was about to end.

The med center complex grounds were bustling with emergency vehicles and people standing about. Adam stopped at the security kiosk and asked the guard what had happened.

"It's some sort of contagious infection. The area is quarantined. No visitors are allowed."

"That's okay. I work here," Adam said, showing his badge for the first time in months.

"All right, doctor. But only emergency services are in effect. All med school classes are canceled."

The guard then gave Adam a brief status summary.

The med center was two hours into emergency countdown because of the strange infection. No patients were being admitted, and the hospital was closed to vehicle access. The outbreak had started in the immunology laboratory, where Dr. Fred Hamlish collapsed after handling a vial of experimental virus. He was in the contagion ward experiencing high fever and breathing difficulties. Dr. Hamlish's research assistant was also there with the same symptoms.

As Adam entered the building, a group of staff members were clustered, talking excitedly.

"I hear somebody dropped a vial of Ebola virus," one nurse said.

"I hope not," a bearded African-American medical student replied. "We don't have funding for Ebola experiments. But we have a laboratory strain of a virus more virulent than Ebola. It's reputed to be unstoppable, a killer on the scale of AIDS, except it would all take place in a week. Whole tribes in Africa have been wiped out by the less infectious Ebola. Hamlish was working on the experimental virus."

"Does anybody know what the symptoms are?" Adam asked.

One resident recognized Adam. "Hello, Dr. Boatwright. Dr. Hamlish and his assistant are running 105-degree fevers and their lungs are filling with fluid. Several medical staff people have been exposed. Everybody in contact with the original two has gathered in the contagion ward."

"What about Hamlish's lab?"

"Sealed tight," a woman lab technician answered. "The ventilation to that part of the building has been shut down."

"Yeah, this virus appears to be an airborne spreader," the medical student interjected.

Compelled to help, Adam entered the hospital and took the elevator to the hospital administration office. There he encountered a heated conversation in the conference room. The hospital chief, Dr. Harold Svenson, and the dean of the medical school were present, along with several department heads and the director of security.

Dr. Svenson nodded at Adam and turned to hear the laboratory director's words. "Apparently, somebody switched labels on all Hamlish's vials. He was exposed to the experimental African strain."

Chief Svenson rubbed his blonde beard and glared at the lab director. "What was Hamlish doing with that mutant virus?"

The skinny, balding man answered sheepishly. "Our researchers need access to all kinds of viruses. That particular strain was on loan from the National Institute of Health. Hamlish was going to test it on rats to assess propagating modes."

"How did Hamlish know it would infect rats?" the chief asked severely.

The director glared back at Svenson. "I suppose he didn't. That was to be determined."

Svenson addressed the entire group. "We need fail-safe procedures to prevent this type of thing from happening again. Are all the exposed people now in quarantine?"

"As far as we can tell," the security head answered.

Adam was finally able to speak. "That's not good enough. Dr. Svenson, do you have a complete list of the people in quarantine?"

"I've got it memorized. Let's see. There's Hamlish and Morrison, the only two physicians. Then there are the nurses, Gonsalves, Eddington, and Mercer. And two third-year medical students, Morton and Burton."

"*Bonnie* Burton?"

"I believe so," Svenson said placidly.

Suddenly, he barked, "Boatwright, are you here to help? If not, get the hell out of the way."

"I'll help in any way I can."

"Dr. Svenson!" yelled the chief of nurses as she ran into the conference room. "Dr. Hamlish has gone into heart failure. A student is administering CPR."

"Oh, God. I need a surgeon there," said Svenson in a panic. "It could be a death sentence for whomever we send."

"I'll go," Adam said, followed by a *lie*. "I'm immune to the Ebola family and similar viruses. I was exposed on rest-and-recreation, during my second tour in Vietnam."

Not asking for the details, Svenson accepted the offer. "You'd better get suited."

The chief referred to an outfit such as those worn by astronauts, containing its own breathing apparatus.

"Forget that. I'll work better without a suit."

Although the super virus in his body was untested, there was no safe way for Adam to verify its workability. But the odds were in favor of his remaining uninfected. Knowing that, Adam was compelled to save those people. He didn't feel particularly heroic and acted totally on impulse, almost reflexively.

It was an eerie walk down the hallway of the deserted wing. Adam's heart rushed as he entered the safety chamber connecting the makeshift isolation ward to main hospital. Taking a deep breath, Adam closed the outside door and walked through the inside doorway. He was now a virtual prisoner in the danger area. Adam followed the sound of voices to a room off the main corridor.

Bonnie Burton was busily pressing rhythmically on Doctor Hamlish's chest.

"Bonnie, I'm here to help," he said from the opposite side of the examining table.

"Hello, Dr. Boatwright," she greeted with a look of shock, not losing her beat. "Thanks for coming."

Adam went directly to work, enlisting the aid of the other staff. Leaving Dr. Morrison to writhe deliriously on a nearby table, he gave Hamlish a shot of insulin directly into the heart, while the others readied the crash cart and monitor. When everything was in place, Adam instructed, "Okay, we're going to use the paddles. I want you all to take a shot of gamma globulin as we work. Nurse Gonsalves, please start administering the injections. Can you do yourself, too?"

"Yes, doctor." She was a big woman, which was why Adam picked her. "Shall we inject Dr. Hamlish and Dr. Morrison?"

"Later. I wish we'd gotten to them sooner. Gamma globulin will slow the pace of infection."

"Don't you want an injection too?" Gonsalves asked.

"No. I'm immune to this virus," Adam answered, wanting to avoid the drug's side effects. He thought: *I hope I'll be protected by the super virus.* "Bonnie, please immerse Dr. Morrison in an ice bath. Then start an aspirator to clear his lungs."

After three shocks, Hamlish hadn't responded. Adam made a quick incision the width of his chest cavity. He then sawed on a rib, breaking it to make room to squeeze in and grab Hamlish's heart. All the while the heart-lung machine was keeping the patient alive. Nurses Eddington and Mercer assisted, separating ribs, clamping bleeders, and handling the instruments.

It had been nearly an hour before Adam could finally grasp the lifeless organ. After a few minutes of direct massage, the monitor began to show a regular heartbeat.

"Okay, let's close him up," Adam ordered. It took over an hour to finish the surgery.

Exhausted from the rushed effort, Adam instructed, "Okay, we have to put Dr. Hamlish in ice and start aspiration. Bonnie!"

With the help of Nurse Gonsalves, Bonnie had earlier undressed Dr. Morrison and had then moved him into a tub of very cold water. Morrison was propped in a sitting position, held in place with a safety strap. The women began to gently prepare Hamlish for a similar bath, securing him with his chest safely above the water line.

As Adam gathered the mobile members of the group, Nurse Mercer started to break under the pressure. "We're all going to die. This disease has wiped out whole villages in Africa. Oh God, I don't want to die!"

"Stop it right now!" Adam ordered. "We're not going to die. I survived this thing, and so can you."

"I believe in Dr. Boatwright," Bonnie said. "If anybody can pull us through, he can."

"Listen to me," Adam said to the group. "We're going to have to wait this thing out. Your bodies should already be starting to fight the virus, and the gamma globulin should keep you a step ahead of it. As soon as Hamlish and Morrison show a break in their fevers, Nurse Gonsalves will administer shots to them too."

"Can't we take a shot of something else or get a vaccine?" Nurse Eddington asked, her small size making her look far younger than her years.

"No," Adam answered. "There's no vaccine for this virus. Antibiotics won't work. All we can do is treat symptoms as they occur and wait it out. Since we've intervened early, all of you will survive. I can't say as much for Doctors Hamlish and Morrison."

It had been five hours since Adam entered isolation. Everyone else was now running a fever. Morton and the three nurses had severe headaches, and two of them were vomiting. Bonnie's body ached severely, but she was still mobile. She and Adam hooked up saline IVs to everybody to prevent dehydration and then administered more gamma globulin all around. Adam finally made Bonnie lie down and connected her to an IV. By that time, Dr. Hamlish had been moved to a bed and covered with blankets. Once he had received his gamma globulin, his lungs had started to clear, and he now was receiving fluids from IV.

But soon thereafter Dr. Morrison suffered heart failure. The small staff was too ill to help, and Adam had to tend him all alone. While Adam was prepping him for surgery, Dr. Morrison died.

Finally, Adam had a chance to call Vera. "Hi, honey," he said in an exhausted voice. "I guess you've heard about the emergency."

"Adam, are you okay? It's been on the radio. There was some sabotage at the med center and there's a terrible epidemic."

"I'm there."

"Where?" asked Vera, frightened.

"I'm in the isolation ward."

"You're the mystery doctor who's been treating the contagious people?" she asked, already knowing the answer.

"Yes," he said in a calming voice. "Everything's under control. I'm okay so far."

"I should have guessed. Oh Adam, I'm so worried."

"I think the super virus is working. I'd better go back to my patients. Talk to you later."

"Goodbye, my hero," Vera said, seeming to struggle and not show her emotions.

Adam had been free of any symptoms so far. The super virus seemed to be doing its job, keeping him free from other viral infections. All they could do now was wait.

Adam had been in isolation nearly twelve hours, when Dr. Hamlish finally awoke from his stupor. Within hours, the symptoms disappeared from the remaining staff. Adam never experienced symptoms.

Taking no chances on the infection spreading, Dr. Svenson ordered the victims to remain in quarantine for three more days, during which they whiled away the time playing cards and chatting.

On the second day of post-emergency confinement, Adam finally spoke with Dr. Hamlish. "I'm sorry about Morrison."

Wincing at the effort, Dr. Hamlish replied in a weak voice. "Yeah. He was a great kid. Lots of potential."

"Well Fred, at least you're back from the jaws of death."

"Boy, have I learned a lesson," Hamlish replied, struggling to control the pain. "I'll never again be cavalier in my research when life and death are in such precarious balance."

"I know what you mean," Adam replied. Only he knew the profundity of his words. No one had ever been so cavalier as himself.

"I wonder how I caught this bug, Adam. My virus was safely stored for future mouse studies."

"Your vials were all mislabeled. It must have been the animal rightsists. They've been causing lots of mischief."

They were interrupted by a call from Dr. Svenson, checking on the group's prognosis. Adam was in the waiting room reading medical journals. Bonnie joined him there.

"Dr. Boatwright, thank you for saving my life," she said, putting her arm around him.

"Bonnie, I didn't really do a lot. You did as much as I."

"It was your quick thinking and firm hand that did it." She caught Adam by surprise, kissing him hard and with passion. Adam responded as he had done months before at her apartment. But Bonnie didn't pursue it. "I love you so much," she said, "in a way that only true friends can love."

"I love you, too, Bonnie—but, as you said, as a *friend*. You know I'm totally committed in my marriage."

"I know," she said, smiling radiantly. "I can't help it. I'll always love you. It's because I do that I want your marriage to continue on a high plain. I couldn't bear to see you unhappy."

"But, Bonnie, you aren't being fair to yourself. You should be dating and enjoying the company of men your own age."

"I don't have time for a relationship. I have my studies, my work, and my son. I couldn't do any man justice. Feel good, Dr. Boatwright. My loving you allows me to avoid relationships and keep my sanity."

"But, Bonnie, you must *not* neglect your basic needs. A loving relationship can only help your work."

"You mean sex," blurted Bonnie, blushing beet red. "I redirect my sex drive, channeling it to my duties and studies. I'm not exactly a dried-up prune, but in my current phase of life, I wouldn't have the energy for good sex."

"I know exactly what you mean," replied Adam, blushing himself. "I went through those periods, too. But, someday you'll have the time and the energy, and you'll find the right man. You'll see how much that relationship will enhance your life. It's wonderful to have someone with whom to share your ideas."

Bonnie and Adam were interrupted by another call from Dr. Svenson. "The Director of Security wants to talk to you," Svenson said. "I'm putting him on."

"Boatwright here. What can I do for you?"

He asked Adam who might have relabeled the vials in Hamlish's laboratory.

Adam was quick to respond. "I think it was an animal rightsist who didn't want Hamlish to inject his rats. I recently had a similar experience with a disgruntled employee." Adam gave the security director a green light to talk to Dr. Hamlish.

Vera was among the boisterous family members cheering as Adam led the staff out of isolation. Bonnie was last, pushing Dr. Hamlish in a wheelchair.

"Congratulations, Dr. Boatwright," Svenson said, grabbing Adam's hand and patting his back. "You've saved six lives."

"Sorry about Morrison. These guys deserve a reward."

"I'm giving them a week off with pay. Adam, you deserve a greater reward, anything within my power."

"Can you persuade the med school dean to give me a sabbatical?"

"Done!" Svenson gratefully replied.

"Darling," Vera squealed as she brushed past Svenson to embrace Adam. "You brave thing."

"I've missed you, Vera," Adam said before kissing her tenderly.

"Me too. I'm so proud of you," she said lovingly.

"I didn't do it alone. The whole staff was heroic, especially my third-year student, Bonnie Burton."

"Isn't she also your research assistant?"

"Yes. And what an amazing coincidence. She also helped us track down Itzak's murderer."

"I've never met her. Is she the one pushing the wheel chair?"

"Yes."

The evidence was compelling that the super virus had worked.

Adam was virtually immortal.

36

Putting the Genie Back into Its Bottle

President Wentworth hosted the dinner in honor of Dr. and Mrs. Adam Boatwright. Attending with their wives were Dr. Svenson, Adam's two department chairmen, and his two school deans. After dinner, Wentworth made a congratulatory speech announced that Adam could have a year's paid sabbatical leave as reward for his unselfish efforts with the emergency.

Adam was anxious for the dinner to end. He disliked ceremony and especially being the center of attention at a banquet. As the speeches droned on, Adam's mind was preoccupied perfecting a new plan to change the super virus project into a positive experiment. He would meet with Dave Wiley the next day to set it in motion.

Two busy minds were at attendance at the banquet, dwelling at opposite ends of the greed–altruism spectrum.

Also suffering through speeches was Dave Wiley, who stared at Adam Boatwright, jealous of his notoriety and newfound political influence. Throughout the dinner ordeal, Wiley sat like a grinning owl, scheming and plotting how to best prey on Boatwright's new status in the pursuit of virtual immortality.

Just as Adam entered Wiley's office, the department chairman received a phone call. Adam waited, again admiring the red-haired dancer in the wall art. The image reminded him of Mildred Rose, who had helped assuage his guilt and gather strength for what he was about to do.

"Sorry about that," Wiley said. "It was the FDA calling about Epstein's project."

Mentally crossing his fingers, Adam began. "We need a basic strategy for our human super-virus project. As I see it, this will involve a bit of backpedaling on our part."

Wiley was all ears. "What do you have in mind?"

"We can't announce that we've stopped mouse *aging*. That'll give hot shots an incentive to duplicate what we've done."

"I've been worrying about the same thing. I agree 100 percent. What's your plan?"

Adam sensed he would soon have Wiley eating out of his hand. "Let's say nothing about cessation of *aging* in any communication about the mouse super virus. Our reports should avoid the term 'super virus'—just 'B13G.4 virus' will do. Our quarterly report to National Cancer should say only that the Dirty Dozen mice had no tumors. We won't even mention virus immunity."

"Wonderful!" Wiley said, pushing up from his chair. "It'll be years before anyone puts two-and-two together. By that time, we should be in business with a human super virus."

Adam held up his hand to stop him. "But there's more," he said, as Wiley started to pace. "What if the wrong people discover anti-aging properties of the mouse super virus *before* we develop a human counterpart?"

"Then we're screwed. That'd put us in a race with every genetic engineering outfit in the world."

Adam threw a curve ball. "Is it even desirable to link fighting cancer with stopping the aging process?

Wiley sat and grinned at Adam for a moment. "Not at all. These are two different things. There's a big constituency for fighting cancer and—ironically—none for becoming immortal. But the latter is infinitely more attractive."

"Then you're in favor of de-linking these two things?" Adam asked.

"Damned right I am."

Adam almost couldn't believe his ears. Vera was right when she said Wiley would be a tremendous ally.

Adam hid his excitement. "I have a way to separate fighting cancer and achieving virtual immortality."

"Let's hear it," Wiley said.

"I want to re-engineer the mouse super virus so it'll self-destruct over time. It'll fight cancer over a mouse's normal life span and then cease to function. The mouse will die naturally shortly thereafter."

"What about the *human* super virus?" Wiley asked impatiently.

"We'll apply what we learn to the experimental human virus. But that one will eventually have to stop reproducing too."

"And we'll have *two* versions of the human super virus, right?"

"Exactly," Adam *lied*. "The public one will be temporary, just to fight cancer. The second one will be permanent, stopping the aging process."

Wiley's happy face became a scowl. "I like your objective, but I see problems with that. Young-looking mice will suddenly die of flu after living long, cancer-free lives. Some genetic engineer may prolong the virus lifetime, leading him to pursue a *human* anti-aging version."

"We have a dilemma here. But it could take years before they realize our mice die mysteriously in young bodies. Someone would then have to discover it was all due to *death* of the super virus."

Wiley was smiling again. "Go ahead and monkey with B-13G.4. Keep any hint of anti-aging features out of all literature, letters, and reports. Don't talk about that property with your staff."

Adam congratulated himself. He got exactly what he wanted, and now Wiley would be working with him.

But that was not exactly true.

It was Dave Wiley who had Boatwright just where he wanted him! Boatwright would now cooperate in keeping anti-aging potential a secret. That would make it easier to gain a monopoly position for selling immortality. They would peddle the full-strength super virus to the highest bidder.

Wiley planned to keep a close eye on Boatwright. Maybe his clandestine human super virus was working after all. Nothing in Boatwright's documented past could verify earlier exposure to African viruses. Why would Boatwright willingly expose himself to horrible infection during the hospital emergency? He was certainly not suicidal and he didn't want the glory. Could his heroics really be a guise for testing his own immunities?

Boatwright must be host to a working human super virus.

But for some reason, Boatwright did not want him to know. He would have to find out why.

Adam wanted to put the immortality genie back in the bottle. But doing so would contradict the entire anti-cancer thrust of the project. A self-destructing super virus might be unworkable with humans. How odd it would be for a person to live 80 cancer-free years—the last 60 in the body of a 20-year-old—only to quickly die of some exotic flu strain.

To complicate matters, Adam did not know the effects of a self-destructing super virus. Under another scenario, the self-destruction mechanism would cause the super virus to mutate into a monster doing unimaginable harm to its host.

He now had a preventive for cancer. The whole premise of his research, indeed of medicine itself, is that this treatment must be made *available*. But he could not let the world have it, because doing so would grant humankind virtual immortality, which would accelerate the destruction of Earth itself.

37

Here We Go Again!

Adam was mortified as he entered his LSB study to find somebody snooping around. The trespasser was a heavyset, long-haired man, wearing a yellow shirt and black pants held up by red suspenders embroidered with pink flamingos.

"What's going on?" Adam hollered.

"I'm John Holbrook, Central City Police," the intruder replied.

"So why are you in my office?" Adam asked again, fearing the worst.

"I have a search warrant."

"What for?"

"We're investigating your operation. Where do you store your viruses?"

"In the mouse lab, two doors down," Adam replied, spitting his words. "Would you kindly tell me what's going on?"

"Sorry. Police business. I'll see you later, Doc."

Adam broke into a nervous sweat, unable to decide whether that was a threat or a promise. He wondered if the vials were connected to the emergency, and if he was suspected in the sabotage. Chills ran down his spine at the prospect of repeating the fiasco over Itzak's murder.

Adam met at the Beckwith Ranch with the reactivated super-virus task force. He would set in motion the next phase of that project. The remote site was chosen to conceal as much as possible of the experiments from Wiley's view. In spite of their seeming agreement in goals, Adam couldn't trust Wiley. The chairman's agenda was power and money—a radical departure from Adam's goals of bettering humankind and saving the planet from the ravages of greedy traffickers.

Adam limited the group to the original three—Rita Morales, Jack Chin, and Sandra Wickham. Only they knew the rationale for engineering a mouse super virus to cure cancer. Only Sandra knew the connection between that virus and human herpes, but only as a computer *simulation*. Jack knew only that he had genetically engineered a *mouse* B-17 backup candidate for a *mouse* super virus. Adam had never revealed to Jack that he had instead modified Adam's own *herpes simplex*. Adam would maintain those deceptions—too much was at stake if he did otherwise.

Adam began with an opening statement. "Thanks for coming. I'm reactivating the task force for the next phase of our cancer prevention project. I want you to stop calling Methuselah by that name. It has too strong a Biblical connotation with long life. Dave Wiley thinks it's unwise to advertise anti-aging properties. We'll have to de-link anti-aging and anti-cancer."

As usual, Jack was first to speak. "But the whole premise of the super virus is to prevent cancer by maintaining faithful cell division, and the agent for that is I-complex, a chemical I don't fully understand. That miracle substance automatically brings the other benefits, most notably disease avoidance and youth."

"True, but there'll be tremendous problems with that. It'll be impossible to control this research if outsiders grasp that it also stops aging."

"I don't see it," said Jack.

Adam aired his primary concern. "To stop aging is a universal desire; it has been for thousands of years. Many legitimate researchers, plus charlatans and hacks, would be compelled to duplicate what we've done. Some would even take it to the next logical step—a human super virus. Someone might even succeed. Imagine the mischief they could cause."

"Yeah," Rita added. "Quacks and criminals could peddle the stuff and make billions."

"Trillions!" Adam corrected.

Jack continued. "But think about the benefits from cessation of aging."

Sandra then got right to the heart of the matter. "And how long, Jack, do you want people to live? Would you stop at five hundred years? At a thousand years? Never? And who decides? And what happens to the planet with all these old farts crowding out the young, making it impractical for new children to be born? The planet is already enormously overpopulated."

Rita took a turn next. "Sandra, you're thinking about the developed world. Here we practice birth control, and there would be economic pressures against new lives. But the third world knows no such limitations. They'll keep on having babies, but nobody dies. What kind of world will that be?"

Adam shook his head. These were Vera's exact arguments.

"I see your points," Jack admitted. "In the abstract, stopping the aging process seems good. The reality would be horrible. The planet could not sustain the huge new population."

The entire group seemed to be against virtual immortality, for very much the same reasons as Adam's and Vera's.

Elated at how easy it had been, Adam directed the meeting toward specific action. "We all want to fight cancer. But eliminating it stops *aging,* as we know it. My solution would be to attempt to engineer a self-destruction gene directly into the super virus."

"So the super virus itself will die of old age?" Rita asked.

"Yes. Doing so would still prolong life, but not indefinitely, since people would have immunities and be tumor-free while the super virus still works."

"That seems like a reasonable compromise," Jack agreed.

"Let's play this out," Sandra suggested. "A person takes the super virus at age twenty. She gets no more colds, flu, or other illnesses, and so on, until she is sixty. Then she starts to go gray, her body falls apart, and by ninety she dies of old age, probably from some form of cancer."

"That's the way it looks to me," Adam said. "We could work on a delay for cancer, but we couldn't eliminate it without granting immortality."

"This is one hell of a dilemma, isn't it?" Rita asked rhetorically, expecting no answer.

"This sort of thing is exactly what medical science has been seeking for the past hundred years," Jack said. "I think we should go for it. People lead healthier lives, cancer-free for their biblical allotment, senility is eliminated, but they eventually die at a natural age."

"Tell me, each of you, how do you personally feel about death?" Adam asked. "Jack, you start."

"Let me be totally candid. I'd love to live forever, but not in a deteriorating world. If I and my loved ones and friends could be the only ones having immortality, I'd take it."

"But that'd be impossible," Adam responded. "It has to be shared with everybody."

"Well—then I wouldn't want it," Jack concluded.

"Me neither," Rita said firmly.

"It would be fascinating to watch the world change," Sandra said, "but I'd probably commit suicide after fifty years of it."

"And you, Adam?" Jack asked.

This was going to be a hard one, Adam thought. He realized he would have to answer with the truth. "I feel like Jack and like Sandra. I'd like to sample immortality for a while. But I wouldn't want everyone on the planet to have access to it."

Adam gave instructions. "Okay, back to reality. Sandra, I want you to work up the DNA coordinates in the mouse super virus for potential self-destructing genes. We want to make the host's entire virus population age. We want a half-life of about six months, so that a young mouse would live maybe nine to twelve months before I-complex output becomes too weak to ward off disease or cancer.

"Jack, you'll take Sandra's coordinates and engineer the actual viruses—just like before. Clone sufficient quantities for Rita to infect her mice with each variant form of the super virus."

"Do you want me to hide this?" Jack asked.

Adam took the opportunity to set the policy. "It's paramount to keep secret our *motives*—finding a virus *self-destruction* gene. Only you three and Dave Wiley will know about our new goal. If outsiders find out what we're doing now, they might deduce we already have a mouse super virus that does *not* self-destruct. We don't want to encourage anybody to engineer a full-blown super virus of their own. We can't trust anybody to keep secrets, so we must spare our colleagues most of the details until we're ready to start human research."

Adam continued to instruct. "Rita, you'll prepare the test mice. We'll try each of Jack's DNA mutations of the super virus and track what happens. As you monthly administer killer virus cocktails, we'll see how long it'll take each mouse to die."

Adam was paying a visit to police headquarters, lucky to find Dick Reilly sitting at his desk entering a computer report with two fingers.

"Hello, Detective Reilly."

"Dr. Boatwright. What brings you here?"

"I had a visit from John Holbrook. But he won't reveal anything. Can you tell me what's going on?"

Reilly looked very flustered. After a moment, he said, "There's a coffee shop, the Blue Bird, across the street. Meet me there in ten minutes."

Adam entered the old-fashioned cafe, sat down in a booth near the back, and ordered a cup of coffee. He picked up a newspaper from one of the nearby tables. He was busily reading the sports pages when Reilly slipped into the booth and muttered, "Those jocks and their fancy salaries. It makes me sick."

"Yeah," Adam replied, "and they know how to spend it."

Reilly switched to the matters at hand. “I’m not supposed to say anything, but I owe you from before.”

“Thanks, Dick. What is it?”

“It’s about the sabotage at Central University Medical Center.”

“Holbrook was interested in vials,” said Adam. “Do the police think I had something to do with Hamlish’s lab vials?”

“Your fingerprints were all over them,” Reilly answered with a pained expression.

“Oh, God, here we go again. They must have been planted.”

“Knowing what I know about you, *I* tend to agree. But you’re a prime suspect.”

“How much time do I have before formal proceedings?”

“Since they haven’t brought you in, I guess you have a few days.”

Adam stared at the newspaper for a long time without turning a page, without even reading an entire sentence. He just couldn’t believe all this was happening.

38

The Plot Thickens

Vera had fully recovered from the breast incision, which never cramped her violin playing. Worries over her possible cancer were totally eclipsed by apprehension over Adam. Although anxious to hear about the task force meeting, she put up her guard when she saw Adam's haggard expression.

"Hi Honey, you look tired. Rough Day?"

"Hi Dear. Only the last part was tough," Adam replied with a smile, giving her a light kiss.

On the spur of the moment, Vera decided on a change of scenery. "I haven't had a chance to go shopping. Let's go to Trader Vic's. Hope you're in the mood for Polynesian."

The restaurant was within walking distance. She waited until they were on the Falcon Tower elevator before asking Adam about his day.

"Something's not right. Tell me what's bothering you?"

Adam took a couple of deep breaths before answering. "The cops are on my tail over the African virus sabotage."

Vera's jaw dropped. For once she was at a loss for words.

"My fingerprints were all over Hamlish's vials. I'm being framed for another murder."

"It's outrageous! You saved Hamlish's life and the lives of the others. You risked your own life doing that."

"I'm supposed to be immune to African viruses, remember? In their eyes, I was not at risk."

"We know you didn't switch the vial labels. The question is: who did?"

"Hamlish was testing the African virus on rats. I suspected the animal rightsists from the first."

"And now?"

"Saul Lowenstein! I think he changed the labels. Saul wouldn't want Hamlish killing mice. But something doesn't fit. Saul was very protective of his own animals, but he willing sacrificed rodents belonging to other researchers."

"Don't animal rights people have special attachments to research animals?"

"No. They want *all* animals free regardless of ownership. Zoos and circuses, even pet owners, have to deal with their shenanigans."

"You mean they'd kill *people* to save mice?" Vera asked in disbelief.

"Yes, I'm sure some of them would," Adam replied, a bad taste in his mouth.

"Good God! Then we have a nut case here?"

"Not at all. They're rational people, blinded by an almost religious zeal. Lowenstein might be *too selective* to be an animal rights advocate."

Vera gave her husband a puzzled look. "There's a contradiction here. Why do you suspect Lowenstein, if he isn't one of them?"

"His quirkiness doesn't follow the pattern, but I can't exclude him. Lowenstein was bitter over the Little Oscar incident and must resent being fired. This might be his ultimate revenge."

"But you have doubts."

"Yes. Saul Lowenstein is not a killer."

"And how well do you know him?" You're going to have to confront Lowenstein. Pry the truth out of him."

"I need this diversion," Adam said as they entered Trader Vic's. "Let's not talk shop anymore."

A tall, dark-haired woman, wearing a Hawaiian muumuu, led them to their seats.

Early the next morning, Adam knocked loudly on Saul's apartment door.

"Adam!" Saul said, in shock as he opened the door. "What are you doing here?"

"We need to talk, Saul."

Saul invited him in. "I read about your exploits at University Hospital. You've become a local hero."

"And what am I in your eyes, Saul?"

"Until then, you were my worst enemy. But I've changed my mind. You're a very good person. I admire and respect you."

Adam hid his surprise, glaring like an eagle about to grab a salmon. "So you think I did the right thing, firing you?"

"Yes," Saul answered, pleading with his eyes. "I deserved what I got. But I have regrets and would love my old job back. I don't much like cleaning up after pet-shop canaries and puppies."

"What do you know about the sabotage in Dr. Hamlish's lab?"

"Just what I read in the papers. Somebody moved labels on the virus vials."

"Did you know my fingerprints were on the vials?"

Saul's jaw dropped. "They were? That must have been be a frame-up!"

"Saul, be honest with me. What do you think happened?"

Saul was clearly alarmed. "It looks like they want to get you, but they're really framing *me*. They want to get me through you. They knew you'd come after me and that I'd have a weak case. Kill two birds with one stone. Save rats, get Saul."

"Why would someone want to get you?"

"To shut me up," Saul answered with the precision of a twelve-year-old reciting his lines from a school play. "I'm a fellow traveler with the UFFASE—the Underground for Freeing Animals and Saving the Earth. My former girlfriend is a member."

Adam looked at the man with disgust.

"I couldn't agree with their violence and indiscriminate mischief. We broke up. But I know some of their plans. The African virus thing was long in the works. But there was no conspiracy then."

"Why *my* fingerprints?" Adam asked in disbelief.

"Publicity. You're a 'name.' Tangling you in this mess would help the cause by intimidating other researchers. If you go to jail, so much the better. But they were really after me."

"Why didn't they just kill you? After all, you know some of their secrets."

"They want me to suffer, not die," Saul answered nervously. "The vial sabotage is the main secret, but they know that nobody's going to believe me if I disclose it. The cops would think *I* planted the vials and that UFFASE was my invention. The group is extremely secretive. Few people even know it exists."

"And how were they going to get you by getting me?" Adam asked, fighting off his fear.

"They know you fired me for switching mice. They must've deduced that you'd try to implicate me."

"So how did my prints get onto Hamlish's vials?"

"I don't know exactly," Saul replied, again as if he were in rehearsal. "But I have suspicions. The planted vials would not be Hamlish's original stock. These guys are creeps, but they're not suicidal. They wouldn't pour contents from one vial to the other. The vials were handled by you elsewhere and then planted."

Adam made a rare call to the concertmaster's secretary, asking that Vera meet him at Father Nature's at 10 a.m.

He was sitting in a corner table sipping a cup of espresso when she arrived.

"Hi honey," she greeted. "What's up? I feel like I'm part of a spy movie."

"Not far from the mark," Adam said, glancing around as if he suspected they were being filmed for some terrible version of *Candid Camera*.

"What's going on?"

In a quiet voice, Adam related the conversation between him and Saul Lowenstein. "The whole thing just doesn't ring true."

"I agree. It seems a bit too pat. Ever since Itzak Friedman, your life has been one long Humphrey Bogart movie."

"I know. Two murder frame-ups in six months defy all the odds."

"Let's brainstorm this thing out," Vera suggested. "Maybe you weren't the first person to know Itzak's secret. After all, Little Oscar was already six years beyond a normal rat's lifespan. Could somebody have guessed the secret earlier, before you found out?"

Adam smiled widely. "Yes. You're very good."

"Saul Lowenstein is no dummy. Itzak would never hire a nincompoop. I'll bet he knew more than you were led to believe."

Adam was beginning to get excited. "Okay, so now we have Saul knowing about rat virtual immortality many months before I did. That makes sense."

Vera asked another leading question. "And you made human application viable. Curious, isn't it, that Itzak was killed just after you joined his project?"

"Oh Vera, you should write Hollywood scripts. Go on."

Not missing a beat, Vera incorporated the movie analogy. "You were stepping into *his* role. We'd just started worrying about me getting the familial breast cancer. That follows exactly the Friedman script."

"Yes. But that wasn't public information."

"Maybe our apartment or phones have been bugged. Let your imagination run wild. We're dealing with highly improbable circumstances. While you do that, I'll go call the concertmaster."

While Vera was at the pay phone, Adam played his guessing game with people's occupations. He started with a well-groomed man, about thirty-five and wearing a stylish suit, who reminded Adam of a marine in civvies. He was reading the sports section of an already-read newspaper. A *salesman*, probably used cars. At the opposite corner was a twenty-something man wearing a Baltimore Orioles hat, beak pointed back. He had a scraggly beard and wore a student "uniform"—jeans and Deadhead T-shirt. He was reading a paperback book, about halfway through. A *liberal arts major*, reading a reprinted novel. Adam was about to analyze the middle-aged woman in the other corner, when Vera arrived back.

A fresh thought suddenly flashed through his mind. "Okay, play it out, Madame Sherlock. But first, why would somebody want me to play Itzak's role and then have me charged with his murder?"

Vera resumed her rhythm. "It's a red herring. What a wonderful way to divert your attention from some underlying conspiracy over virtual immortality."

"But conviction for Itzak's murder would have prevented me from following my plans—plans unknown then even to *me*—to engineer a human super virus."

"We're dealing with extremely clever, devious persons. They would've gotten you off. They probably planned to have the Palestinian group expose itself. But you beat them to it. Whoever they are, they used the PPFA like they used Friedman. Like they've been using us."

"And like they're using Saul!" Adam added.

"Bingo!"

Adam took a minute to assemble his thoughts. One point had to be resolved. "I originated the super-virus ideas. How would grand conspirators know where everything was heading?"

Vera was uncanny in the quickness of her answer. "They must've gambled. All the ingredients were there. You knew how to map DNA. You directed software to accelerate that process. You'd successfully accomplished germ-line intervention on mice. And, you had a staff capable of pulling it off. You're unique in this world. They knew that if it could be done at all, you'd be the one to do it."

"And who could've realized all of this?"

"You tell me."

It took Adam only an instant to think of the answer. "Oh, my God, *Dave Wiley!* Of course, he must be in on this!"

"Bingo again! He might have prodded you if you hadn't taken the initiative."

Adam squirmed in his chair. "It's odd that he knew about the B-17 batches. Did you know Wiley was connected with Millner Laboratories?"

The man at the counter interrupted. "Ma'am, the phone is for you."

Vera stroked Adam's arm. "It's the concertmaster calling back. Give me a couple of minutes."

Adam resumed his guessing game. He glanced over to the corner where the student sat. The man was staring at Vera's behind. Horny little twerp! When the student resumed his novel, he read from near the beginning. That cued Adam that he might be prepping for a lit exam. The middle-aged woman, her clothes hopelessly out of fashion, was reading a letter. Her face was fully made up, giving her an older look. An *actress*, a one-time leading lady who hadn't aged gracefully.

The student's eyes followed Vera all the way to the table. Adam now noticed that he had then been reading from the *back* part of the book.

"I moved my solo to the end of rehearsal."

Uneasy about the student, Adam positioned himself so the man couldn't see Vera's face. "I may be paranoid, but I think we're being watched. The guy in the hat might be reading our lips. Where were we?"

"You told me that Wiley was connected with Millner Labs. That puts a sinister twist to all of this."

"How's that?"

Vera rubbed her chin up and down with fingers extended vertically. "Didn't you tell me that Millner destroys all remnants of clonings after each job?"

"Yes, for safety reasons."

Vera stared down at the menu, letting her hair flow to the table. "Do you believe Millner destroyed the human super virus after duplicating yours?"

"My God, what a thought! They'd have the super virus and know how to make it. They could manufacture unlimited quantities!"

They stared at each other, speechless.

Rubbing her chin like before, Vera broke the silence. "Let's continue our nerve-wracking game. Let's assume they do have your super virus. But they don't know it works. Right?"

"I'm not so sure. Wiley might have deduced that it worked on me. I gave him the opportunity with the emergency. My feigned Ebola immunity was all a hoax."

Vera stared down at the menu again. "Okay, suppose they do know it works, or suspect so. Only you and I *really* know. And, we know it works on you, not on me."

"I've been wondering why it doesn't work on you."

"We'll get to that later. Wouldn't they be testing it right now?"

Adam the scientist replied, "That would violate all ethics and protocols, and it would also be against the law."

"Come on, Adam. They've committed two murders. Be realistic."

Adam reached for the creamer on the table behind him, sneaking a glance at the student, and turned back to Vera. "They're probably testing it, then, giving it to human Guinea pigs."

Vera vigorously rubbed her forehead with both hands as if trying to erase wrinkles. "I think your super virus won't work for them, for the same reason it didn't work on me. It was created from *your* herpes virus. You probably have a strain that has mutated in your body. Maybe it won't take with anybody else."

"That sounds plausible."

The student changed seats, getting a better view of Adam and Vera. Adam stood up suddenly, whispering into Vera's ear. "He's definitely watching. Let's get the hell out of here."

They left Father Nature's, walking toward the park. "It's safe to talk now," Adam said.

Vera served her next round. "Let's suppose our scenario is true. Then why would these conspirators cause the African virus outbreak?"

Adam snappily returned her volley shot. "Because it would be a sure thing for testing the super virus. They must've presumed I'd eagerly jump into the fray."

"Bingo!"

"If you keep saying that, I should win a prize."

"You will. Okay, does it matter what you would've done if the super virus didn't work? Or what would've happened if you didn't go to the isolation ward?"

"Most likely I'd be dead if it didn't work. I didn't want the gamma globulin for myself. And if I hadn't gone in, I don't know if Svenson would've ordered the substance in time."

Vera served again. "Okay, so you've survived the test of fire. Planting your fingerprints proves they didn't really need you anymore. They have all they require, and you're now their potential enemy."

"Why would they think I'm an enemy?"

Vera made a logical quantum leap. "Because of your feelings toward Wiley and selling virtual immortality. You proved that by destroying all evidence of how to formulate a human super virus."

Adam stifled a gasp. "They could only know that if our apartment has been bugged! They must have been listening. They're probably tailing us too!"

Adam turned around, pulling Vera with him, as they reversed directions like two ballroom dancers, passing the man in the Orioles hat. As they went by, he stared, holding his Harlequin romance book. The man was no student.

39

Playing Cop

Bonnie Burton was surprised when she opened the door and saw Adam. For a moment she wished she hadn't answered the bell, embarrassed that her hair was in curlers and that she was not even wearing makeup.

But Adam was not paying a social visit. "Bonnie I need your help."

"Dr. Boatwright! Please forgive my appearance. Come in and tell me what's happening. I'll make you a coffee or whatever you'd like."

He told her about the virus vials and about some of his suspicions.

"I think somebody at Millner Laboratories has stolen my secret research. I need to plant a mole in the company."

Bonnie was puzzled. "Secret research? I thought all of your stuff was public."

"Tell no one what I'm about to say," Adam said, knowing that he had to trust her.

"You know I could never betray you," Bonnie replied, gazing at him with adoring eyes.

Leaving out most details, Adam then told Bonnie an abbreviated story about human virtual immortality and about the suspected conspiracy.

"That explains why you volunteered to save us from the African virus," Bonnie said. "You're immune to *all* viruses."

"I believe I am, but only temporarily. I wasn't sure until I actually got past the emergency."

It didn't take Bonnie long to deliberate. She would walk over hot coals if Adam asked. "Okay, I'll do it. I know quite a bit about pharmaceutical companies."

Adam told her his plan. "You've proven that to me. But you also know a lot more about what we need. You're a perfect fit. I think I can get you placed in a summer internship, through the medical school. That'll be our first shot. We'll have to tell Millner that you're a PhD candidate in pharmacology, with an emphasis in genetics."

"Do you think I can pull off the masquerade?"

"I'm positive you can. The hard part will be getting you in."

Detective Reilly was quite surprised to see Adam sitting beside his desk.

"Adam! It looks like I'm in for a wild ride."

"Hi Dick. It's going to be a very wild one. Is there somewhere we can talk very privately?"

Reilly led Adam down the hall to an interrogating room, one that didn't have a one-way glassed viewing window.

"I think I know who switched the vial labels," Adam began.

"Great," Reilly said with relief. "I wanted to give you some incentive to solve my case for me. You're going to make me sergeant."

"*Your* case? What about Holbrook?"

"I requested the case. Detective Holbrook will be working for me now."

"That's an incredible relief. Thank God. You should get lieutenant from this. I spoke to an ex-employee fired for substituting experimental mice."

"Saul Lowenstein," Reilly said, smiling knowingly.

"Right," Adam said, appreciating that Reilly had been doing his homework.

Adam then told Reilly the details of that conversation.

"So, who switched the virus labels—Lowenstein or his girlfriend's animal rights group?" asked Reilly.

Sparing the detective any hint about his suspected conspiracy over the super virus, Adam answered. "I don't think either one did. I don't believe the girlfriend's group exists. The people who did this don't give a damn about animal rights."

"Okay. So where do I fit in?"

"I want you to grill Lowenstein. I think he knows who switched the virus labels. There's an outside chance he did it himself. But his story is bogus."

"We could never do that here. But I'm intrigued by this whole thing. I'll try to think of something."

Adam managed to pull some strong strings to get Bonnie into Millner. On unofficial leave from her regular job in genetics, Adam had also arranged her temporary release from summer hospital rounds. Since the commute was a long one, Adam authorized funds to send her son to camp.

Adam warned Bonnie not to disclose her true student status or any connection with him. She also should avoid being seen by Dave Wiley or anybody else who might connect her to the Genetics Department.

Bonnie was assigned to Millner's animal research division in the Genetic Engineering Department, where she would be helping with development of synthetic hormones for organ regeneration.

Saul Lowenstein entered the dark med center lecture hall, waiting for his appointment with Adam. But Adam apparently wasn't in the dark auditorium, illuminated only by a floodlight aimed down at the podium.

"Saul Lowenstein?" a strange man asked, his voice echoing slightly.

"Yes," Saul replied. "I'm here to see Dr. Boatwright."

"He sent me in his place. I'm Dick Reilly, Central City police."

"What business do you have with me?" Saul asked as he scratched his bearded face, trying to calm a nervous tick.

"I only want to ask you some questions. What do you know about UFFASE?"

"It's a super-secret animal rights terror group," Saul replied, starting to play with a strand of his long grayish hair—another nervous habit. "You've spoken to Dr. Boatwright?"

"Only briefly. My colleague is interviewing him at the station. I wanted to speak with you first. Did the animal rights people transfer labels on the vials in Dr. Hamlish's lab?"

"Yes, they did it."

"Didn't you switch some of Dr. Boatwright's mice a few months back?"

Saul's nervous ticks returned. "Yes. They terminated me because of that. It was a stupid thing for me to do. So what?"

"You don't like Dr. Boatwright, do you?"

"He often rubbed me the wrong way," Saul replied, looking up at the floodlight.

Reilly glared at Lowenstein. "Is that why you set him up by putting his own vials in Dr. Hamlish's lab?"

"I didn't do that."

"Who did? I need their names."

"I don't know. Maybe the tooth fairy did it," Saul said sarcastically, his words sounding stronger than he seemed.

"Don't get cute with me. We know you did it."

"Bullshit!" Saul said, gaining psychological strength.

Reilly turned up the pressure. "You want to know how we know? Because *your* fingerprints are there too! Boatwright didn't set up this meeting. I did. I brought you here because we're going to go upstairs and you're going to show me how you did it."

"I can't. I don't even know where Hamlish's lab is," Saul said, in a whiney voice.

"Then what are *your* fingerprints doing on the vials?"

"They must have been planted."

"The same way that Dr. Boatwright's fingerprints were planted?"

"Yes," Saul said. "I guess so. How would I know?"

"Who really did it?" asked Reilly, his voice becoming animated. "It wasn't the animal rights people, was it?"

"I can't say. I'm afraid," Saul replied, vigorously rubbing the sweat from his hands onto his pant legs.

"Whoever they are, they must want to get you."

"I know, and I'm afraid."

"The way I see it, we can indict you for murder and conspiracy for planting false evidence. I don't believe you. I believe you did it."

"No. No. It was the *cartel*," Saul blurted out.

"And who is this cartel?" Reilly asked, keeping up the pressure. "Are they Colombian drug people?"

"No. They're based in Singapore. They can't touch narcotics. Over there that's a hanging crime. They're into drugs, though—the conventional kind."

Reilly spoke cordially. "I think we can work out some kind of deal. If you help us get to this cartel, we might be able to lose a few vials, severing your connection to this case."

"They'll get me," Saul wailed. "I'm a goner."

"We have a witness protection program for you. We can get you a good job working with animals. A safe place."

"Okay. I have nothing to lose. The bastards are out to get me anyway,"

Reilly stood up from the chair. "Okay. Continue with your life as if nothing happened. I'll be in touch."

After Saul left, Adam marched triumphantly out from the equipment closet. “I heard it all. This confirms my suspicions. You’ve got one hell of a case on your hands.”

Adam had been watching Dave Wiley for anything unusual. Fortunately, he could always enlist the support of Jill Yamamoto. He went directly to see her.

“Hello Jill,” Adam greeted. “What’s happening with the boss?”

“He’s got a golf match tomorrow afternoon. He’s having a busy day, starting with a big morning meeting at Millner.”

“I wish I could have a day like that. Party time and playtime.”

“It’s hardly a party. Dr. Wiley has been fretting about that meeting.”

“Well, I guess I’ll have to see him another day. I’ll talk to you later.”

Adam strode into his study and called Dick Reilly.

“Hello, Dick. Adam here. Something big is going down at Millner. Dave Wiley is upset about a meeting in the morning.”

“I think I can help,” Reilly replied confidently.

40

The Bleached Blonde

Bonnie Burton met Adam at O'Connor's Tavern, after spending her first full day at Millner's suburban headquarters. She had learned a great deal about the Singapore company, Vita Helix Ltd., which had recently became Millner's major stockholder. Bonnie had eavesdropped, finding that Singapore executive Ming Koo was meeting at Millner in the morning.

Adam disclosed his plan. "Wiley was agitated about a meeting, probably with this Koo. We want you to help us eavesdrop."

Reilly had loaned Adam a small microphone and transmitter, which Adam inserted in the lining of Wiley's briefcase that afternoon. Reilly had coordinated the action with the district attorney, who obtained a warrant permitting electronic surveillance at Millner.

Adam handed Bonnie what looked like a book, only heavier. "The police have given me this receiver and tape recorder. The transmitter will be inside the meeting room. You must position this within fifty feet. Make sure the recorder is ready when Wiley's there. I'm guessing the meeting will last about two hours. After you retrieve the tape, leave the facility immediately and don't worry about ever going back. And be careful. It could be dangerous if anybody connects you with me."

Walking down the hallway alongside the Millner main conference room, Bonnie glanced inside and glimpsed Dave Wiley looking right back at her. Certain that she was recognized and that they would soon be looking for her, Bonnie's heart started to pound.

Bonnie entered a women's restroom near the meeting place and dragged the trashcan into a stall. She placed the inverted waste receptacle on top of the toilet and used it as a ladder to climb high enough to reach the ceiling. She pushed up an acoustic ceiling tile and slid it over an adjacent one, making a hole through which she slipped the recorder. Bonnie rested the device on top of another tile, and aimed it directly at the conference room. She then slid the first tile back into place, jumped down, refilled the trashcan, and repositioned it.

She couldn't hear the voices inside the conference room that activated and were taped by the miniature tape recorder.

They would be looking for Bonnie during these last hours at Millner. She would have to avoid detection until Wiley left. Fearing that the restroom would soon be checked, she remained in the stall, thinking what to do. In minutes she had a plan.

Bonnie went down the hallway of the research wing, opening each door, until she found an empty chemistry lab, where she went directly to the supply cabinet. Rummaging, she grabbed a bottle of hydrogen peroxide and a pair of rubber gloves. Slipping on a fresh lab coat, Bonnie hurried to a private place where she could use the bleach unseen—the nearest women's restroom.

Two gabbing employees were standing by the sinks having an illegal smoke. Sparing no time to wait, she went to the far stall and locked the door. Remembering that toilet water was clean enough for her cat to drink, Bonnie kneeled down and put her head into the bowl, soaking her long brown hair. Her scalp began to sting as she worked dabs of peroxide into the strands. When she had thoroughly mixed in the bleach, she agitated her hair in the toilet bowl and flushed. The itch was nearly unbearable as she waited for the bowl to fill. She then rinsed her hair, flushed the toilet, and rinsed again, flushing the toilet several more times.

When the two women left, Bonnie went to the sink and wringed out her ragged locks. She then turned the spigot of the stationary blow dryer to the up position and let it blow onto her itchy scalp. After a vigorous brushing, fluffing, and more blow drying, she produced a pair of scissors and cut off about four inches. She then tied her still damp hair into a ponytail. The mirror now reflected a very *blonde* woman.

Bonnie always wore contact lenses, but had found it professional to wear glasses when making pharmaceutical sales calls. Her purse still contained two pairs of vision-neutral eyeglasses. She put on the horn-rimmed pair, slipped on the lab coat, and applied a heavy coating of lipstick. Bonnie was awestruck to see a very different woman staring back from the mirror. She could hardly recognize herself. Overall, she was pleased with the change. Her disguise would have been good enough to pass as a character from *Grease*.

Behind closed door, Wiley's meeting began with a financial discussion involving a cacophony of accountants' and analysts' voices. All was transmitted to the hidden recorder.

The central focus was on the visiting director; Ming Koo was a heavy man with a pasty complexion. He lit a fresh cigarette every few minutes, using the butt of the nearly spent one. Still suffering from jet lag, Koo yawned between puffs, showing everybody his badly stained teeth. He frowned as a young financial analyst droned through his status report.

Impatiently, Koo announced in an Oxbridge English accent, "We're done bean counting today."

It took about a minute for the room to clear.

Ming Koo looked expectantly at a large crew-cut man, about fifty years old. "Well, Jerry, let's have your report on the super-virus test."

Jerry Tomason, the laboratory director, spoke. "We've administered it to two dozen employees, using the same doses ordered by Boatwright. Depending on their immunity histories, we injected them with a variety of viruses likely to cause an infection. We chose diseases with obvious symptoms, such as chicken pox and German measles. Each person became sick."

Koo glared at Dave Wiley. "What the bloody hell is going on here? Isn't this super virus supposed to give immunity to these?"

"Yes," Wiley said, red faced. "It's supposed to protect against all viral infections."

"Somebody fed you a line of crap," bellowed Tommy Lee, a short Chinese American. "Now that we've implicated Boatwright in murder, the stuff doesn't work!"

Wiley had not been party to any criminal activity. "What murder are you talking about?"

"The outbreak at Central," Lee said, sneering. "We snuck some vials into the researcher's lab with Boatwright's fingerprints on them."

Wiley couldn't contain himself. "You Cretan! Now we can't use Boatwright to work bugs out of the super virus." He threw up his hands and looked at Ming Koo, anticipating fireworks.

Koo glared at his henchman. "Tommy, I agree with Wiley. Why did you mess with the vials?"

"To start an epidemic. It was a great way to test the super virus. Our intelligence indicated Boatwright would try to become the hero."

"Why did you act so precipitously?"

"Surveillance indicated the super virus was working. All conversations between Boatwright and his wife pointed to that. You already decided you wouldn't need him again."

"I see, Tommy—an unforeseen turn of events," said Koo dismissively.

They all watched while Koo removed another cigarette and lit it. "Well, Wiley, what do you recommend?"

"We can genetically engineer our own super virus, one that works," Wiley said, grasping at straws.

Koo frowned at Wiley. "That is crap. After you've given Jerry all documentation on the super virus, I'm releasing you from the project. I want our crew in Switzerland working on this. Okay, Wiley, you're done."

Wiley pushed back his chair and slunk out of the room. He felt like he had been slapped in the chops. Until now, he still had hopes of working independently on the super virus with Boatwright. Those plans were in jeopardy because those imbeciles had implicated Boatwright in a murder, and now he, Wiley, had been cut off completely.

Bonnie remained incognito. As insurance against discovery, she pinned her photo badge backside out, making it look like she had carelessly attached it to her lab coat. She walked past the conference room, its door propped open to ventilate Ming Koo's cigarette smoke. She glanced inside without breaking her pace, seeing no trace of Wiley.

There was a "closed for cleaning" sign outside the women's restroom. She would have to wait to retrieve the recording tape. As she turned the corner, Bonnie passed a uniformed security guard walking in the opposite direction. Her heart jumped when he called.

"Just a minute, miss," he said, smiling flirtatiously. "You must be new. My name is Freddy."

"Hi Freddy," Bonnie smiled. "I'm Bonita. I work with the monkeys."

"You don't look like a scientist."

"I'm just a tech. I just feed animals and clean cages."

"Do you ever monkey around?" he asked, winking.

"That depends," she said, walking away. "See ya."

Bonnie went to the cafeteria and bought a coffee and Danish. Nervous as a kid at a dance recital, she sat down at an empty table, and began reading a wrinkled newspaper. It was impossible to concentrate, so she read anyway without comprehending, thus killing fifteen minutes.

From the opposite direction Bonnie walked again past the conference room, its door now shut. The sign was still outside the restroom. She took a chance and went inside, finding the place was untouched from before. Quickly, she pulled the trashcan into the stall, positioned it as before, and climbed up. She slid back the ceiling tile and reached for the tape recorder. As she grabbed it, the wobbly receptacle crashed to the floor, making a terrible racket.

Bonnie prevented her own fall by grasping the rough tile tracks that lined the false ceiling. That left her with feet dangling directly over the toilet. Fortunately, the recorder was hanging by its strap, secure around her neck. She took a small swing and dropped to an open spot. She placed the tape recorder in her purse. She then repositioned the trashcan and climbed back up to straighten the ceiling tiles. She put everything back in place and entered the hallway. There, Bonnie bumped into a female guard.

"Can't you read?" the guard asked, referring to the closed sign.

"Sorry! Nature called and I just couldn't wait," Bonnie blurted in a croaking, laryngitic voice. I'm feeling slightly ill today. I probably shouldn't even be at work,"

"Your badge is backward."

Bonnie turned so that her breast was out the guard's line of vision, fussing with the badge. "I told you I'm sick today. I guess I was clumsy," she said, her voice rasping as she stumbled away.

She had to leave the building as quickly as possible. Her badge now picture side out, she went to the main lobby. The duty guard was the flirtatious man from before.

"Hi Freddy," she said, hoping he wouldn't notice the dark hair in the photo or the name on her badge.

"Hi Bonita. Going home early?"

"Yeah. I'm feeling sick today. I have a doctor's appointment. See you tomorrow."

As soon as she passed the guard, Bonnie pulled off her badge, put it in her pocket, and walked to her car. She noticed two guards sitting in a nearby van, keeping surveillance. She kept walking, past her car. She wanted to leave on foot. Unfortunately, the exit from the fenced parking lot led directly past the main gate. Bonnie feared they would check any pedestrian. She reversed course, walking directly to the patrol van.

"Hi," Bonnie said, again in a croaking voice. "I can't find my car keys. I'll have my husband drive me back after my doctor's appointment. Could you give me a lift to the bus stop?"

"Sure thing, ma'am," the balding guard said. "I'll drive you."

They rode in silence out of the Millner grounds to the main road, where Bonnie gratefully left the guard van. She sighed with relief when she finally caught the bus back to Central City.

Adam and the detective listened to Bonnie's tape.

"Bonnie, you're astounding. I can't believe you accomplished all this," Adam said with admiration. "Besides, you look cute as a blonde," he joked.

"You're totally in the clear, Adam," Reilly announced. "There's an obvious conspiracy to commit murder here. I want the DA to indict Koo and Lee."

"The FDA should get after Millner," Adam added. "They can get Tomason for violating drug laws. The cartel conspiracy will set an example to discourage this sort of thing."

"I'll contact the proper authorities. I'll need corroborating testimony from Saul Lowenstein. Do you think he had anything to do with the sabotage at the hospital?"

"Possibly. He's a wriggler who can't stay still. He lied through his teeth to me."

"I can make Lowenstein tell the truth," Reilly said with a smile.

Adam didn't find everything to his satisfaction. "Saul's just small potatoes. It would be nice to get Wiley too, but it seems he's landed on both feet."

"You'll have to deal with that sleaze. Although he was in thick with the cartel, we can't tie him to the hospital sabotage."

Adam puzzled over the taped meeting. He wondered why the super virus had failed on Millner's human Guinea pigs. Maybe Vera was right. Maybe his own virus was now specific to him. The parent herpes strain had probably mutated years before.

Even if other scientists tried to duplicate his own super virus, Adam now knew they wouldn't succeed. And if someone figured out how to do it from scratch, each candidate virus would require complex customizing. The effort would be prohibitively expensive.

Adam vowed to keep his secret about virtual immortality.

41

Agonizing over the Universal Attractor

The Central City Police found and removed several listening devices from the Boatwright's Falcon Tower apartment. Snooping devices were also found in phones, throughout the LSB, and in Adam's med center office.

Adam and Vera were at home having their first dinner since the mystery had been solved.

"I feel violated," Vera said in disgust.

Adam smiled at his wife. "Your good thinking brought everything to a head."

"So what's going to happen now?"

Adam summarized the status. "Millner's lab director and security honcho have been arrested. The FDA inspector general has sent a team to Millner. Big boss Ming Koo has fled the country."

"What about Lowenburg?"

"Lowen*stein*. He had nothing to do with the African virus incident and will testify against the cartel. He knows a lot, going back to Itzak's time in Israel."

"But who switched the vials?"

"One of Tommy Lee's people. He's Koo's henchman. The cast of characters is long."

Vera smiled at Adam as she placed a piece of homemade apple in front of him. "Your student, Bonnie Burton, was really heroic. She must love you very much."

Adam had anticipated this. But the apple pie was almost too much to take; that was Bonnie's dessert, at her apartment. Adam started to feel a little edgy, even though he gave the truth. "Yes, she told me so more than once."

"I empathize with her. Too bad you can't return her affection."

"I've been sorely tempted a couple of times," Adam confessed, wondering how Vera knew about Bonnie and him.

"I guessed about her after seeing the look she gave you that night at the hospital. Oddly, I don't feel jealous or resentful. She ratifies my good taste in selecting you. And that has increased my self-confidence. That you didn't fall for that stunning beauty, one whose interests closely matches yours, strongly endorses our relationship."

"Bonnie's a lot like you in many ways. Maybe that's why I grew so fond of her. I'm so glad we can be totally open. How did you know I had feelings for Bonnie? Are you a mind reader?"

"I know you. You couldn't be cooped up with somebody who loved you—a smart, beautiful woman, your student, your employee—without feeling more than simple friendship. But if you loved her, it would've been all over your face. You haven't displayed any guilt whatsoever, so I knew she was no threat. But, watch out! I can be nasty if I feel threatened."

"You're my whole purpose for being," Adam said, bending to kiss her.

After dinner they read different sections of the paper. Adam saw a piece on the local zoo featuring Ernie Dickson, their caving companion. The article described his work to collect animal embryos from a worldwide network of zoos.

"Did you read this article about Ernie?" Adam asked.

"Yes. Maybe you ought to work with him on your sabbatical."

"I was thinking the same thing. I'll go see him today."

"Speaking of the future, Adam, what'll happen with Wiley?"

"Temporarily, he'll be less of a threat than before. The cartel investigations will keep him jumping. Unfortunately, he spotted Bonnie at Millner, so he knows I was involved in the investigation. I'm meeting with Wiley first thing this morning."

Adam confronted Dave Wiley, who was not his usual cocky self. "I know about the Singapore cartel. I only know because they framed me for murder."

"I'm so sorry. I had no choice about dealing with them. When Vita Helix bought into Millner Laboratories, things went to hell fast."

"Why did you stay involved?"

Wiley looked like a kicked puppy. "They enticed me with irresistible rewards and coerced me with blackmail and physical threats."

"What kind of blackmail?"

Wiley made a rare confession. "When I was still a researcher at Central University, I developed a vaccine. I sold it to Millner, and they patented the process. I received royalties that should've gone to the university. The new owners threatened to turn me in unless I cooperated."

Adam stared coldly at his boss. Adam thought Wiley was pathetic as he squirmed while making that confession. "And what were the physical threats?"

"That I might end up like Itzak Friedman."

"From what I can tell, you weren't involved in the murders."

Wiley put on his good face. "Yes. But I did make a deal with the devil. These guys at Vita Helix followed Itzak Friedman here. That's when they bought controlling interest in Millner. They wanted to exploit his aging prevention and your follow-on research."

"How far did you go in your cooperation?"

"I was ready to treat you like a marionette. But I didn't have to do anything much. You were always a step ahead."

"And you knew nothing about Itzak's murder?"

Wiley began to look more like an owl than a pussycat. "That's right. I only realized their involvement during my last meeting with Koo. I'm so ashamed. Adam, can you forgive me?"

"I'll think about it. But you did share information with the cartel, didn't you?"

"Minimally," Wiley replied, in hushed tones. "I wanted to commercialize virtual immortality on my own. Now I've lost my appetite."

"Don't you still want to go into business with me?" Adam asked.

Wiley now seemed fully composed. "No, Adam. I've been agonizing about it for weeks. My meeting with Koo was the nail in the coffin. I don't think the world is ready for this."

Adam treaded carefully. The man was sounding a bit too much like Adam himself. "So, where do we stand?"

"We should continue research on a tamed-down mouse super virus. We'll play it by ear from there. Now tell me, Adam, how did you make the connection with Millner?"

"I didn't," Adam lied. "My fingerprints were not the only ones the police found. Other fingerprints led to the culprit. I don't know his name. He turned state's evidence for asylum and protection. I helped the police by planting Bonnie Burton at Millner."

"Thank God, Adam," Wiley said, sounding sincere. "I'm eternally grateful."

Adam was very tired of lying and deception—weary of keeping secrets. He had always been such an open person—until he'd met Itzak—until he'd begun messing with immortality, something he had never sought. In the abstract, stopping the aging process was wildly appealing. And yet everyone who had seriously contemplating unlimited life had rejected it.

He would talk with Ernie about the wildlife project. The diversion would be a good change of pace.

42

Maharani

Adam arrived at the Central City Zoo before opening time. He hadn't been to a zoo in over twenty years, since his last vacation with his late wife Judy and the kids. Although he loved animals, the zoo setting had lost its appeal.

Ernie was attending to a problem with one of the elephants, and they would be meeting outdoors. Adam strode toward the pachyderm pavilion, passing through the primate collection.

The mountain gorillas were huge, much bigger than he remembered—but so gentle, so graceful. One large male was cradling a sleeping newborn while the mother sat passively nearby. The orangutan complex was directly opposite the gorillas. There, a hyperactive youngster was doing acrobatics on an apparatus made from steel tubes, chains, and wood. It appeared to be an orphan, since the species almost never bred in captivity. Sitting in the corner was a solitary, grotesquely obese male. He reminded Adam of a caged person depressed from confinement with bratty kids. The last complex contained the chimpanzees.

Of the three commonly-known primate groups, even a layman could tell chimpanzees were nearest to humans. Closeness of species can be measured by time since common ancestry. Since genes mutate at a nearly constant rate, scientists count the number of major DNA differences between two related species. The fewer the differences, the shorter the time span since the evolutionary chains parted. With chimpanzees and humans that was some ten million years before. Adam recalled that the human and chimpanzee genomes are about 98 percent in agreement, making the two DNAs much more alike than with most primate pairs.

One female chimpanzee stared intensely at Adam, causing chills to run down his spine. Was she somehow reading his mind? How could that be? A clairvoyant chimpanzee! His mind fell into a strange fantasy about living among chimpanzees.

The daydream was interrupted by a loud trumpeting sound.

As Adam rounded a bend in the path, he saw a parked zoo ambulance with lights still flashing. The air was pierced by a rumbling sound, followed by a high-pitched scream. Adam approached an unconcerned zoo worker standing by the bridge into the pavilion.

"What's happening?"

"Maharani is in labor. Her water has broken, and the baby elephant's coming out."

Adam walked toward Ernie, who was standing outside of a barricade separating him from the mother elephant. "Hi Adam. You're witness to a rare blessed event."

The baby elephant had begun to emerge from the severely stressed mother, who growled loudly in low frequencies, punctuated by an occasional bugle call. The baby's head and dangling trunk poked all the way out of the standing mother. Adam watched in awe as the front legs emerged, then the torso. Suddenly, the entire body dropped into a pile of hay.

The mother turned around and began to massage the calf with her trunk. The newborn flapped its ears and flailed its legs. The mother then scooped him up with her trunk and helped him stand. The calf's first steps brought him to her teats, and within seconds he was having his first meal.

Adam was speechless.

"Pretty fascinating," Ernie said, smiling. "I love this part of my job. Did you know it took twenty-two months for that baby to develop inside his mother? That's over twice the human gestation."

"I knew it was about that long. These are Asian elephants. Is it the same for Africans?"

"Almost identical. The two species are closely related. Closer, I think, than donkeys and horses. But Africans misbehave in captivity. Zoo babies from that species are orphans picked up in Africa. They're fostered by easily controlled *Asian* mothers."

"Can't you get an African baby naturally?"

"We've never bred Africans in captivity. Few zoos have a male African in their collection. We'd have to do an embryo transplant. But sadly, there are plenty of orphans, what with the ivory trade. We won't confront propagation issues until wild populations dwindle to practically nothing. That's going to happen much sooner than people realize."

They talked as they walked back to the offices. The same female chimp was standing by the fence. She gave Adam a longing look, reminding him of glances from some female students. Adam shook his head in puzzlement.

Adam turned toward Ernie. "I'm very interested in embryo transplantation—what is popularly called making a 'test-tube baby.'"

Ernie gave a detailed response. "So-called test-tube embryos are created outside the uterus, using an egg and sperm. Much cattle breeding is done that way today. But our embryos are natural ones. They're removed from the mother, either through live surgery or after she succumbs early in pregnancy."

"I'm familiar with the artificial process. How extensive are cattle applications?"

Ernie seemed to enjoy the direction of their conversation. "Artificial methods predominate in dairies."

Ernie gave a capsule summary of the process. He said that in traditional cattle breeding, good genes were passed from the father through artificial insemination with his sperm. That way, a good bull could sire more offspring than by natural sexual intercourse. However, using embryo transplants, dairy breeders could get a hundred offspring from a good mother, too. Veterinarians would surgically remove a cluster of her mature eggs, which were inseminated in vitro. Then they would transplant the embryos. That way they could exploit genes from both sexes.

"So, you have lots of surrogate mothers with cattle?" Adam asked.

"Yes, especially with dairy cattle. Genes of the cow surrogate herself are unimportant as long as she can deliver a healthy calf. Breeders can create a purebred herd with mongrel birth mothers and embryos created from the egg and sperm of aristocratic parents."

Ernie was interrupted by an assistant. Adam found the whole concept of artificial pregnancies fascinating. "Will you do embryo implants with wild animals?"

"Yes and no. We'll use surrogates primarily to test viability of the procedure. In an emergency we would use surrogates to propagate our embryos."

"How long does a frozen embryo last?" Adam asked.

"We have no idea. Theoretically, there's no limit."

"What if there's no surrogate for an embryo you want to grow?"

"We could use another related species. Recently a horse served as the birth mother for a zebra. Domestic cats have carried embryos from small wild cat species. That's called interspecies surrogacy."

"That means you could implant an African elephant embryo into an Asian elephant mother."

"That would probably work. They're closely related."

"How close do you suppose two species ought to be?"

"Nobody has done the research. It boils down to physiology and anatomy."

Ernie told about the process. He said that it would be impossible for a domestic cat to be surrogate mother to a lion—just because of size incompatibilities. By the same token, a tiger female could probably carry a lion. But even though it would be small enough, a lion fetus wouldn't develop in a cow because of radical differences in body chemistry.

An odd thought jumped into Adam's consciousness.

"A human could even be surrogate to a chimpanzee."

"Yes, indeed," Ernie replied, smiling. "That seems like a plausible possibility."

When they reached the office, Ernie gave Adam a formal presentation about the International Wildlife Fund's frozen embryo program.

Ernie then made his pitch. "Adam, we need to maintain genetic diversity in the collection. That's why I wanted to talk to you."

"I'm fascinated. There are software possibilities for keeping track of things. Let me think about it."

"I just wish we had more money. We have to compete with other programs, such as restorations to the wild. We need something to capture donor imaginations."

"If I come, you can have me for free," Adam promised. "It would be a sabbatical project."

Then a flash of inspiration brought an image into Adam's mind.

"I have something! It just popped into my head. It was inspired by our surrogacy conversation, my own fantasies about prehistory, and the elephant's birth."

"Out with it!" Ernie said excitedly.

"Okay. But first, a question. How closely are mammoths related to elephants?"

"Very close. The mammoth is really an extinct elephant. It may be closer to either modern elephant than those species are to each other. But we don't know. You geneticists have to get mammoth DNA and tell us."

"Another question. Occasionally we hear about somebody finding a mammoth carcass spit out from a glacier. The Explorer's Club once served mammoth steaks to a gathering. Could a mammoth embryo have survived ten thousand years in its mother's frozen body?"

"Yes," Ernie replied, his eyes gleaming, "it's possible. Some tissues are well preserved. I see no reason why, under proper conditions, an embryo couldn't survive. Although it may be damaged."

"Bingo!" Adam said, emulating Vera. "We look for one. We implant it into an elephant. We deliver a live mammoth!"

"Beautiful! My God, Adam, you're a genius," Ernie said enthusiastically. "That would certainly capture the world's attention."

Adam reflected on various details from such an undertaking. "I'd like to do that. You know I crave adventure. I might even be able to use my skills to repair a damaged embryo, possibly by extracting the DNA and inserting it into elephant embryo cells."

"My mouth's watering with excitement, Adam."

"We could even use this to bring back the species."

Ernie made Adam a promise: "I'm going to ask our network to alert me to any findings of frozen female mammoths in good condition."

The day had been a productive one indeed. The wheels were set in motion for changes that would benefit the world.

43

Protector of the World

When Vera left rehearsal, Adam was waiting, eager to discuss his plans. As they walked to Father Nature's, he told her about his zoo visit and the meeting with Ernie Dickson.

They passed a mother pushing a toddler riding in his stroller and holding a stuffed Babar. The elephant toy reminded Adam of his brainstorm, which he immediately shared with Vera. "This is the most interesting part. We plan to make a mammoth. More accurately, I mean bring to *life* a baby mammoth."

"How will you do this?" Vera asked. "Are you going to alter elephant DNA?"

"Not if I can help it. That'd be very difficult and there'd be little chance of success. But we think the mammoth genome is very close to the elephant's—either Asian or African."

After seating and ordering, they resumed the conversation where they left off.

"Okay, Adam, how are you going to do this mammoth thing?"

"We're going to transplant a mammoth embryo into an elephant."

"You've got to be kidding! And where are you going to get the embryo?"

"From a frozen mammoth. Several are found every year," Adam replied, happy for a change to be sharing something positive with his wife.

"Sounds like *Jurassic Park*," Vera said, seeming surprised at Adam's new direction.

"No, that was total fantasy. This can actually be done. We have to find the remains of an adult female. We need one that became pregnant just before she died. If the carcass is in good shape, the embryo might still be viable."

Adam retold Ernie's story about cow surrogate motherhood and the recent success of interspecies embryo implants.

"How exciting! You'll certainly get the world's attention."

"That's the whole point. Ernie thinks it'd be a great fundraising gimmick. But I think it'd be great science."

"I suppose you can learn a lot from doing this."

Adam felt lighthearted, like a kid planning his summer. "Oh yeah. The same methods might bring back other extinct species, such as the woolly rhinoceros. This could also generate interest in all kinds of genetic experimentation."

"You're moving back to *Jurassic Park*."

"In a way, I am. But in that story, dinosaur DNA was supposedly complete, saved for millions of years inside amber. It was pure science fiction, involving procedures totally debunked by real biologists. I want to take the DNA of preserved *living* animals. Then, in very small steps, I'd introduce changes that would carry to the offspring. A series of small changes to any animal's DNA might reverse its evolution—allowing us to approximately recreate its ancestor species."

"I'm not a big fan of science fiction," Vera remarked impatiently.

"It'll only be fiction until somebody does it. I'm talking pure *science*, but controlled and directed in a new way. This is possible!"

Vera seemed relieved to see Marty Sweet walking toward their table.

"Hi Vera. Hello, Dr. Boatwright. Mind if I join you?"

"Hello Marty," Vera said. "Take a load off."

"I've done it! I am going to perform as soloist with the Boston Pops," Marty said proudly.

"Oh Marty, I'm so happy for you."

"It's your wife's fault," Marty said to Adam. "She encouraged me to follow her example."

"So you're flying to Boston?"

"No. I'm taking the train—Amtrak."

Adam looked inquisitively at Marty. "What are you going to play with the Pops?"

"The Dvořák cello concerto," Marty beamed.

"That's my favorite cello piece," Adam replied admiringly.

"Whoops," Marty said, looking at his watch. "Got to run. See you."

Vera smiled at Adam. "Aside from you, he's the sweetest man I know."

Vera changed the subject. "You've obviously planned how you'll spend your sabbatical. With Ernie, I suppose?"

"Right. My university pay will continue. I'll donate my time to Wildlife."

"What about your research projects?"

"They'll run themselves, more or less. I'll still have control and keep my pulse on them. But I won't have to punch the clock. I may ask Ernie to buy moonlighting time from the Crunchers. We could use their help developing software for the embryo collection."

"And what about Wiley?"

"I think he'll continue working on virtual immortality, but he'll strike out on his own. He's released me from commercial venture plans. I think he doesn't trust *me*."

"I think you're powerless to stop others from chasing this thing."

"Right," Adam replied, trying hard to remain cheerful. "That'll be especially true after the news media cover the cartel story. It may rival the infamous Scopes monkey trial, the one over firing a teacher for teaching evolution. But I can't help feeling responsible."

Vera must have seen Adam starting to slip into a morass, and she responded positively. "But in the eyes of the cartel, you were an innocent pawn. They knew where you were going before you did."

"I'm glad to let it rest a while. I welcome the diversion of working with large animals."

As they left Father Nature's and walked back to Falcon Tower, Adam could feel his psychic energy level rising. He looked forward to positive activity, after so much skulking and intrigue.

44

Enclosed in Blue Ice

It was now early fall. Adam still had control of his three projects, which needed little of his time. Now on sabbatical and released from medical school classes, Adam spent most mornings at the Central City Zoo.

The cartel murder conspiracy trial would soon be starting. To Adam's relief, the press never acknowledged the true cause of the conspiracy. Amazingly, nobody was speaking of virtual immortality. But he was certain the story would eventually come out. It was too juicy to remain suppressed.

Ernie Dickson was beaming when Adam arrived at the zoo office.

"I just read a Fax from Russia. A well-preserved female woolly mammoth carcass has been discovered on the Kamchatka Peninsula. We should be there to supervise dissection."

Adam couldn't contain his excitement. "This is what we've been waiting for!" he said.

Ernie had made all the arrangements. "I want to leave today. We'll fly via Alaska, puddle-jumping across the Aleutians to Kamchatka in two small pontoon planes."

"Why two planes?"

"The National Geographic Society is sending a camera crew to record the event, just in case."

It had been only hours since Ernie had announced the find. Now the two men were flying at low altitude above Kodiak Island. The weather was crystal clear for early fall.

Adam wondered about the cold weather in the coming months. Woolly mammoths had been well adapted to harsh winters. Unlike their tropical cousins, they had extra fat reserves and heavy fur coats. Although the last Ice Age had ended at about the same time as the mammoth's decline, the warming didn't cause its extinction.

The cause was man.

When men first arrived in North America, some fifteen or twenty thousand years before, the mammoths were common in Alaska and remote parts of Siberia. Fossil evidence showed man and mammoth coexisting for several thousand years until their numbers dwindled too low for the species to survive.

Ernie was excited like a boy with new toys. Adam was infected by his enthusiasm, and they competed to see who could spot the most wildlife species. Over islands, they saw brown and black bears, moose, and caribou. On the shores, they spotted walrus and several species of seals and sea lions, plus an occasional sea otter. The smaller animals were seen during water takeoffs or landings, near refueling stations. Over open-ocean they saw humpback and blue whales, plus nearly every other type of dolphin and whale indigenous to those waters.

Adam was fascinated with cetacean evolution. Sometime around twenty or forty million years before the present, the whales branched off from land-based mammals. The primary ancestor was once believed to be a cowlike grazer. Later DNA evaluations showed whales to be more closely related to carnivores, having wolflike creatures as ancestors. Some scientists were of the opinion that they descended instead from hippopotamus cousins, but nobody knew for sure.

Adam ran a hypothetical sea-mammal evolution through his mind, as if he were watching an animated film.

He started with a four-legged land carnivore that took long swims in the ancient sea, where fish were easier to catch than terrestrial prey. One pup was born with webbed feet, a random mutant genetic event. Not very mobile on the land, she performed better in water and outdid her siblings catching fish. Her own pups also had webbed feet. Over the span of several hundred years, the web-footedness gene spread throughout the original population and became more prevalent.

Adam spotted several isolated locations on lonely island shores that seemed ideal places for the next evolutionary stage. Over thousands of years, several more random genetic events created a race of better swimmers. Those aqua "wolves" resembled modern otters. Some migrated to new locations, losing all contact with the original web-footed group.

Adam's mind wandered, letting the process continue through tens of thousands of years. One group did not change much, and adapted well to its environment. It separated from another group, which was changing to resemble modern seals as their pups became more streamlined and better suited for longer open-water living. A third group could survive without touching land. Some of their pups were born with nasal openings higher in their heads, becoming better breathers in rough seas. A further evolutionary milestone had been met.

Some of those animals bore offspring with extra surface body fat, giving them better protection in cold waters. Their fur was an impediment to fast swimming, and furless pups experienced slightly higher survivability than their hairy cousins. Over hundreds of thousands of years, the small, gradual changes accumulated, as the dominant furless group became more and more fishlike in form.

At that evolutionary milestone, Adam's mental image had moved millions of years beyond that first web-footed "wolf." The proto-whales had now spread around the globe. One family evolved with strainer plates in their mouths, allowing them to skim the ocean for food. They were primogenitors of modern baleen whales. Another group kept their teeth; their descendants evolved into today's toothed whales and dolphins.

Of course, the exact ancestral lineages and relationships were just idle conjecture. The whales and dolphins might have begun much earlier, with ancestors to the modern hippo. Adam would make a hobby of investigating those issues further. He would also explore applying his genetics expertise in new ways.

Adam fantasized participating in a directed evolution, making changes millions of times faster than historically. He was especially intrigued with reversing evolution. He daydreamed of starting with a modern species like the pigeon. He might make step-by-step genetic changes, bringing descendants ever closer to their ancestral form. Possibly, he could direct evolution forward from that "ancestor" to a live and functioning approximation to the dodo—an extinct cousin of the pigeon.

At last they saw the Kamchatka Peninsula. The planes turned north, following the coast of that huge finger of land, nearly half the size of Alaska. For hours, they passed numerous volcanoes punctuating the rugged, glacier-coated mountains that formed the western edge of the Ring of Fire.

It had been almost forty-eight hours from the start, when the pilot pointed to a small lake. They would land there, beside a large glacier.

Adam's excitement matched Ernie's as the plane touched down on the glass-smooth lake. The plane floated toward a small pier, where a group of Russians were waiting. They included two English-speaking members of the Russian Academy of Science who had arrived earlier from Vladivostok.

In the morning they would take a two-hour hike to the site, where the glacier was still holding the partially exposed mammoth in its cold grasp.

The scene was unimpressive. The mammoth carcass looked like large cowhide wrapped around a barrel, half of which was enclosed in blue ice. Part of the body was exposed and had been thawing for several days. The entire area was permeated by the odor of rancid rotting flesh. The still-frozen fleshy body parts were nevertheless well preserved. But the animal's shape had been lost from centuries of crushing ice pressure.

"It doesn't look good," Adam said sadly.

Biologist Olga Lupitov was more optimistic. "We won't be able to tell until we chip the ice out around the hips. If they aren't badly smashed, the uterus might be in good shape."

"How are you going to remove it?"

"With saws and axes," answered Vladimir Splinsky, the tall Russian veterinarian.

All four began carving an ice cavern around the mammoth, while photographers took stills and shot a video of the entire operation. Everybody puffed cigars to camouflage the stench. Not habitual smokers, Adam and Ernie rested occasionally to recover from bouts of nicotine-induced nausea.

"I wouldn't have come," Adam complained in agony, "if I'd known about this."

"Sure you would've," Ernie replied, chuckling.

The hindquarters were in much better shape than the rest of the carcass. The woman asked Vladimir to cut out the uterus using a chain saw. It took a solid hour for Vladimir to cut into the solidly frozen rear half of the mammoth and remove the uterine cavity. The surgery was not clean; there were pieces of fur, frozen bone, and muscle tissue protruding out of the fifty-pound mass.

It would be impossible to tell if there was an embryo inside. That would wait until Adam and Ernie performed delicate surgery back home.

Leaving the Russians hacking away at the carcass, the two Americans tied the blob onto a travois and pulled it back to camp. There they transferred the bloody and smelly mass to the traveling container and smothered it with dry ice.

Adam and Ernie remained only long enough to eat a quick meal of fresh salmon served by the pilots. They took off in a hurry as a storm approached.

The weary travelers slept for much of the trip back to Alaska

When their flight arrived home from Anchorage, the press was waiting. Although the two colorful characters were disheveled and unshaven, they gave a successful television interview. They also spoke with radio and newspaper reporters. Those encounters were the first steps in Ernie's lengthy publicity campaign.

All the while, Vera and Jayne waited impatiently to greet their husbands.

Alone with Adam at last, Vera spoke first. "Now I know how you feel when I travel—I missed you."

"Next time, I'll take you. This was the most gorgeous excursion of my life. But I'm very glad to be back."

Vera held tightly to her husband's arm. "Will you know tomorrow if you have an embryo?"

"Yes. But a lot of things could've gone wrong. Our mammoth might never have been pregnant. Even if she was, the embryo might have grown into a fetus too advanced to survive the freeze."

Vera was fascinated by the details. "How could an embryo survive for over ten thousand years?"

"Vets can freeze cow embryos and store them indefinitely. But our mammoth didn't freeze under controlled conditions. It's still a long shot."

"So you'll go back again."

Adam told her that many more trips might be needed to get a viable embryo. But they could achieve a mammoth restoration with much less. Only a complete strand of embryonic DNA would make it possible. By exchanging that with contents of an elephant's stem cell, they could jump-start the mammoth's life. Adam had already done that with mice. He noted that at the cellular level the technology would be the same with an elephant.

Vera prodded again. "Don't you think the DNA would change over thousands of years?"

Adam took a moment to put it together. "Ancient animal DNA has been obtained in various forms, sometimes fairly complete. But even if there was some decay in the ancient cells, we could patch together several incomplete DNA strands to make one good whole. We could even splice elephant segments to fill any remaining DNA gaps."

"I never realized what was involved—spare me the details. It sounds very complicated."

"The DNA repair work and molecule cloning can take weeks," Adam continued.

"A mere tick on the geological clock," Vera concluded.

45

Just Desserts

Jack Chin and Sandra Wickham had worked with elephant DNA since before Kamchatka. Ear size and other exterior features indicated that Asian elephants were more closely related to mammoths than their African cousins. Once they had actual pieces of mammoth DNA, they would use special software to systematically determine the differences.

Genetic repairs were simulated by converting the DNA of one elephant species to the other's. Beginning with an Asian molecule, they inserted carefully chosen African elephant DNA segments. When that artificially patched and spliced helix was compared to genuine African DNA, there were no serious errors.

They were now capable of piecing together a complete mammoth DNA molecule, if necessary.

Adam and Ernie began surgery on the thawed mammoth flesh. They carefully carved away the exterior layers, organizing the tissues to be refrozen for later research. When the uterine walls were finally exposed, Ernie identified two blistery spots as attached embryos, which he removed for microscopic examination. To their astonishment, the first cluster's embryonic cells were still viable.

"I think the cells from the first blister are female," Ernie marveled. "We won't be able to sex them until we do a chromosome count."

"That's great," Adam replied. "Is it ready for implantation?"

"Almost. I want to split the embryo into two. We'll grow one for immediate implant, and keep the other in reserve."

Ernie examined the second cluster, saying excitedly, "She must've been carrying fraternal twins from different eggs and sperm. Only one of these could have survived a complete pregnancy."

"Is this one viable?"

"I don't like the color. It'll need work. There's an even chance it's the opposite sex."

The damaged embryo was given to Jack and Sandra. Jack had found the first blister to be female and quickly confirmed that the second was a male. Although the males' DNA had deteriorated, Jack would patch together remaining DNA pieces from other original cells. After those repairs, there was a good chance for reconstructing a viable embryo.

It took only a few hours in a special culture to grow the female embryo to optimal size for implantation.

Ernie had already arranged for the surrogate mother. She was the Asian elephant Rani, the teenage daughter of Maharani. That same day—all recorded by National Geographic photographers—Rani was sedated and the female embryo was surgically implanted. It would be several days before it could be determined whether the pregnancy would develop normally.

Adam was awakened at 3 a.m. by the sing-song tune of his cell phone. A croaky voice spoke. "I'm dying, Adam. You're the only one who can help." He took only a moment to realize it was Dave Wiley.

"Dave," said Adam in a groggy voice. "Are you at home?"

"Yes," Wiley replied, sounding like he had a mouth full of saltine crackers.

"I'll be there in ten minutes," Adam said with the reassuring tone of a family doctor.

"Who was it?" Vera asked sleepily as Adam turned on the lights.

"Dave Wiley," answered Adam, fear in his voice. "He sounds like hell."

Adam drove to Wiley's, searching his mind for explanations. Had he tried to experiment on himself with his own super virus? Adam hoped not, but he had to plan for such a possibility.

Wiley may have followed Adam's lead and engineered a herpetic virus. The man was impulsive and impatient, and wouldn't bother with a stopper gene. Wiley didn't have sufficient time for animal preliminaries. He didn't have Sandra Wickham to suggest likely changes, nor did he have Jack Chin to execute them.

Adam felt no guilt over leading Wiley to try for virtual immortality. The man had been unstoppable—until now.

Adam nearly choked when Wiley answered the door; he looked like some cartoon character stung by a thousand bees. The man was covered with pustule mounds from some gigantic pox.

"What virus did you use as the seed?"

It was hard for Wiley to form his words. "I had some skin eruptions, probably a reemergence of childhood chicken pox. It was stress-induced, probably because of the Millner fiasco."

Adam recalled that chicken pox, a member of the herpetic family, can sometimes be aroused after many years of dormancy, much like *herpes simplex*. Physicians commonly misdiagnose adult flare-ups of that innocent childhood disease as genital herpes. But chicken pox caused serious problem for adults. It had almost been responsible for nearly wiping out American Indians and Hawaiians.

"So you took fluid from the pox and re-engineered it?" Adam asked.

"Yes," Wiley gasped, continuing his answer in spurts. "My colleague wanted to make small changes until we had continuous infection. This is the result of the first change."

"Did you engineer a stopper mechanism into your virus?"

"No. What's that?" Wiley croaked.

Adam didn't answer, hoping that this infection could be driven into dormancy. The pustules would be highly infectious. He shuddered at the horror of innocent persons infected with this thing.

"Where's your wife?" Adam asked, hoping she was not affected.

"She's been visiting her mother."

"When did you inject yourself with this virus?"

"Yesterday."

Adam was amazed at the disease's fast action. It reminded him of the mouse that had to be destroyed. Wiley would likely reach the same fate.

"I'm taking you to Central Med."

By personally intervening, Adam would save time and avoid endangering an ambulance crew. On the way he called ahead and arranged for isolation.

Wiley could barely walk to Adam's car, moaning loudly when he tried to sit down. He sobbed all the way to the hospital. Adam guessed that Wiley was running a fever of over 106, near the threshold for brain damage.

When they arrived, a special gurney was sitting beside a deserted hospital entrance. Adam had warned that all personnel be kept away. Wiley could barely get out of the car, and Adam had to manhandle him onto the gurney. He closed a hood over Wiley and then spent ten minutes rubbing all surfaces with alcohol. He then stripped naked and gingerly climbed into an isolation suit the staff had place at the curb. He threw his clothes into the car, locking it, and then washed his gloved hands with alcohol. By himself, Adam pushed the gurney into the hospital.

"Stay away from my car," he told security staff. "It's contaminated."

Adam pushed Wiley to the isolation ward and entered a compound similar to the one occupied during the African virus emergency. He stripped the now unconscious Wiley and immersed him in a cold bath; he then injected him with gamma globulin.

But it was too late—Wiley died minutes after reaching isolation.

Adam struggled to get Wiley's body back onto the gurney, which he swabbed again. He wheeled it to the ward entrance, where an orderly was waiting to take Wiley to the morgue. Adam warned the technician to take extreme caution in avoiding possible contamination.

Adam thoroughly bathed, washing his arms and hands as if he were going into surgery. He took the deserted stairs back to ground level and returned to his car, retrieving his street clothes. He placed those and the isolation suit into the burn bin. Now totally nude, Adam scrubbed the car's passenger compartment with alcohol. After that he walked naked back into a hospital side door near the showers, where he bathed all over again and then changed into a surgical costume.

Vera was in a fretful sleep when Adam returned to the apartment at seven o'clock in the morning. He was too strung out to sleep, so he busied himself preparing a breakfast of pepperoni and mozzarella omelets. The smell of cooking rousted Vera, who rolled out of bed and stumbled into the kitchen.

"How's Wiley?" she asked groggily. "Did you do surgery?"

"He died two hours ago," Adam answered, feeling a mixture of sadness and guilt. "He experimented with a lesion from flared-up chicken pox and tried to create his own super virus from it. But instead, he engineered a mutant monster pox that killed him in less than twenty-four hours. Wiley took no safeguards—he didn't prepare a stopper-gene vaccine—and must've had incompetent genetic engineering to boot."

Vera was shocked. "This is hard to believe," she said. "God has had his vengeance."

"Maybe I'm next. I'm responsible for all of this."

Vera almost screamed at him. "No, you're not! Even if you hadn't done it, Wiley would've manipulated you into creating the super virus. He got his just desserts."

"Some dessert," Adam replied sadly.

Vera did not dwell on the past. "So what happens now?"

"I haven't given it a thought."

"You'd better," Vera said, taking over and becoming strong for him. "Somebody has to talk to the press. You must get your story straight."

"I don't want to deal with it."

"You have no choice. Let me help."

Vera and Adam planned a public relations campaign to deter the world from questing after virtual immortality.

46

The Most Convoluted Story

Adam returned to Central Hospital to sign Dave Wiley's death certificate.

"I'm Adam Boatwright," he said, greeting the chief resident for internal medicine with an extended hand.

"Hello, Sir," I'm Aharon Zeissel," the tall young doctor said as he shook Adam's hand. "The pathology report on Professor Wiley indicates chicken pox. We entered that onto the form."

"Close enough," Adam said, signing the paper. "A mutant form, highly infectious, I suspect."

"I've never seen anything like it," Zeissel said. "The poor man's insides were full of the same lesions as his skin's. What a way to go!"

"Yeah, I feel the same way. I'm sorry to rush off—the hospital chief's waiting. Thanks."

Dr. Svenson was in the staff conference room along with a reporter from the Central *Clarion*. Adam had called her earlier, offering an interview.

"Hello, Adam," Svenson greeted. "You've had more than your share of horrible diseases, and you're not even in active practice."

"Stick around. The story is an incredible one."

"Dr. Boatwright, I'm Lisa Cantouros of the *Clarion.*" She was a striking red-haired woman, wearing a brown suit. Her small size made her look much younger than her age, which Adam guessed to be about thirty.

Adam greeted her with a smile. "Are you ready to interview me?"

"Yes sir," she said, barely able to hide her excitement.

Dr. Svenson sat off to the side of the large table, while Adam and Lisa took facing chairs.

"I'm ready to tell the whole story," Adam said, anxious to begin. "Where do you want to start?"

"Let's start at the present and sort of work our way back. What did Professor Wiley die of?"

Adam took a deep breath and began. "He died of a massive infection from an altered chicken pox. He genetically engineered that in an attempt to create a super virus."

"What do you mean, *super* virus?"

Swallowing hard, Adam paused a moment to compose a fitting explanation of his staff's special jargon. Adam and Vera had conferred and decided to tell the world about super viruses, because it was now impossible to hide them.

"A super virus gives its host immunity to all other viral infections and also delays the aging process."

That wasn't completely true. It *stopped* the aging process, not simply delayed it.

"How does the super virus do that?" Lisa asked.

Adam gave a simple answer. "A super virus keeps the body continuously infected, forcing it to constantly produce *defensive chemicals*. Those key body chemicals naturally conquer most viral infections."

He went on to talk about chemicals generated to ensure that cells divide properly, and that those were generated by the body in response to a virus infection.

"What do dividing cells have to do with aging?"

Adam continued, bothered by the half-truth just presented. "Animals and people age because mistakes are made when their cells divide to create new ones. For example, the wrinkles in older people's skin are caused by errors in the new skin cells. The accumulation of errors gets progressively greater as we age. Ultimately, skin loses its elasticity and shrivels."

"But the super virus only *temporarily* stops aging, right?" Lisa asked, giving Adam a hook onto which he would hang his next fabrication.

"Yes," he replied, reinforcing the half-truth. "The super virus itself ages. Eventually, it becomes so weak that the body stops making I-complex chemicals. Then the host animal's aging process accelerates, and the animal generally dies of cancer."

The mouse super virus was being engineered to *force* it to age. Nobody really knew how long coexisting viruses, like herpes, would faithfully duplicate themselves. Adam guessed that herpetic viruses had a far slower natural mutation rate than more mobile viruses, such as those for influenza.

But Adam continued with the party line he and Vera had developed. "But the super virus was only partially successful in mice."

That wasn't true. It worked for Adam *and* mice, and both versions were permanent.

He continued his explanation. "Dave Wiley jumped the gun. He went directly into human experimentation, without waiting, and treated himself. He died a horrible death, less than twenty-four hours after injecting a mutant virus. Luckily, we've prevented it from spreading."

"You mean this might have been another Ebola?" Lisa asked, prodding for a broader story line.

"Far worse," Adam said emphatically. "Ebola is not nearly as destructive as Wiley's monster pox potentially would have been. For all we know, his pox could have spread like a wildfire, and like the virus that decimated Australia's wild rabbit population, it might have killed millions of people within days."

"How did *you* manage to avoid catching Wiley's pox?"

"I was very careful and very lucky," Adam replied with another half-truth. "I was called to help him and put myself in jeopardy before realizing what had happened."

"By coincidence, weren't you involved in the recent African virus outbreak?"

Adam gulped and gave another lie. "I only assisted the patients. I volunteered because I'm *immune* to the Ebola family of viruses."

Adam didn't disclose that he was immune only because the super virus protected him from to *all* viruses.

"I was exposed in Africa years ago," he said, telling another outright lie.

Although Adam had never before been exposed to Ebola, he needed the world to believe in his prior immunity. That lie would deter guessing that his own super virus had protected him.

"Did Wiley have anything to do with the accident?"

Adam took advantage of the reporter's attempts to broaden her story.

"It was no accident. Drug cartel employees are under murder indictment for switching labels on virus vials. One of those vials contained the deadly African virus. A researcher mistakenly administered that virus to animals. He got infected in the process and spread it around."

"And what was Wiley's role?"

"Wiley was a consultant to the cartel. But the police don't believe he was connected to the murder conspiracy."

"Wasn't Wiley also your boss?"

"Yes," Adam answered before shifting the interview back on a helpful course. "The police believe the hospital sabotage was an attempt to discredit me."

"I don't understand."

Adam continued with his own interpretation of things. "The drug cartel was pushing Wiley to prematurely transfer mouse super-virus technology to human beings. I resisted Wiley's pressure to join them."

Actually, Adam had never been asked to join them.

"I was simply in the way."

"So they tried to kill you?"

"It was more subtle than that," Adam answered, building a public version of his story. "They arranged an epidemic, knowing that I was immune to that type of virus. They wanted me to volunteer to help. But the conspirators were very diabolical. They stole empty vials carrying my fingerprints and mingled them with the researcher's lab supplies."

"So that *you* would be accused of murder?"

"I think so," he answered. "But I'm mystified by the whole story."

Another lie—he actually knew the whole story.

"Regardless of what happened, I would either be accused of murder or have my credibility severely compromised. I would be neutralized from interfering with the cartel's human experimentation."

That cartel story was not totally true—but neither could it be disproved. Adam needed to obscure the cartel's true motives, since doing so would help him keep the vital secret about virtual immortality.

The truth was a bit more convoluted. Wiley had informed the cartel about Adam's self-injection of an untested super virus. Wiley apparently never believed in Adam's previous immunity, and the conspirators enticed him to test his own super virus by causing the African virus outbreak. They believed he would likely help in that crisis. Although Adam had other reasons for helping in the emergency, not getting infected *did confirm* workability of his super virus.

Lisa fired her next question. "So what was *your* connection to the cartel?"

Adam replied with another half-truth. "I became aware of their existence just weeks ago. I was only a source of information regarding mouse super viruses."

Adam did not share that the cartel suspected he had a human super virus.

"They spied to get that information, bugging my home and offices. With the help of Wiley, they wanted to exploit my mouse research in an attempt to make a human super virus. They actually engineered and then tested an ineffectual virus on several people."

In truth, the cartel had engineered nothing and had tested stolen copies of Adam's own human super virus, one that seemed to work only on himself.

Adam continued, with the slightly embellished truth. "They were lucky it didn't cause symptoms similar to Wiley's. The FDA shut them down."

Lisa listened, furiously taking notes, pausing to shake her arm and ask further difficult questions.

"But Wiley has just died," she said, "and the conspirators were arrested weeks ago. How did he get his mutant virus?"

This was Adam's opportunity to make a key point, and in this case he was able to answer factually. "Wiley was an impatient man. The cartel had been broken, so he struck out on his own. It's obvious he didn't come close to getting a human super virus. He was killed by the monster of his own creation."

"When did Wiley join the cartel?"

Adam again gave a true answer. "It began with the arrival at Central University of Dr. Itzak Friedman."

"The Israeli scientist murdered by the Pan Palestinian Freedom Alliance?"

"The same," Adam replied, happy to have such a smart and knowledgeable interviewer. "The police now believe the cartel was also partially responsible for the death of Dr. Friedman. He had outlived his usefulness to them, and they disposed of him."

"Weren't you once charged with Friedman's murder?"

"Yes, but the perpetrators were found and confessions were made. They're both dead now. Only recently, we learned that the cartel probably caused Friedman's murder by bribing members of the PPFA. I believe my connection was due to some sort of mix-up between the PPFA and the cartel."

"So the cartel followed Friedman here?"

"Yes. They bought the nearby pharmaceutical firm Millner because it was connected to Wiley. Friedman was working with his department at Central University. And I got involved because Friedman wanted me as his consultant. I suspect that Wiley arranged all of that. My active involvement in the cell-division project started with Dr. Friedman's death. I extended his project into live experimentation with mice. The concept of a mouse super virus was my own."

"This is the most convoluted story I've ever heard," Lisa Cantouros marveled.

Now it was Adam's opportunity to make the universal attractor more remote. "Yes indeed. Wiley tried to do fifty years of research in weeks. We're nowhere close to getting a human super virus."

Adams's thoughts were going in two directions He wanted no super virus for others, though he was infected with it. He had vowed to keep that secret as long as he lived.

"Do you think we ever will have such a virus?"

"Perhaps some day," Adam answered, knowing there would inevitably be attempts to create a super virus. His new goal was now to discourage that.

Adam told Lisa that Wiley's experience should be a warning to the world. There were terrible dangers lurking for anyone careless with viruses. Wiley took no precautions whatsoever, and his research ended in a quick and hideous death. He could have taken millions of innocent people with him.

"I hope you can spread that message."

"May I call you if I have further questions?" Lisa said in response to Adam's subtle signal to end the interview.

"Of course."

Lisa thanked Adam and Dr. Svenson as she left the conference room.

Svenson stared at Adam for a few seconds, struggling to speak. "You're right about viruses. You're an amazing man, Adam. I'm proud to know you."

Not wanting to prolong the discussion, Adam excused himself, hoping to assuage his guilt over having told a pack of lies.

The crushing weight of his secret and his new mission—preventing the spread of virtual immortality—was taking its toll.

47

A Modern P.T. Barnum

Vera's press strategy was working as intended. The conspirators' stories received worldwide attention, and their trials would further discourage super-virus pursuits. Wiley's horrible death strengthened that deterrence. Those were formidable weapons in Adam's undeclared war against virtual immortality. Perhaps his biggest guns were FDA's disciplinary actions against Millner. Those would discourage hasty human experimentation.

Vera's sister Nora passed away from her cancer just before Christmas, making the Boatwrights' holiday a subdued one.

Among the bright spots was Rani's pregnancy with a female mammoth fetus. Adam's team had also successfully reconstructed DNA for the male mammoth. From that, an embryo had been artificially formed, grown, and duplicated. The original had been placed into the womb of elephant Regina, Maharani's younger sister.

Both pregnancies had progressing successfully for six months. In about sixteen months the world would have brother and sister baby mammoths.

Like a modern P. T. Barnum with his gigantic elephant Jumbo, Ernie Dickson created a flurry of interest in mammoths. Adam joined him in their first media event since arriving from Kamchatka. Over a hundred reporters and photographers presented a scene reminiscent of presidential news conferences. It was held outdoors, around the zoo's pachyderm pavilion.

Ernie made the opening statement.

The International Wildlife Fund welcomes you to Central City Zoo. You see before you a group of Asian elephants. Few of these creatures remain in the wild. Their habitat is being eliminated to make room for crops. Their African cousins are disappearing for the same reasons, but even faster due to ivory poaching.

These animals resulted from tens of millions of years of evolution. It's sad that within our lifetimes elephants will disappear from the wild. They and hundreds of familiar species pictured in children's books will be history.

The culprit is man. People are causing mass extinctions on a scale rivaling that of the dinosaurs. But man can do something about it. Today, you'll see how we can mitigate the damage brought by ourselves and our desperate brothers.

Meet Maharani and her calf. Shiv was born six months ago. Until then, he spent twenty-two months in his mother's womb—over twice the human gestation. To her left is Maharani's daughter. Rani is now pregnant with a very special calf.

Rani's calf originated from an embryo implant—a sort of test tube baby. Rani is just the surrogate mother. Her baby is of a species related to the Asian elephant. That species hasn't walked the Earth for ten thousand years. Rani's calf is a female woolly mammoth."

Ernie's speech was interrupted by a buzz of side-talk among the startled audience. After about a minute, he was able to continue.

The calf's biological mother died some ten thousand years ago. During all that time, that real mother was encapsulated in a glacier in Kamchatka, Russia. The calf's embryo was safely ensconced in the mother's womb, frozen all those years.

Frozen embryos have been used for years in cattle breeding. As we have proven with our baby woolly mammoth, a frozen embryo can remain viable for a very long time. The inspiration for regenerating the mammoth came from my colleague, Dr. Adam Boatwright.

The International Wildlife Fund is forming collections of embryos from species—worldwide. We're their repository of last hope. Someday, when men have learned to better coexist with animals, those embryos will regenerate whole populations. Hundreds of years from now, we may be able to reestablish elephant herds in their native Africa and Asia.

Meanwhile, the collected embryos will help zoos maintain viable populations, ensuring genetic diversity through scientific breeding. But all of that is expensive. The Fund needs help.

Now that I've made my pitch, I want you to meet the surrogate mother of a second woolly mammoth. To the right of Maharani stands Regina, her little sister. Regina is carrying a baby male woolly mammoth. The two mammoth fetuses are fraternal twins.

The male is special. His embryo was damaged during a hundred centuries of cold storage. Dr. Boatwright and his team were able to patch together a complete DNA strand and insert it into an emptied elephant egg. Dr. Boatwright has done something never before attempted in genetic engineering.

In closing, I'm announcing a contest to the world's children. We want your help finding very special names for the girl and boy mammoths. Entry forms for this contest will be available in the schools. To submit a mammoth name, a child will fill out the form and enclose a dollar registration fee—lesser amounts will be accepted from poorer countries. The schools will collect the entries and send them to us. The money will help implement the frozen embryo collections.

It's now time for questions.

A reporter from a popular tabloid asked the first question. "Dr. Dickson, will embryo transplant eliminate the need for sex?"

"Yes and no. All embryos are formed by the union of an egg and a sperm. The mammoth embryos were created through natural intercourse. But natural sex is not needed to get an embryo. Transplantable embryos are ordinarily created by removing sperm mechanically from the father. That is used outside of the womb to fertilize the mother's egg, which has already been surgically removed."

"Dr. Dickson, How can an elephant be a surrogate for a mammoth?" a reporter for the *Clarion* asked.

"They are very closely related species, with similar size and body chemistry," Ernie answered.

"What will you do in five hundred years when there are no surrogate mothers?"

"I hope zoos will still have some females of the target species. But we could use surrogate mothers from cousin species. For example, a goat might serve as birth mother for a small deer, or a dog for a bear."

"What about behavior? How will a reintroduced elephant learn to eat or find water?"

Ernie had to dig hard for the answer. "There are limits to what we can do. It's possible that may have to be relearned by the new animals, in a sort of cultural re-evolution."

A woman reporter asked Adam's first question. "Dr. Boatwright, you've made genetic repairs to woolly mammoth DNA. Do you know how to make a Tyrannosaurus Rex?"

Adam waited for the side-talk to subside. "No. We didn't *make* the DNA. We just patched together partial strands of DNA to make one good whole. If you gave me similar strands from a T. Rex, we could do it for that species as well. But only tiny DNA remnants from that dinosaur have been preserved in bone marrow. Re-engineering T. Rex DNA from those pieces would be like recreating the Last Supper from random paint chips swept off the floor beneath the original work of art."

Building on the momentum, a male television reporter went next. "Dr. Boatwright, does that mean it's impossible to recreate a dinosaur?"

"No, I didn't say that," Adam answered professorially, as if still in lecture mode. "Modern birds and dinosaurs have common ancestors. It might be possible to achieve an approximation of the ancestor by a process of 'reverse' evolution. Each step would involve a small change to reproductive DNA.

"It might take one hundred successive generations to go from a turkey to the ancestral version of all related birds. A further hundred successive generations could bring us back to the primordial bird. A final hundred iterations could end with an approximate bird-dinosaur primogenitor. All of that might take five hundred years and cost billions of dollars. Then we could reverse the process, aiming to create a descendant having characteristics ascribed to T. Rex. That would require perhaps another thousand years and more billions. But when we're done, we wouldn't have T. Rex. We would have a phony that just looks and acts like him."

"You mean you could actually create a *Jurassic Park*?" The earlier woman reporter asked.

Adam thoroughly enjoyed the opportunity to expound. "Eventually we could. But we wouldn't live long enough to see it. However, we could reverse in one year what nature took ten thousand years to do in normal evolution."

"Dr. Boatwright, could you make a man from a chimpanzee?" asked the same reporter, obviously relishing the added drama.

"Not exactly," Adam replied. "Chimpanzees and man are very closely related species, though not nearly as close as the elephant and mammoth. I would skip getting the common ancestor. I would make obvious changes to the chimp DNA, trying to remove body hair and increase brain size. Then I would try to get offspring having a human-like mouth and jaw. But not all changes would result in a viable creature. What do we do with our mistakes? There would be tremendous ethical implications."

Ernie showed no irritation at the turn taken by the questions. Dinosaur and evolution talk would strengthen the world's interest in his project. Nevertheless, he seemed grateful when the questions returned to the immediate concerns.

A *Clarion* reporter asked, "Dr. Dickson, when do you expect the mammoths to be born?"

"In about a year. In a couple of months we'll take sonograms, photos of which will be released to the press."

"How much money do you think you'll raise?"

"That depends on the interest generated. There are about a billion school-age children in the world. If one out of ten sent a dollar, we could raise one hundred million dollars. We only need a fraction of that to implement our embryo banks. Some of the rest will fund genetic research."

The press conference was a huge success. Coverage would eventually saturate all the media, spawning further stories about evolution and genetics. The school kits were expected to be a very effective in generating funds.

"I didn't know you were going to attempt to fund genetic research," Adam said.

"That's for you," Ernie replied. "Without your help, we'd never raise funds. I think we'll have more money than we can handle."

"I gratefully accept. Who was the genius who came up with the naming contest?"

"Our wives dreamed it up!"

"That figures," Adam said, once more amazed by Vera's skills.

"Will you try to create the dodo we discussed returning from Kamchatka?"

"Birds would be easy to do," Adam replied. "We could get a new generation every six months. If I went directly from pigeon to dodo, I might have something in about five years."

"I want you to do it. Whatever you learn with the dodo will apply to species lost in the next fifty years."

"But Ernie, you'll need permission to spend the funds."

"No, I won't. The children's money will go to a foundation directed by you and me. We'll only be associated with International Wildlife, not controlled by them."

Adam was about to live Dave Wiley's wildest dream: plenty of money to do whatever research he wanted. All would be done with the blessing of the world's children.

He felt good about himself in ways not experienced for months.

48

A Warning to the World

Adam and Vera were having Sunday brunch. Adam opened the Central *Clarion* and nearly jumped when he saw the headline for a story by Lisa Cantouros. Adam read the story with fascination.

Key Witness Implicates Conspirators in Virus Sabotage

CENTRAL CITY, January 17. *The trial of the African virus epidemic perpetrators took a surprising turn today. One of the accused, Saul Lowenstein, read an amazing statement tying the conspirators back some five years, to Israel.*

The chain of events started with Dr. Itzak Friedman, the famous Israeli scientist murdered a year ago. Lowenstein served as an undercover "mole" for the pharmaceutical drug cartel believed responsible for Friedman's death and for the sabotage leading to the aborted epidemic at the Central University Medical Center.

Lowenstein became Friedman's lab assistant shortly after arrival in this country. Former colleagues were shocked that Lowenstein has a PhD in pharmacology from the University of Wisconsin, a fact hidden from his employers, who thought he was a gifted college dropout.

Dr. David Wiley, late chairman of Central University genetics, was drafted by the cartel and served as Lowenstein's main contact for passing sensitive data about Friedman's research. That role continued through Dr. Adam Boatwright's accession to head of the hush-hush project. Boatwright was a major victim of the cartel. Lowenstein arranged his own firing by sabotaging Boatwright's mouse study, substituting one rodent strain for another.

Lowenstein confessed to later helping frame Dr. Boatwright for murder. He planted some of Boatwright's own vials in the laboratory of the researcher doing studies with African viruses. Lowenstein's ex-girlfriend, med center technician Tamara Chung, switched labels on the original vials of virus. Lowenstein, along with Wiley and Chung, had been blackmailed and threatened by Billy Cantrel. Lowenstein identified Cantrel's boss as Tommy Lee, an employee of the Singapore firm serving as front for the drug cartel.

"That wretched scoundrel was the spy, or at least one of them," Adam blurted to Vera.

"Who?"

"Saul Lowenstein," Adam said in disgust. "He had a PhD in pharmacology. It was all a masquerade. He must have slaughtered hundreds of mice to get his dissertation."

"I might have guessed that if I'd met him face to face."

"I'll bet you're right," Adam said, adding one more item to his growing collection of regrets.

"Here's my story!" Adam said, spotting the companion article. Adam read the second Cantouros article.

Famous Scientist Warns World over Mysterious Death of Geneticist Wiley

CENTRAL CITY, January 17. *Geneticist Adam Boatwright, also a medical doctor and surgeon, explained the mysterious death of David Wiley, chairman of Central University's Genetics Department. Wiley, implicated in the infamous drug cartel responsible for two murders, died of a mutant form of chicken pox.*

> *Wiley had engineered this virus from one taken from his own body. He was attempting to make a super virus. According to Dr. Boatwright, that super virus was supposed to maintain a continuous infection in Wiley's body, generating* I-complex. *That substance group would prevent any other viral infections from occurring and temporarily stop the aging process.*
>
> *The quest for a chemical temporarily slowing the aging process brought the murderous drug cartel to Central University. When the key conspirators were arrested, Wiley struck out on his own. He violated all protocols and laws. He took no precautions. According to Dr. Boatwright, Wiley tried to invent a super virus by himself, hoping to become very wealthy in the process.*
>
> *Wiley died of a monster pox, less than twenty-four hours after injecting himself with the mutant strain.*
>
> *Dr. Boatwright had been working on a mouse version of a super virus for some time. He said that it was not even ready for mice, and that human research could not even begin until the mouse studies were finished.*
>
> *Boatwright went on to say that Wiley's pox had the potential for killing millions of people within hours after infection. He added that this mutant chicken pox was far worse than the infamous Ebola.*
>
> *Ironically, it was chicken pox that decimated Hawaiians and other Native Americans. Even in its normal form, this children's disease is very serious in adults. Wiley gave that pox a lethal twist. Dr. Boatwright stated that Wiley's tragedy must serve as a warning to the world. Extreme caution must be taken when genetically altering viruses.*

"Nice story," Adam said, passing the front section over to Vera, who read the articles with fascination.

"Maybe we've finally put the virtual immortality genie back into the bottle."

"It can come out at any time. It's a universal attractor, and researchers will not stay away."

"Are you well prepared for tomorrow?" asked Vera.

"I'm to report to the court clerk at ten o'clock. They assure me that I'll give testimony right away—medical privilege."

"Adam, you have to be agile and support our 'party line.' Reporters from the world press are covering the trial."

"I'll do my best."

Adam was about to be questioned by the DA, Marvin Smithline, who had been in charge of the Itzak Friedman proceedings in which Adam had been accused of murder. That case had been solved before ever going to trial.

Now, Adam was on the prosecutor's side, and the defendants were employees of the cartel.

"Dr. Boatwright," Smithline started, "when did you first become aware of the conspiracy to cause the outbreak at Central med?"

"It was after the emergency, after the police told me *my* fingerprints were on the vials in Dr. Hamlish's lab."

"What did you do after the police informed you?"

"I did my own investigating. I went to Saul Lowenstein."

"Why him?" Smithline asked, putting on a puzzled expression for the jury's benefit.

Adam then told the story of Lowenstein's original mouse sabotage and how that was similar to switching the African virus vials.

"What did he tell you?"

"Lowenstein said animal rights people did it. He said they wanted to frame him."

"Didn't that sound odd to you?" said Smithline, looking at Lowenstein.

Adam frowned at Lowenstein. "Yes. I wondered if he was telling the truth."

"And what did you do then?"

"I went to Central City Police to see Detective Reilly. The detective interrogated Lowenstein, getting a completely different story. Lowenstein disclosed the cartel's existence."

"And that was your first knowledge of this cartel?" asked Smithline, looking at the defendants.

"Yes. Detective Reilly told me afterward."

"And what did Lowenstein tell Reilly?"

"Objection! Hearsay!" the defense attorneys shouted, almost in unison.

"Sustained," the heavy, balding judge ruled. "Mr. Smithline, you know better than that."

It was not hearsay. Adam had heard it directly while hiding in the closet. But he kept silent, not wanting to hurt the prosecution's case.

"Dr. Boatwright, how did your fingerprints get onto the vials in Hamlish's laboratory?"

Adam truthfully replied, "I think the impressions were on empty vials stolen from one of my labs and filled later. I believe the vials must have been planted there by someone, before Hamlish's lab was sealed."

"Dr. Boatwright, why were your prints planted?" asked Smithline dramatically.

Adam answered with the party line, as established with Vera. "To discredit me. I had unwittingly supplied the cartel with all that they thought necessary to make a super virus—a virus that would temporarily stop aging. I wouldn't take my research the next step, *human* experimentation. They didn't need me anymore, and I had become an obstacle."

Smithline continued his examination. "Dr. Boatwright, please explain your theory as to why the cartel would find it advantageous to do so."

Adam answered, using his cover story. "I now know they were spying on me. They knew I developed immunity to the virus in Africa. It's common knowledge this particular virus is highly infectious and often fatal. They guessed I'd volunteer to treat infected people, since I was likely the only doctor around who had immunity."

"Isn't that a lot of conjecture?"

"Yes, but these clever people are capable of almost anything."

"Objection!" shouted one of the defense attorneys.

The judge responded. "Sustained. The jury will disregard the last statement."

Smithline was done. It was now time for cross-examination.

Anton Crosskey, the cartel's impeccably dressed defense attorney, began. "Dr. Boatwright, who is Itzak Friedman?"

This launched a series of questions and answers regarding Adam's relationship to Itzak. Then Crosskey dropped the first bombshell. "Why did you slit Dr. Friedman's throat?"

"I did not slit his throat," Adam protested adamantly. "I performed an emergency tracheotomy. I found him in my office, struggling for breath."

"Weren't you indicted for Dr. Friedman's murder?" Crosskey asked, gesturing dramatically.

Smithline jumped out of his chair. "Objection! Dr. Boatwright is not on trial here."

"Sustained," the judge ordered. Turning, he added an instruction: "The jury will disregard the last statement." The judge glared at Crosskey. "Counselor, no more of this."

"Didn't you steal his project?" Crosskey asked.

"No. After Dr. Friedman was gone, Dr. Wiley arranged for me to take over."

Crosskey aimed the next barb. "You found out that Friedman had discovered how to stop aging, and you wanted it for yourself. Right?"

"Wrong," Adam replied truthfully. "Itzak Friedman had never discovered a viable way to slow aging, except in rats. He injected cloned I-complex intravenously for that purpose. I found a way to accomplish the same thing in mice through a viral infection. We call the infective agent a *super virus*. But its effect is only temporary."

"Didn't you find a way to do it with humans?"

"We tried, but it never worked," lied Adam, faithful to the Boatwright party line.

"And who did you try it on?"

Adam made the first public admission of self-experimentation. "My wife and myself—we wanted to prevent cancer."

Vera and Adam had argued long about such a confession. But Vera finally convinced Adam that Wiley's death would take the sting out of admitting to self-experimentation.

"Don't you know it's against all scientific ethics and research protocols to experiment on yourself?" Crosskey asked smugly.

"Yes," Adam answered, unable to hide his guilt. "But many medical pioneers tested on themselves. I was desperate to save my wife from getting cancer. I committed a cardinal ethical sin, yes. I regret that."

"Didn't you volunteer in the African virus emergency as test of your super virus, to see if it was actually working on you?" Crosskey asked, not disguising his cockiness.

Adam took a big breath, about to perjure himself again. "No. During rest-and-recreation during the Vietnam war, I went to Africa to translate a negotiation between Sudanese and Israelis. In southern Sudan there was an outbreak of Ebola. I caught the disease, but through early treatment with gamma globulin, I survived. I'm now immune to the Ebola disease family."

"You speak Arabic and Hebrew?" Crosskey asked sarcastically.

"Yes. I'll show you. Let's take the words, 'It's most dangerous to tinker with viruses.' First I will restate them in Arabic." Adam spoke the sentence in fluent Arabic. "Next, the same words in Hebrew." Adam then translated out loud the sentence into that language.

Shocked by Adam's impromptu answer, Crosskey asked, "Then why did you volunteer to assist in the recent emergency?"

Adam answered with the half-truth, "I knew I couldn't catch it, and somebody had to help. I was there."

"Where did you meet Saul Lowenstein?"

"In Itzak Friedman's lab."

Glaring at Adam for effect, Crosskey asked, "Did you kill his pet rat, Little Oscar?"

Indignantly, Adam replied in the same tone he would use scolding an animal rightsist, "The pet rat belonged to the project. He was a research animal."

"Please answer the question." Crosskey demanded.

Adam began to give his answer: "I cut down his I-complex and administered a mega dose of vitamin C, hoping that would be sufficient—"

"Please answer yes or no," Crosskey almost shouted, visibly irritated.

"No," Adam answered, having great difficulty restraining himself. "After giving Little Oscar vitamin C, I injected a mouse virus cocktail. I wanted to see if he'd maintain the immunity, as he had with large uncut I-complex doses. He died in service. I used similar cocktails on my mice."

"And later, when Lowenstein tried to get revenge, you fired him. Right?" Crosskey asked, gesturing to the jury as if offering Adam on a platter.

"Absolutely. Lowenstein substituted one set of mice for another, sabotaging our research."

Then defense attorney Crosskey painted himself into a corner. "Dr. Boatwright, tell us what you think of a substance that prevents aging."

"Your Honor, relevance?" Smithline protested.

"I'll allow," the judge ruled. "Dr. Boatwright, please answer."

Now was Adam's chance. "Cessation of aging would be a disaster for the world. We have tremendous population pressures. Imagine a world where people don't die—except by accident. That would put pressure on new births. The world couldn't handle such a population explosion. And where would new ideas come from?"

Adam continued with a second rhetorical question. "And who decides who gets the magical potion? Those controllers would be unimaginably rich. That is what the cartel was trying—"

"Enough, Dr. Boatwright," Crosskey cried, realizing he had made a terrible mistake.

"No counselor," the judge interrupted. "You started this. Now you let Dr. Boatwright finish."

Adam continued. "The cartel was trying to get a monopoly position on a universally attractive substance. But they couldn't make it work. They ran over anybody in their way. They had Itzak Friedman killed. They pulled the plug on Dave Wiley. They set me up for two murder charges."

"Dr. Boatwright, keep it general," the judge ordered. "The jury will disregard comments about the cartel and the other allegations. Okay, Dr. Boatwright."

Realizing that he was addressing the world, not just the jury, Adam unloaded his bombshell. "We all know about cocaine, a substance that only makes people high. Imagine a substance that might allow people to live for five hundred years! A thousand years! If cocaine is worth billions, the magic potion should be worth trillions. If cocaine can corrupt governments, imagine the power of such a miraculous elixir in the hands of a not-so-benign, greedy monopolist."

There was a roar from the gallery. "Order," the judge yelled, striking his gavel again and again. But the excitement did not stop. "Recess!" he finally called. "Bailiff, clear the courtroom."

Adam left the courtroom. As he entered the lobby, the press mobbed him. He didn't really have anything new to say. But he answered all questions, careful to stay within the guidelines he and Vera had established. Since he was outside the court, Adam held nothing back regarding what he knew about the cartel and Wiley. He took the opportunity to reinforce his warnings to the world about messing with viruses. He told the press what he could to deter further research on virtual immortality.

49

Brunhilda

After only three weeks, the African virus sabotage and conspiracy trial came to its predictable end. Saul Lowenstein received a light, plea-bargained sentence, with much heavier penalties for the other conspirators. Ming Koo had never been found and brought to trial. The charges against the Millner officers resulted in probation sentences.

No agencies took interest in Adam's own confession of self-experimentation.

Press coverage of the trial led to a continuing interest in Adam and his research. He was granted several interviews with reporters, reinforcing the Boatwright party line: the *temporary* nature of the mouse super virus, the need for complete animal research before human trials, the disastrous failure of actual human experiments, the vast potential for corruption by groups connected with an anti-aging substance, and the terrible dangers of genetically engineered viruses. When given the opportunity, Adam emphasized that prolonged lifetimes would be disastrous to society and the world.

In spite of his desires to the contrary, Adam was becoming a media celebrity. That was only partly due to the trial and interest in postponing aging. The public was now interested in genetic engineering and recreating extinct species.

Adam and Vera were taking stock of their situation during one of their visits to the zoo. They decided to stroll around the park.

"It just won't end," Adam complained to Vera. "This virtual immortality stuff seems to be running my life."

Ever the helpful soulmate, Vera replied, "Few people live according to a predetermined script. You'll just have to take what comes."

"I've apparently become the Carl Sagan of genetics."

"That's not so bad," Vera consoled him. "You're doing a tremendous amount of good. You may have saved the human race from megalomaniacs. And, you're instrumental in preserving wild species."

"But I'm not a publicity hound, I'm a doer."

"You *are* doing. You're directing five projects, if you count the new ones here."

"Yeah, that's true. The frozen embryo project is going well. Sandra Wickham has been consulting here for extra money. She has assembled a great software package."

They walked into the primate area, pausing to watch the gorillas. Adam envied those peaceful animals. A large male and female, sitting arms with around each other, watched their baby frolic. Across the way, as usual, the bratty orangutan youth were annoying an old male. Adam shuddered at the thought of being locked up in a cage with a bunch of two-year old children.

Adam stopped suddenly as they rounded the turn by the chimpanzees. The young female was there, obviously pining. Adam waved at her, and her face became animated. "What's going on here?" Vera asked, her question almost a visceral reaction.

"I have a new girlfriend. Meet Brunhilda!"

"Brunhilda?" asked Vera, surprised.

"My name for her. I always think of operatic tragedy when I come here. I don't know why. She seems so lonely, like Violetta's doomed love from Verdi's *La Traviata*."

"I don't like how she reacts to you—she seems like a lover of someone she can't have. I suppose I'm envious that a chimp would fall in love with you."

Adam was surprised at Vera's reaction; it wasn't like her at all. She seemed like a jealous teenager. But Adam didn't see what happened next, while he turned to look back at the orangutans. As Adam looked elsewhere, Brunhilda turned toward Vera, giving the woman a frightful grimace. When Adam turned back, Brunhilda's expression instantly changed to one of innocence.

As they continued their walk, Vera turned back to Brunhilda, noticing the chimpanzee's heartbroken expression.

"Brunhilda is in love with you," Vera said stoically.

"Yeah, lots of animals love me."

Vera stopped and again looked back at the female ape. Then she skipped to catch up with her husband. "I don't mean like a dog or cat becoming affectionate with their owners. I mean like a *woman*. Brunhilda is like a woman scorned."

"That could be," Adam said, trying to stay clinical. "You may recall that chimpanzees and humans are very closely related."

"Yes, I know," Vera said, seeming irritated at Adam's obtuseness. "I heard your little speech about making a human being out of a chimp."

"Not a single chimp," Adam corrected, missing Vera's point entirely. "We take the DNA and modify it over a long series of generations. It would take hundreds of years. In the end we would have something that is human-*like*, but not human. The genomes would be quite different."

"You could do that, Adam! You know you could." Vera said, turning a fiasco into something positive. "You might live long enough to see your synthetic human."

Adam was taken aback. He'd been attempting to remove all thoughts of himself being virtually immortal. "I don't want to talk about that now. Besides, I already have plenty to do."

They walked quietly for several minutes. Vera broke the silence. "And how's your second new project going?"

"Oh, yes, the birds. This was Ernie's inspiration. I'd told him about one of my fantasies—you know the one—pigeons to dodos. He asked me to actually do that. Right now I'm establishing a viable population of pigeons, one not reflecting human breeding. More moonlighting money will be coming to Sandra and Jack when we begin the genetic engineering."

"I can just see the show—you and Ernie presenting your prize to the world—a fat dodo."

They both chuckled.

Adam grinned widely. "You and Jayne dreamed up the mammoth show, contest and all. Ernie will be after you two again, wanting you to put on a mammoth and dodo show."

"I can just see the little mammoths running around, each with a dodo on its back," Vera laughed, Adam joining in.

"What's the response been to the name contest?" Vera asked.

"Spectacular, so far. Over 90 percent of the schools in the test area ordered posters and entry forms."

"Who's paying for the printing?"

"We have lots of printing companies lined up to do it for free. We license them free rights to use our copyrighted mammoth logo in all their advertising. That's good promotion for them and for us."

"Ernie's a marketing genius. And now the printers will be advertising for him, too. How about the kids? Are they filling out the forms?"

"Yes, almost 100 percent in the test schools."

"And how much do you think you'll collect?"

"Ernie thinks it'll be over $50 million, just from the U.S. and Canada alone. Possibly $500 million, worldwide."

"Well, thank God. I'm getting back some of my faith in the human race."

Adam smiled at his wife. "The best part is that we have absolute control of the money through the World Species Preservation Society. Ernie is the chairman of the board, and I'm one of the directors."

Vera's admiration for her husband knew no bounds. "Clearly, the animals are in very good hands." Vera replied.

They continued their walk in contented silence.

50

Aurora Borealis

Adam's sabbatical ended in August, when he returned to teaching. He was still managing his three projects in the Genetics Department, where Dean Boucher had been serving as interim chair until a replacement could be found for Dave Wiley. Adam had been offered the job, which he politely declined. Adam's formal connections with the Wildlife Fund had been transferred over to his and Ernie's World Species Preservation Society. When that was combined with his public speaking demands, he was a very busy man indeed.

The Crunchers carried through the DNA mapping software development with only minimal guidance from Adam. They had managed to shorten the effective mouse lifetime to three years, more than double a normal life span. The new plan was to re-engineer the super virus to further to hasten its die-off.

Adam had adapted the mouse germ-line findings to pigeons. That effort was funded by their personally directed society. After two generations, starting with the generic rock pigeon, the impromptu team had already obtained a transient bird with a larger beak. Adam predicted a reasonably approximate dodo within five years.

Vera had experienced no new breast growths, and her monthly mammograms remained clear. She was traveling less than before, focusing on a series of recordings with the Central Symphony. Her initial albums had been well reviewed, and she was happy at the prospect of less travel and earning a royalty income surpassing her concert fees.

It was now late March, and the two elephant surrogates had reached full term. The time was coming for the two new baby mammoths to join the outside world. The winning names had been selected: Aurora for the female mammoth and Boreal (Bor-ee-al) for the male. They were symbolic for the northern latitudes where the mammoths once roamed and were inspired by the Aurora Borealis, or Northern Lights. Of the millions of entries, several hundred children had chosen Aurora for their girl. Only a handful picked Boreal for the boy; two children gave the exact pair of final names. Each child who picked a winning name would receive a special engraved commemorative plaque.

The funds were still trickling in from schools, then to banks, and from the banks to the international financial network and, finally, to the World Species Preservation Society. So far, over half a billion dollars had been received by the WSPS. The money had been invested in dozens of mutual funds. Over a million of those dollars had already been spent on preliminary research for the frozen embryo project.

It was five o'clock in the morning when Adam received a call from Ernie Dickson. "Rani is in labor. Can you come?"

Adam wakened Vera, who wanted to witness the rare event.

The grunts, groans, and trumpeting could be heard all the way to the parking lot and probably for a mile or so further. Adam and Vera hurried through the zoo to the pachyderm pavilion. Two television crews were already there, one from WCC news and one from National Geographic, which also had two photographers taking high-resolution still pictures. Ernie was assisted by the female pachyderm keeper and a veterinarian woman specializing in large mammals.

Rani's cervix was now fully dilated, and she was extremely agitated because the baby Aurora was going to emerge any time. "This is very much like Maharani's delivery," Adam said quietly to Vera. "It should be just minutes before the baby literally drops to the ground."

Aurora's head emerged. At first she looked just like a baby elephant. In just seconds her torso started to exit the birth canal, with front legs folded back and still inside the mother. Rani was screaming in a wide range of frequencies, but now she was very careful in her movements. Seconds later the front legs emerged and unfolded, feet down. Rani started to undulate rhythmically from side to side. The force of gravity steadily pulled Aurora all the way out, and she gently dropped onto a mound of straw.

There was a collective gasp from the witnesses, followed by a boisterous cheer and then by clapping. "She is definitely not an elephant," Vera exclaimed to Jayne and Adam. "Look at her head. Doesn't it seem to be taller and narrower than an Asian elephant's baby?"

"Yes," Adam replied, "even after accounting for the babyish look. But I don't see any fur."

"I think there's fur," Jayne said. "But it's all wet and obscured by the amniotic fluid and blood."

Rani began messaging Aurora with her trunk until the baby started kicking with all four legs. The mother gently positioned her to stand and then levered her up with her strong trunk. The crowd gasped when the baby stood. Ernie and the other staff had been standing back all this time, patiently waiting until the photographers had fully digested the scene. Ernie and the keeper slowly approached Aurora and with towels briskly wiped her dry.

"Oh—look!" Adam said. "She has long reddish brown fur, similar to a bear's."

The attendants then left mother and daughter alone. Rani gently prodded Aurora toward her teats. Everybody clapped when Aurora began to suckle.

"What a beautiful scene," one of the women photographers enthused, her eyes filled with tears of joy.

Two days later the whole scene was repeated as Regina delivered a healthy male calf, Boreal. Although not identical twins, without their collars it was difficult to tell them apart. Even the keepers had to feel for Boreal's tell-tale bulges, hidden under his covering of fur.

Worldwide television news showed pictures of the baby mammoths. It was one of the biggest news stories in history. The newspapers carried many articles, including features on Adam and Ernie. They were continually amazed by the world's reaction to the mammoth restorations. Unsolicited donations continued to pour into the World Species Preservation Society.

Shortly after the babies were born, Ernie broached future concerns. "Adam, we should plan reintroducing mammoth into the wild."

"But Ernie, be realistic—it'll be years before we need that. These guys can't breed for fifteen or twenty years."

"Close enough. And that'll be after us. But we must plan for it now. I'm thinking about a cooperative arrangement with Alaskan Native Americans for some land."

"Yes, but there's plenty of time," Adam argued.

"I want to build on the momentum of public interest. These mammoths can fire-up enthusiasm for other species reintroduction projects."

Adam liked hearing that. "It's okay with me, but that'll be hard with just one pair. It could take centuries to build a self-sufficient breeding population."

"I want to lift some of Aurora's eggs and fertilize them with elephant fathers," Ernie continued. "Maybe the hybrids won't be sterile. Maybe we can cross breed the daughters with Boreal, just like they do with cows, ending up with a third generation that is three-quarters mammoth."

Adam was still skeptical, but he couldn't let go of his genetic passion. "I think we'd do better with the DNA replacement we talked about before," he said. "I'm willing to give that a try."

51

Just an Ordinary Guy

Finally, the day arrived that Adam had been dreading. It had been five years since infecting himself with the super virus. Vera was turning forty-two, for her not a very happy human milestone. Adam was now fifty-two. As he had predicted, Vera was cranky and not too terribly excited about her birthday card and necklace. She also knew her menopause was approaching. Adam feared what was about to come.

"I'm thinking about retiring," she said. "The regimen of concerts is telling. I'm getting so sore after a long solo performance."

"But you've never been in such demand," Adam protested. "You're one of the few woman violinists compared to the greats."

"I'm probably the only woman dumb enough to stay in this racket so long. Look at my head. My hair is riddled with gray."

"Heifetz was totally gray at his peak," Adam protested, knowing where all of this was heading.

"But he was a man. Gray-haired women are not glamorous like gray-haired men."

"Nonsense!"

"It's true," Vera continued stubbornly. "Take films. I know of no gray-haired leading ladies, unless the main theme is geriatrics. A man can be the lead in his sixties or seventies. After forty, actresses are cast as mothers, aunts, and old maids. They're not lovers. They're not sexpots. They never appear in bikinis or in the nude."

"You're my sexpot. I still letch over you."

"I'm over the hill. It's a bumpy downhill ride from here."

"I disagree," Adam said, futilely trying to stem the tide. "For one thing, why don't you have your hair colored with blonde highlights? Thousand of women do it. And they look years younger. There's also the idea of Botox—if you're really concerned about your facial appearance.

"You have a point, but you shouldn't talk! Look at you! You don't have any gray hairs, and you're fifty-two years old—"

"Okay, said Adam, "I'm *never* going to get gray. Maybe I should inject the stopper now and kill the super virus. Then we can grow old together like a normal couple.

"Oh, Adam, I'm so sorry," she apologized, suddenly reversing roles. "I've been so selfish. Of course I can get my hair done—and I will. But I won't impede your research. No! You have too much to do."

"Why not? What's so special about me anyway? I'm just an ordinary guy, lucky at research."

Vera gave him a tender look. "You're a very special man indeed. Somebody has to be here to pick up the pieces when Ernie's gone. You'll need to keep watch for the Dave Wileys. Somebody's got to try to save this crappy world. You're specially endowed to do that."

"I admit my tremendous curiosity about the future, but it's going to be terribly lonely."

"I know."

"Oh, Vera, "Adam choked, almost sobbing, "how can I survive without you? You've been much more than a wife to me. You've been my alter ego. You're the only person I can really talk to."

"I'm not dead yet! I'm only forty-two years old!"

"Okay," said Adam, a bit testily. "Then, stop talking like you have one foot in the grave."

They stopped talking at all for a long while. Both of them moped through the rest of the day, going through the motions. Vera finally regained her tremendous psychic strength.

"Adam, we have to plan. We've done very little of that since the cartel conspiracy. Start by giving me a progress report."

Adam was relieved to hear those words. She was back!

Adam started. "We've managed to do a lot. Every day I read about a new genetic disease that's being cured. Genetics is in its golden age. Ernie has managed to stockpile a stupendous collection of frozen embryos in every major zoo in the developed world. Over ten thousand animal species have been included, with hundreds being added every month. My dodo is about ready to meet the world. Only minimal tinkering is needed now. I think we can genetically engineer replicas of almost any species, living or extinct, from a nearby relative."

"Bravo, Adam," she said, respecting Adam's superior mind. "None of that could've happened without you. But what about your mouse super virus study?"

"We have it under control. I'm afraid of going human with it—for all the reasons we've gone over again and again. I think National Cancer will stop our funding. They're making great headway in direct treatment of cancers as they occur. There's a great deal less interest in nipping all cancers in the bud."

"So what's in the hopper?"

"Ernie's concerned about cryogenics. He's afraid of some accident, such as a major earthquake, flood, or fire. Any of those may interrupt cold storage, destroying embryo collections. He wants another storage medium. I'm thinking about that one."

"Interesting. Anything else?"

Adam gave a long reply. "As an extension of that, he wants a national embryo repository, along with an extensive plant seed collection, so that in case of an unimaginable disaster—such as a nuclear war—the animals and plants could someday be brought back."

"Wow!"

"You may remember that he wanted to use the yellow chimney rock cavern complex as a storage and livable space," Adam continued.

"Didn't he map that place?"

"Yes. But he's been keeping it secret all this time. He's purchased a nearby ranch and has grazing rights all around it."

"So, where do we go from here?"

"I'm plenty busy," Adam answered, smiling. "I love my work. I'll just keep going as before."

"People are going to wonder about you. In ten or twenty years, you're going to have real problems keeping your virtual immortality secret."

"Maybe I ought to go public."

"You've got to be kidding! And open Pandora's box again!" Vera protested.

"Of course, I can't. I know. I'll dye my hair, as you suggest. If those guys on TV can wipe away the gray, I can wipe *on* the gray. That should keep me out of harm's way for a while."

"That would buy you a few years, but gray-haired men don't have gorgeous complexions."

"Then I'll use makeup. I can buy lots of time."

"And what will people say about that nonagenarian who has such a quick mind, who walks to work, who goes caving, and who still leers at pretty women?"

"I've never thought that far ahead."

"Adam Boatwright, the identity, will have to *die*," Vera insisted. "That's the only way. You're going to have to fake your death—over and over again. You're going to have to assume new identities."

"How can I do that? Geneticists are a pretty close-knit and small group."

"You cannot remain a geneticist, at least not a public one. You can reincarnate yourself as a doctor, perhaps in Canada. Then you become a doctor in Israel. Then work as a geneticist in Mexico, and so on. Luckily, you're a linguist."

"So, my projects can only last twenty or thirty years."

Vera looked deeply into Adam's eyes. "Take the knowledge you've gained to the next place. You'll have a very long time to complete your projects."

Adam gave a facetious reply. "But I'd have a hard time making a T. Rex."

"You don't want to do that, anyway!"

"Right. That's just an example of a long genetics project."

"Adam, you could have a public persona and do your evolutionary research in private."

"I don't want to live like a spy, like some eternally young science fiction freak."

"Honey, you don't have a lot of choice in the matter. It's your *body* that will not age. But your *mind* will be getting older, and, luckily, you'll keep your memories. You'll be unique in human history. Your accumulated knowledge will make you very powerful."

"I don't want power, Vera. And I'll lose everything in the process. I'll lose you."

"My physical presence will be gone, yes, but you'll have your memories of me."

"I want more."

"I know, Adam, but all long-lived people face the same types of losses. That's a natural part of the human condition. But you'll be young in body, with unprecedented continuity. You'll be a tremendous force for good."

"I'm just a man. I'm not a deity."

Vera clasped Adam with both arms. "I worship you. I'm so proud to be part of your life."

Adam embraced her with all the love he could muster. But he still could not accept losing her. As long as he lived, Adam would never accept being immortal.

The Story Continues

Super Virus is the first book in the *Boatwright Chronicles*. This series of four books carries Adam Boatwright through his adventures as a virtual immortal. The present book brought Adam from his role as a genetics researcher and teacher of medicine to the point where he has found himself in a quandary: either take the stopper vaccine and live through old age within a normal lifespan; or continue a very long life punctuated by changes in his own identity. At the end of this book, Adam has chosen to live on, applying his genetics knowledge to helping wildlife, now in serious jeopardy from mankind's relentless population growth and consumption of all the planet's resources.

The next book in this series has the main title *Boundary Layer*, a geological term for the rock formation delineating two long epochs. That book takes its title from the K-T boundary layer that separates the Cretaceous and Tertiary Periods. The first epoch ends with the demise of the dinosaurs, some sixty-five million years ago. The layer contains a rare element iridium, now believed to be of extraterrestrial origins. That deposit was attributed to a giant meteor that impacted near Mexico's Yucatan Peninsula.

The subtitle of the second book is *Restoring Life to a Dead Planet*. The story begins with the history of the dinosaurs' demise combined with Adam's and Ernie's concerns over a pending nuclear war to be launched by third-world countries. They want to save the planet, and must collect and store seeds and embryos as insurance against a nuclear winter resulting from such a conflict. They take on the huge responsibility of saving as much life as possible.

I won't spoil that story for you now. But *Boundary Layer* has been written and will be available in bookstores sometime within a year, plus or minus a few months, of the publication of *Super Virus*. If you like the present book, you will find an equally good read with its sequel. Borrowing from Adam's love of movies, I am pleased to present this "preview of coming attractions": Chapter 1 of *Boundary Layer*.

Lawrence L. Lapin

The Boatwright Chronicles Book Two

BOUNDARY LAYER

Restoring Life to a Dead Planet

L A W R E N C E L.

LAPIN

Breedwell bwp Press

Lincoln, California

1

A Thin Dusting of Iridium

Boundary Layer: Restoring Life to a Dead Planet
Book 2 of The Boatwright Chronicles

Adam Boatwright's jet-black hair framed his ruggedly handsome face. The medical professor's attention was focused on his younger wife, who was brushing her long blonde hair, heavily threaded with silver strands. Vera still had the beauty and energy of a younger person and enjoyed the inevitable surprise when a new acquaintance learned she was a famous concert violinist.

Vera looked through the mirror at Adam's admiring eyes. "I'm flattered you still look at me that way. Soon, people are going to mistake me for your mother. They won't believe I'm ten years younger."

Dreading another painful spat over aging, Adam said nothing. But the troubled man's silence only aroused pangs of sadness at the prospect of losing Vera. That emotion morphed into anger as Adam raged at the unfairness of outliving his companion. As always, his anger brought instant relief from the premature mourning. The nerve-wracking merry-go-round only stopped spinning at the realization it was his fault, and seas of guilt then flooded all other emotions.

Adam was grateful at the ringing telephone's interruption. It was Ernie Dickson, inviting them to a lecture associated with their wildlife preservation projects. Like aspirin for a headache, thinking about work brought quick relief from emotional turmoil.

But there was something odd about Ernie's urgency. Strangest of all was the presentation topic.

"We're in for a treat tonight." Adam smiled at his wife as he poured morning coffee.

Ordinarily the Boatwrights' evenings were spent watching a couple of movies from their extensive collection. Films provided Adam a perfect antidote to the scientist's intellectually challenging life and relieved his eyes from the daily stress of working with microscopes and other biological research instruments. It also provided necessary counterpoint to the frustrations of dealing with a hundred medical students at Central University, where he was a joint professor of medicine and genetics. Vera enjoyed the movies mainly because they added precious moments of companionship to their busy, career-driven lives.

"What's it going to be?" Vera teased. "*Abbot and Costello Meet Frankenstein* or *Rocketship XM*?"

"I've got a change of pace in mind," Adam answered, enjoying the non-threatening word play with his wife. "Dinosaurs."

"Not *Jurassic Park* again, please," Vera groaned. "We must've seen that one twenty times."

Adam gave a light-hearted reply. "We're doing the original *Lost World*."

"That stop-action film from the forties. Yuck. Can't we do better than that?"

"Yes. That was Ernie Dickson inviting us to a live show. A paleontologist is speaking tonight at Murphy Hall. He'll tell us about extinctions."

Vera was glad for Adam's company on the sinister nighttime walk through the Central University campus. The shadows and blackness starkly contrasted with the more familiar lively daytime setting, when young people were scurrying about. She enjoyed morning visits to Adam's office complex in the Life Sciences Building, where he directed research on genetics. Murphy Hall was on the opposite side of the huge campus. Vera had last been there to see a revival of the musical *Li'l Abner*.

The speaker, Bruce Kincaid, was a big man with sparse gray hair pushed back to frame his large, balding head. His face was dominated by a large mustache and bulbous nose, reminding Vera of the General Bullmoose character seen on the same stage. But with his Oxford-British accent, Kincaid sounded nothing like the play's right-wing industrialist.

The professor spoke about how the Alvarezes, a father-son research team, had proposed the now widely accepted cause for extinction of the dinosaurs. Dominating the world during the Cretaceous era, those creatures had suddenly vanished at the onset of the Tertiary period, about sixty-five million years ago. Nobody had known why.

A solution to the great mystery separating the two epochs was suggested by the respective rocks from each, which were separated by a layer of iridium everywhere on the planet. The Alvarezes declared that the rare element had extraterrestrial origins, since only atmospheric fallout could have become so widespread.

"The Alvarezes claimed the iridium—the K-T boundary layer—was compacted dust from Earth's collision with a large meteor," Kincaid said in his sonorous voice. "But their case was weak. Corroborating evidence was needed."

That evidence was provided when satellite radar located the K-T meteor impact site. Kincaid showed a slide of Mexico's Yucatan Peninsula.

"Here's the spot," the professor announced, his mustache bouncing with excitement as he pointed to the peninsular coast. "It's hard to see, but there's a crater here, about fifty miles wide and just the right age. Investigators believe the meteor was about one mile in diameter. The oblong shape tells its direction of impact after zooming down at thirty thousand miles per hour."

Adam and Vera listened in awe as Kincaid told how the meteor had hit at the worst possible angle. Coming from the south, the collision's blast virtually scorched the Northern Hemisphere.

With sad eyes, Kincaid looked at the audience. "Winds of several hundred miles per hour pushed hot, vaporized debris all over North America, so that all plants burned and all animals cooked."

Kincaid paused to rub his eyes. "So nearly all of North America was on fire. The smoke blackened the sky, adding soot to the dust and debris skirting the atmosphere, like the belching from a thousand Mount St. Helens volcanoes.

"The fires explain the disappearance of many plant families from the Northern Hemisphere. Notable among them were early conifers, such as the Norfolk pine, a New Zealand native. But the fires were only the initial phase of the catastrophe."

Vera's eyes teared as Professor Kincaid soberly explained what had next befallen the entire planet. Creatures and plants of all types had perished as the Earth became dark and cold. Massive die-offs took place in the sea and on the land. The few survivors from the years-long night inhabited a hostile, cold world. Large animals and uncloaked terrestrial creatures could not thrive in such an environment. Dinosaurs were the most well-known creatures to die off, but entire families of other animals and plants had become extinct too.

After the lecture, the Boatwrights sat in a corner booth at Father Nature's, having coffee with their hosts. Vera admired Jayne Dickson's beauty, enhanced with wisps of gray in her blonde hair. Equally handsome was Ernie Dickson, despite the bald dome of his head sitting above thick sides of blonde-gray hair that framed his thin face.

Vera looked at Jayne, launching conversation. "I had a slight inkling of why dinosaurs became extinct. But I'm only a violinist. What are your scientific insights?"

"It was like a new world starting over," Jayne said while stirring her herbal rain-forest tea.

"That's the part that intrigues me," Adam said. "Jayne, you've spent your life digging for relics of the past. How did ancient creatures cope in their new, hostile environment?"

"I'm a professor of anthropology, not zoology," Jayne gently corrected. "I dug for pottery shards, not fossils."

"Of course," Adam said, blowing on a teaspoonful of hot espresso. "But you've sifted through evidence showing how civilizations came and went. Animals must go through similar adaptations in coping with changed environments."

"I'm sure that's true. Unfortunately, animals leave no trinkets or writing, just their bodies. And we're talking millions of years into the past, not just a few centuries."

"How long do you think it took for the dinosaurs to die off?" Vera asked.

Jayne smiled at her friend; people, not dinosaurs, were her academic specialty. "It probably took several thousand years. But it might've happened much more quickly, within a couple of years. Who knows?"

"That's a pretty wide range," Vera objected.

Jayne paused before speaking. "In geological terms, it was just an instant. Imagine the time since the Cretaceous period as a full hourglass. Human history took about as long as the last grain of sand to slip into freefall."

"Of course," Adam said, bubbling with enthusiasm like a bright college freshman. "But imagine what the hardy mouselike early mammals endured, surviving in a hellacious new world."

All talk stopped as the waiter brought the desserts.

Ernie resumed exactly where they'd left off, mirroring Adam's enthusiasm. "We've seen modern equivalents of epic survival. Hawaii comes to mind. Those islands are only a few million years old."

"That's a great analogy," Adam said, almost choking on a quick swallow. "A new volcanic island was similar to a devastated Earth with pockets of lifeless land—"

"Come on!" Vera interrupted, squeezing her crumb cake all over the placemat. "I love Hawaii. Are you saying such paradise rose from barren rock?"

Adam grinned at his wife. "I am. What you see today is the result of millions of years of ecological evolution. Remember Michener's *Hawaii*?"

"I love that movie, but I don't remember any ecology."

"Not the movie. The *book*. The movie left out the best part, right from the beginning of his story."

"That's right!" Jayne continued. "I remember the plot. Hawaii is one of the remotest spots on the planet, thousands of miles from the nearest land. Every twenty thousand or so years a new plant or animal would arrive by accident. To be precise, not to the Hawaiian Islands we know, but to an earlier island, now worn away and under the sea."

"Yes, yes," Ernie continued the story. "A log from South America would land on the island shore, and a coconut would sprout. A stowaway bug would establish itself on the same land, living off the new plant growth. Slowly, very slowly, new plants and animals would arrive by accident."

"And living things would easily island hop to their new neighbors," Adam added, "evolving over millions of years of continuing volcanic renewal."

"Did you know Hawaii has dozens of birds seen nowhere else on Earth?" asked Ernie.

Vera was skeptical. "Come on," she said. "I've seen the pictures. You mean those delicate little curved-beak things flew thousands of miles over the sea?"

"Their ancestors did. But those early birds were far hardier than today's sapsuckers. Take the case of the nearly flightless nene goose. That curiosity resembles the more streamlined Canada goose. We think the nenes descended from one female Canada, blown off course during migration."

"Yes," said Adam. "The nenes can't fly far because they landed in paradise and didn't need to flee winter. There were no predators to hound them, and they didn't have to migrate to nest. They were fat and sassy, and eventually their dominant descendants could only fly a few miles. We see today the results of that evolution."

The foursome watched in silence while the waiter replenished their beverages, then Vera resumed playing student in the impromptu seminar.

"But the nenes are rare. I've only seen them in cages."

"It was man!" Jayne said. "Humans brought dogs and pigs to Hawaii. They've caused a lot of extinctions of bird life."

"Somehow it all boils down to man," Vera lamented. "Can paradise survive the human race?"

Silence ensued for the first time. Finally Jayne said, "That's the million-dollar question. I'll give you another one. Can Earth itself survive man?"

"The planet can, of course." Adam answered. "But living things are being irrevocably changed by man every day. Nobody can predict the direction of that change."

"I've fantasized about a future without human-caused ravages," Ernie said. "This touches on our work, Adam. Suppose we had a virgin world, like the first Hawaii, into which we introduced our animal collections. If we could then travel in time, millions of years later, would we even recognize the place?"

Adam paused and collected his thoughts. "No. The animals would occupy new niches, evolving in new ways. It would depend on the mix of the first animals and the manner of their introduction."

On the drive home, Adam let his mind wander. He imagined the impact of African fauna inhabiting North America. What would happen to elephants loose in the Mississippi Valley? Giraffes in Georgia? Hippos in Louisiana? Ostriches in Oklahoma? What would happen to the deer population if they were the prey of lions and hyenas? Would crocodiles migrate from the southern waters and eventually inhabit the Great Lakes?

Adam's head was swimming when they arrived at Falcon Tower.

LaVergne, TN USA
01 October 2009
159530LV00004B/5/P